CLOSE CALL

CLOSE CALL

Vivien Armstrong

This first world edition published in Great Britain 1994 by
SEVERN HOUSE PUBLISHERS LTD of
9–15 High Street, Sutton, Surrey SM1 1DF.
First published in the USA 1995 by
SEVERN HOUSE PUBLISHERS INC., of
425 Park Avenue, New York, NY 10022.

British Library Cataloguing in Publication Data
Armstrong, Vivien
    Close Call
    I. Title
    823.914 [F]

    ISBN 0-7278-4708-2

Typeset by Hewer Text Composition Services, Edinburgh.
Printed and bound in Great Britain by
Hartnolls Ltd, Bodmin, Cornwall.

CHAPTER ONE

It was six o'clock on the evening of Easter Sunday before Judith had put the finishing touches to the paintwork. By then even the varnish on the lavatory seat had dried. For three days the mahogany had been sticky as a jam butty and feeling as if it might stay that way for ever.

Detective Sergeant Judith Pullen was absolutely cock-a-hoop with her first solo flight with a paint roller. Admittedly there had been one flash of sheer panic when it transpired just how tricky it was to paper a ceiling, working from a plank balanced between two chairs. But a knight errant had come to the rescue. Dave Barnes was errant all right and his ripped T-shirt and baseball cap were hardly shining armour but nevertheless the analogy was spot on.

Dave occupied the basement – or Garden Flat as the late Mrs Juniper used to call it. He lived rent free in exchange for certain caretaking responsibilities, these dovetailing nicely with his spasmodic employment as a tenor sax player in a jazz quartet called Tears. His odd jobs about the bedsits and flatlets in the house in Rectory Gardens gave Dave access to all the proper gear: decorator's steps, dust sheets, you name it. Papering Judith's ceiling was a piece of cake. Mind you, the guy wouldn't have responded so smartly had the distress signal been hoisted by Mavis Clements, the middle-aged librarian on the first floor.

That Easter Saturday the poor bloke fairly bounded up the stairs behind Judy Pullen, eager to press himself into service. Operation Revamp as she called it had turned out nothing like the doddle the man in B & Q had promised when he had sold her all that paint.

"Why didn't you give me the buzz you wanted to do the place up, Ju? I'd have polished it off in a couple of days

1

while you were at work." He surveyed the shambolic state of Judith's new place, his ponytail swinging like an admonishing finger. "Take all bleeding night just to clear the muck off the floorboards now."

Judy bridled. "I was doing fine till I got to the ceiling."

"Why leave the bloody ceiling till last?"

She shrugged. "Saving the best bit for you, Dave."

He laughed, which only goes to show that paint splotched dungerees on a pretty girl with a tumble of baby-fine blond hair bundled under a knotted fishnet stocking could solve any amount of labour disputes.

He went down to the basement for the decorating paraphernalia and they worked hard for the rest of the day. Dave went off to work that night and didn't surface again till lunchtime on Easter Sunday but by late afternoon the miracle was complete. Judith's large airy second floor flat was immaculate.

Ellie Juniper called in on her way upstairs, curious to see the effect. She paused in the open doorway, her arms filled with shopping, a lanky girl with big eyes, her face framed by her prettiest feature, blond wavy hair hanging to her shoulders.

"What do you think, Ellie?" Judy crowed, tickled pink with the transformation of the dingy rooms.

"Wow! What a difference. It looks great, Judith. I didn't know you were good at this sort of thing."

"Dave's the expert. Why don't you get him to do up your place?"

The girl shifted the bulging carrier onto her hip, looking furtive. "Oh, it's OK. Really . . . Anyway, I still haven't sorted out all my stuff."

Dave moved as if to take the shopping from her but Ellie dodged back, clasping the bag like a shield.

"You here over the bank holiday?" he asked. "We could get together." His eyes slid over her micro skirt and the long legs in their multi-coloured tights. The girl flushed, pushing back her glasses in a nervous gesture.

"I'm not sure," she stammered, backing out.

Judith called to her as she fled upstairs. "Come down for a coffee later."

Ellie didn't answer and Judy frowned, wishing Dave's sexual

overtures were less explicit. A girl like Ellie couldn't cope with a bloke like that.

Dave wouldn't accept any payment for the rescue operation and settled for a mug of tea, the two of them sitting companionably side by side at the kitchen counter which divided the living area. Judith cradled her mug in her hands, hazel eyes gleaming like trout as they darted round the room in the shadowy twilight, the yellow walls now glowing dimly like a Venetian sunset. It *had* been worth it. She grinned at Dave, placing a smudged hand on his hairy forearm. He jerked away, slopping his tea, asking, "Why bother to move just one floor down, Ju-Ju? Thought you liked being up under the roof?"

"Mm. I did. I'm still not sure it was really such a brilliant idea but Ellie made me an offer I couldn't refuse. As soon as the Brents moved out of here she practically begged me to swop. She seemed desperate to escape that big flat of her mother's. I got the impression all that heavy Victorian furniture was crushing her to death. Ellie said she needed the rent from the ground floor apartment – it *is* the biggest in the whole house, of course. The clincher was her offer to let me have this for the same as I was paying for the attic rooms."

"Did she, by God! Her ma'll be turning in her grave, the old skinflint."

"Mrs Juniper scared the daylights out of me, I don't mind admitting it. You can't blame Ellie for wanting to break out now she's gone. She's almost left it too late."

"Too late? Don't you believe it! Ellie's always had her own slippy detours even when the old girl *was* sniffing round. You ever see Ellie done up for a date?"

"What do you mean?"

"Since the funeral she don't have to sidestep, but old Mrs J. wouldn't have Ellie wearing any mini-skirts or anything. Treated her daughter like a kid. But I bumped into Ellie in Soho more than a year ago and hardly recognised her. Talk about Before and After!"

"She saw you?"

"Didn't have her glasses on. Blind as a bat without them. I didn't say nothing at the time but I've pulled her leg about it since."

"So she wasn't altogether under her mother's thumb?"

"A real Jekyll and Hyde lady, believe me. Seen her going to work of a morning looking like beer gone flat. But Ellie Juniper out on the town's an eye-stopper." He jabbed his finger into Judy's shoulder, perfectly serious.

Judith laughed, refilling Dave's mug. He was an odd bloke. Gave the impression he was hell on wheels in some ways and then pulled up short if anyone got close. She fetched an unopened bottle of scotch from the kitchen cupboard and placed it in front of him.

"Please, Dave. You must take something. Won't you give this poor bottle a good home?"

He threw his baseball cap on the floor and held up both hands in mock surrender. "Give me a break! I've only been on the wagon two weeks." He nodded vehemently. "Go on, laugh, Sergeant . . . But I tell you what. Keep it under the sink for me in case of emergencies."

Judy touched her lips in a gesture of conspiracy and pushed the bottle aside. "Two weeks you say?"

"We've got this regular spot at a Soho club weekends. I need a steady hand. I promised the boys. Just as well Mrs J. kicked the bucket – she was an old cow in some ways but she busted a gut to get some company in that gloomy parlour of hers in the afternoons. Always kept some bottles under the bed even when she was half-crocked after the stroke. Tell the truth, I miss the old witch. Gone six months now."

"Can't you just imagine her up there, Dave, sitting on a fluffy cloud, brandishing her harp in helpless fury at Ellie's pathetic stab at being a landlady? Fancy letting her flat to the Osimas! Africans in her bed was bad enough but a *pram* in the hall! What ever happened to the Empire?"

"Not to mention that flakey waiter in the bedsit up here."

"Oh, Mikki's OK. Never hear him as a matter of fact. Works nights and sleeps days."

"Talking of which, my lovely bit of Old Bill, I'd better make tracks. Big night. Tears is trying out a new singer. Black girl from Brixton called Fizzy. Pretty good I thought. She came in off the street, only a kid I'd guess but a voice to break your heart." He checked his watch and glanced round the room, the furniture still stacked at one end. "Want me to help move the stuff back before I split?"

4

Judith, rinsing the mugs in the sink, smiled over her shoulder.

"Thanks, Dave, but I want to bang the dust off the chairs before my old boss gets here. He's promised to pick me up later. My sister's given me a sofabed and Arnott offered to take me over to Hampstead to pick it up."

"That the Yorkshire bugger who swore at Mrs J. last summer? Wouldn't be surprised if he was the one brought on her stroke."

"You could be right. He's a foul-mouthed devil but there's a heart of gold beating in there somewhere. Arnott's a bit lost since he retired in August. He ought to get himself another job. Looks like something carved in granite but he's only fifty-nine and a ferret when it comes to crime. Spends most of his time now working on an old boat he's restoring at Rye. Mrs Juniper hauled me over the coals about his bad language one time he picked me up here in a squad car."

He grinned. "Yeah, I remember. Got up her nose and no mistake. Took three pink gins just to calm her down enough to tell me the story. Something about mud on the floor."

"She was complaining about Arnott's dirty feet in the hall. He's got a phenomenally short fuse and Mrs Juniper on her high horse was just the sort to blow him sky high."

"Why call on an old guy like that to shift the sofa? What happened to that boyfriend of yours, the Special Branch bloke – can't he give you a hand? Holed up in Sandringham over Easter guarding the corgis?"

Judith followed Dave to the door, loading him up with the dustsheets as he launched into a bitter diatribe against the police in general and Laurence Erskine, Judy's semi-detached man about the house, in particular.

"Oh, Laurence is in Washington for a year. Been seconded to the embassy, lucky devil."

Dave paused in the doorway, wondering why this brainy bird with the long legs ever joined the cops. There was a sort of delicacy about her. Never snobby but giving the impression of slightly distancing herself from the rest of the mob. It was her deportment for one thing. Head erect, long strides, a spine straight as an arrow. It occurred to him that Judy Pullen might have trained as a dancer, just got too tall for it . . .

"Hey, you ever thought of going into show business?"

She grimaced and pushed him out, closing the door and leaning against it, snapping on the light to reappraise the new decor. It *was* a bigger flat than the one upstairs. *And* she had a spare bedroom. But she missed the view: the segment of the dear old Albert Hall, the glimpse of Kensington Gardens over the rooftops. Reluctantly she admitted all that was worth an acre of extra elbow room on a summer evening. She sighed and tossed off her gloom in an energetic assault on the dusty upholstery.

It took another couple of hours to clean up and shove all the furniture back and Judy almost wished she had put Arnott off until next weekend. But it was all laid on now, Pixie's sofabed stacked in her garage ready for collection, Arnott's steak sitting in the fridge as a thank you supper afterwards. Judy was shooting the last of the rubbish into a bag as he rang the front door bell. She propped the broom against the counter and spoke on the entry phone.

"Come up. I'm almost through."

The ex-CID Inspector arrived at her door gasping and wheezing, a flat tweed cap clamped over his beaky nose, his fat jowls dark with irritation. "By 'eck, Pullen, thought you told me you'd moved downstairs. You didn't crack on I had to lug this bloody settee up two flights. I'm not Arnie Schwarzenegger." He spied the unopened bottle of Bell's and made a beeline for it.

Judith watched her ex-boss break open Dave's emergency supply with resignation. "Don't forget you're driving, Arnott."

"I'll need more than a sniff of this to start moving double beds at my age. Any road, no-one's about Sunday nights, 'specially Easter. Dead as mutton this place. Everyone out? Talking of graveyards, Pullen, things've gone down the plughole since the old gel croaked, ain't they? Couldn't abide the churchy bat meself but, fair do's, she kept the place bloody shipshape and no mistake. Had to pick me way round a pile of cat shit on the stairs and the light's gone on the landing."

Judith shrugged into a windcheater, anxious to prize Arnott from the whisky bottle and grabbed his arm. "Sounds like poor old Nelson's been messing again. Dave's supposed to clean the stairs and keep an eye on things and Ellie—"

6

"That the old woman's daughter?"

"Yes, poor Ellie hasn't a clue. She leaves everything to Dave. Apart from the rent books, that is. But you're right. It's all gone to pot since September and the poor cat doesn't know who it's supposed to belong to."

They trooped down the front steps into the street where Arnott had double-parked an old Ford van. It was raining; a miserable drizzle holding out no promise of the "Spring iin Park Lane" the tourists had been promised. Rectory Gardens was abnormally unpopulated even for a Sunday night, and the white stucco terrace gleamed in the lamplight, its Victorian elegance fleetingly re-emerging in the emptiness of a wet weekend in the city.

"Most people try to get away at Easter," Judy said, clicking her safety belt and settling into the tobacco-fumed interior of Arnott's horrible van. "The house is practically deserted – just me and Dave and a Spanish waiter who has the bedsit off my landing. There's a research scientist of some sort but he's never there and Ellie's often away at weekends so I suppose the Nigerians are the only tenants who are always at home. They have lots of friends calling round – you'd think the house was the staging post for a political coup."

"Wasn't there some other old bag, a mate of the Juniper woman?"

"Mavis Clements? Mavis isn't *old*, Arnott, she just dresses like Miss Marple. Mavis still rents the first floor front but I haven't seen her for days. She was awfully good to Mrs Juniper when she was ill those last few months. Dave and Mavis were a lifeline for the old lady. Ellie had to keep on her job and I got the impression mother and daughter didn't get on. Can't think why. I'm probably wrong. Anyway, we had a cleaner three mornings a week in those days. Minnie Mouse we used to call her. Had the biggest feet I've ever seen. But she left when Ellie took over."

"What about the caretaker bloke?"

"Oh, Dave's no earthly use. He takes a swipe with the vacuum cleaner once a week but the whole place is beginning to fall apart. Still, he's been a marvellous help to me with my ceiling. Sober, too, which makes a change. He's a wizard with any odd jobs needing to be done in the house and at least he's there all day when everyone's out at work. Apart from the Osimas, that is."

"The foreigners? Idle bloody bunch."

"Must you be so prejudiced? The Osimas *can't* work, they're refugees of some sort. Mavis told me. But they'd be no use in an emergency. Neither of them speak much English."

Arnott made short work of loading up the sofabed which was stacked in Pixie's garage in two sections. There were no armrests and the whole thing could be assembled as two single beds or a double. It all went surprisingly smoothly and Arnott was so full of himself he even forgot to complain. Judy encouraged him with the promise of steak and chips at Rectory Gardens and the old groaner became positively jovial.

They speeded back through the silent streets and carried each half upstairs between them, reassembling it against the wall of the spare room which Judy had fitted out with her desk and a square of carpet. She expanded with pleasure at the improvement which had been effected in less than three days. Perhaps, after all, the new flat would eventually feel more like home.

CHAPTER TWO

Judith had put on all the lamps and drawn a screen pasted over with a collage of peeling magazine cuttings in front of the window. She had yet to get around to hanging curtains. Arnott was lucky to find himself so comfortable considering the scramble it had been to finish the decorating over Easter. He settled on the sofa with a tumbler of whisky while she changed into a sweater and jeans. It had been quite a day. But the steaks were tender and the bottle of Beaujolais nudged aside her growing anxieties about Arnott's ability to drive back to Mortlake. The irascible old toad had mellowed: it seemed a pity to spoil his mood. She could always order a minicab to take him home.

A year ago she would have snorted in derision had anyone suggested the "Punch and Judy Show" would run and run. But since Arnott's abrupt exit from the Force, she and that terror of the Chelsea beat, Detective Inspector Ralph Arnott, against all the laws of nature, had fallen into some kind of lopsided friendship.

It was an odd relationship. Arnott was rude, foul-mouthed, bigoted and paid not the slightest regard to normal codes of behaviour. Having recently claimed early retirement on a full pension – Arnott was enough of a Yorkshireman to count his brass before throwing it away – he had stumped away from a career path pitted with confrontations. His Superintendent had been relieved to be shot of the out-of-date troublemaker with little regard for the Race Relations Act or the tightening restrictions of police procedure. And Arnott's colleagues had been secretly glad to see him go. Lumbering the old ruffian with a pretty detective sergeant had been manna from heaven in the police canteen and a book had been opened on the time it would take before the girl was reduced to tears in the knockabout Punch and Judy scenario.

Judith herself was the first to admit that working with Arnott had been far from easy. But, determined to last the course, it was only later she learned of the big bets lost on her obduracy. It was only after he had gone that Judith had been willing to admit to herself that the random viciousness on the streets held a terror which seemed only to exacerbate with every investigation. It was akin to being a steeplejack with vertigo. She'd scuttled into the Serious Fraud Office where injuries were inflicted only with paper darts.

Judith watched him roll up yet another home-made cigarette and decided to wind him up.

"It was put to me today, Arnott, that it was your filthy temper pitchforked Mrs Juniper into her stroke. Something about muddy feet on her marble floor tiles."

"What bloody lies!" He choked at the very idea, coughing and spluttering for a full minute before catching his breath to continue. "It was the gin what done her in. Take my advice, Pullen. Stick to whisky. It's a well-known fact that a daily drop of malt keeps the brain in top nick."

"A drop, yes, not the whole bottle!"

Arnott lurched forward, his eyes rheumy and bloodshot. "Who's been toting all this cock?"

Judy laughed, patting his arm. "I'm only pulling your leg. Actually, it was probably Nelson's fault. Mrs Juniper's cat, you know. Have you seen it? Nelson's built like a sumo wrestler. Dave calls it Dump Truck."

"Evil bloody things, cats. Wouldn't give 'em house room meself."

"Well, the story goes the old lady shot down to Harrods to collar the man on the fish counter. She swore Nelson's whiting had been 'off'. Carried on alarmingly by all accounts, demanded the Manager, created no end of a scene in front of the queue then suddenly had this seizure. They carted her off to a rest room while they called the ambulance and she was semi-paralysed for weeks. Her speech was never the same which must have been the most devastating frustration for her of all people. So you see—"

She broke off, glancing up at the ceiling. Strains of a violin percolated from the floor above.

"That's the trouble, Pullen. Like I said, cats cause nothing but grief. And you can't prosecute a bloody cat lover when your motor gets piled up avoiding a pussy crossing the road." He ground out his stub in an ashtray and frowned at the ceiling, his hooked nose and belligerent chin raised in profile like a cartoon cut-out. The chords were barely melodic and worse, the amateur soloist had now become bolder, the strangled dissonance increasing in volume. "Just listen to that racket, Pullen! I've heard better scraping than that down the tube stations. Mind you, that's a grand way of using up cat gut. Thin the buggers out in no time if we was all to take up fiddle lessons."

The gleam of satisfaction which suffused his florid features was suddenly extinguished by Nelson's arrival, right on cue, scratching fiercely at the door and mewing piteously.

Judy refilled Arnott's glass and struggled to recapture their amicable chit chat but the tortured violin strings severed the atmosphere like a chain saw and the cat on the landing was now at full throttle, yowling in unison.

Arnott suddenly leapt up, grabbed the broom propped against the wall and vigorously applied the handle to Judy's unsullied ceiling, bellowing threats and obscenities at the hapless virtuoso. Judith flushed, snatched the broom and pushed him back on the couch.

"For Christ's sake, Arnott! You'll get me thrown out. That's the owner of the house up there. Ellie Juniper took over my old flat."

Arnott blustered, by no means diverted, having crossed swords with the Juniper girl before during the row with her mother about muddy feet in her nice clean hallway. Also, he harboured a deep-seated aversion to young women in glasses, probably originating in some arcane prejudice against feminine "cleverness". Judy rushed from the room before he aimed more pithy expletives at the ceiling. Nelson lay like a booby trap over the threshold and she stumbled, then, sweeping the cat into her arms, pounded up the uncarpeted stairs. She knocked at her erstwhile front door, her mind whirling with apologies. The violin playing abruptly ceased and footsteps pattered to the door. It opened a few inches. Wide eyes, set in a face looped about with curtains of hair, peered from behind huge spectacles. Nelson was purring, a deep throbbing reverberation of pleasure as Judy stuttered her regrets. "I am so sorry, Ellie. It's Arnott, my old boss – he's incorrigible. He'd banged on the ceiling before I could stop him. He's allergic to cats, you see. Nelson's howling . . ."

The excuses petered out; the big grey eyes fixed on Judith now clouded with confusion. The door opened wider and Ellie twitched at her stringy hair.

"S-sorry, Judith. I forget you were here over Easter . . . I thought everyone was out. Did I ruin your evening?"

"Of course not," she lied.

"It was my playing, wasn't it? Anyway, it was probably the violin which set Nelson off – the poor old thing's always hated it, nearly as much as Mother come to mention it. I'm no good. She couldn't bear me to practice and I'm never going to play at the Albert Hall now, am I?" Ellie motioned Judith inside and seemed not at all dismayed by this frank admission. She wore a rust-coloured jumpsuit and slippersocks which was very sensible as the room was freezing.

Judith edged inside, stiff with embarrassment. Arnott was the absolute bloody limit. Ellie had a perfect right to play her violin in her own house at nine o'clock on a Sunday evening. Nelson dropped to the floor with a thud and began kneading a nest for himself in a pile of cushions in front of a two-bar electric fire.

Judith's astonishment at the state of her old top floor rooms overcame her before she had a moment to collect herself. The place was utterly shambolic; clothes strewn on every surface, pictures stacked against the walls, books and CDs jumbled in boxes all over the floor. The only relatively clear space was on an old-fashioned pedestal desk which dwarfed everything else in the room, easily accommodating a word processor and an answering machine. She recognised the desk from previous visits to the Jardines to pay the rent and, sure enough, it was strewn with bank statements and bills. Ellie had probably taken up her bow as a break from an evening's accounting. Goodness knows who had humped the monstrous piece of furniture up three flights of stairs. Undertakers?

Ellie's new furniture was the sort knocked together in situ with the aid of a fiendishly complex set of instructions. Everything was raw pine, a gimcrack sofa heaped with gingham cushions being the only place to sit. Still harbouring a sentimental regard for her old set of rooms, Judy was shocked. It was if she had stumbled upon an elderly relative in drag.

"I'm having a clear out," Ellie said with a wry grin. "There's not enough room up here for everything." She sketched a feeble gesture at the mess. As if to underline the point, Nelson flexed his claws on the legs of a low table in front of the sofa and Ellie swiped at him with the Sunday colour supplement. "Nelson's a real pain these days. He keeps infiltrating the other flats. I can't seem to keep him in."

"Couldn't Dave have him in the basement?"

Ellie frowned, stretching her hands towards the electric fire. "The Osimas complain about Nelson sleeping in the pram. He's so big, that's the trouble. Mother used to give him condensed milk . . ." Her eyes behind the smeary lenses looked drowned, like dead fish in a mucky tank.

Judith scrambled up and, struck by a rush of sympathy, impulsively invited Ellie down for a drink. "If there's any left that is. Arnott's been making steady inroads into my booze all evening. Do come. He's not always so rude. Arnott's like Nelson. Perfectly sweet if you scratch behind his ears."

Ellie followed her to the door, Nelson lumbering along behind like a furry Sherman tank, his vast undercarriage almost touching the floor.

"Thanks, but no. I'm expecting a friend later." Her lips thinned to a weak smile and Judy, sensing a polite brush-off, made a fast exit, their farewells truncated by the urgent need to baulk Nelson's escape onto the landing.

When she pushed open her own door a wall of stale tobacco smoke hit her like motorway fog. Arnott had stretched out on the sofa, the TV at full blast. He'd removed his jacket, revealing a grubby M&S cardigan liberally sprinkled with ash. The bottle of Bell's was well down and his air of beatitude sealed her worst misgivings. Arnott was irretrievably sloshed. The abrasiveness had blunted to a maudlin commentary on the Charlie Chaplin documentary flickering on the box and every so often his eyelids

13

dropped as if he were choosing each word with care. Judy knew better.

She endured the lengthening silences for a while longer and was about to ring for a cab to take the silly old sod back home when the decibels from her own TV were augmented by a full volume retaliation of rock music from Ellie's flat upstairs. Judith leapt at her remote control button and as the sound decreased she sensed a shuffle of footsteps on the landing.

Curious, she opened her door a crack, wondering if Ellie really did have a date. But as the hinges creaked a shadowy figure at the top of the stairs swung round. Arnott was right, Dave *had* forgotten to replace the light bulb; the small square of carpet linking her own entrance to that of Mikki Ferrero, the waiter renting the bedsit at the back, was almost in darkness. She opened the door wide, the light behind her spotlighting the man on the landing. He stood transfixed like a dancing bear, all brown and shaggy, dressed in a scruffy sports coat and corduroys. His hair touched his collar and a gingerish beard concealed a lot of face. He smiled and the penny dropped.

"Oh, it's you . . ." she floundered. "Er – it's Mr Fielding, isn't it? From downstairs?"

"Gus. Yes, that's right." He smiled, apologetic, eyes warm as a spaniel's. "I was just going up to ask Ellie to lend me a tin of tomatoes – sorry. Did you think I was a prowler?"

"No, just nosiness to be honest. I was hoping to catch a glimpse of Ellie's date." They chatted on the doorstep for a minute then Judy asked him in. In an undertone she explained her difficulty in getting rid of Arnott. "Could you come in and have a glass of wine or something? Help me get him into a cab? I shouldn't have left him alone with the whisky. I was upstairs with Ellie for a while and he seems to have gone overboard quite suddenly. I've got a tin of tomatoes I can let you have, there's no need to bother Ellie – she's probably trying to clear up before her bloke arrives – she's having a struggle settling in, finding a home for all her bits. And I really could do with a hand, Gus. Arnott can be quite a bundle. My name's Judith by the way. We've only passed on the stairs before."

She closed her door quietly, glad of his company. After a few hours of Arnott someone of her own age was infinitely desirable. Magnus Fielding seemed a pleasant chap, thirtyish but, Judy guessed, a bit of a young fogey at heart. An academic of some sort, researching a book on rocks or fossils or something according to the Mavis Clements News Service. "Awfully clever, Judith," Mavis had assured her in reverent tones. "Needs looking after though, never gets a decent meal for himself if you ask me."

He looked quite hunky, in fact. Not in the least undernourished. Five foot nine or ten but muscular, his nicest feature an appealing diffidence as if every sentence culminated in a question mark. But this impression might have been occasioned by an accent which was hard to place, East Anglian perhaps. Or Cornish? Judith wasn't any good with accents. She introduced Fielding to Arnott who had got his second wind, exhaling a heady mixture of whisky and chips as he pumped Gus's hand and magnanimously emptied the last of the scotch into three clean tumblers he fetched from the kitchen. Arnott playing *mein host* was a new one. Mind you, it wasn't his round, was it?

The two men got on like a house on fire. Arnott never ceased to amaze Judy; brusque with one person and chummy as a gnarled old character actor with someone else. Trouble was one could never tell which way he'd jump. Arnott drunk was no insurance against irascibility either. Arnott in his cups could turn quite nasty.

Far from dislodging the man, Gus's arrival seemed only to revive him. The two lolled on the sofa, locked in cameraderie, Arnott totally ignoring Gus's polite efforts to include Judith in the lively geological discussion, a subject with which, mysteriously, the old fraud seemed quite conversant. The younger man made spasmodic efforts to escape and even got to his feet but Arnott continued firing questions with the rat-a-tat of a sub-machine-gun. After an hour their captive geologist was entirely at his ease, an underlying vein of humour glistening through as he warmed to his subject, unaffected by the continuing rock music pulsing upstairs.

Judith went into the bathroom to fetch another bottle from her wine rack under the hand basin. She paused to brush her hair and jeered at her reflection. Who are you trying to kid, Judy Pullen? Never bothered to look at yourself when Arnott

15

arrived, did you? Vaguely registering bouncing footsteps on the attic stairs she snatched up the bottle of wine, wondering if Ellie's date involved clubbing. It was pretty late for anything else and Dave had darkly commented that since Mrs Juniper's demise her daughter had "branched out".

It was almost midnight before Gus started to make a final move and the Beaujolais had taken its toll. Arnott was going under for the third time. Edging to the door Gus almost got clear away on his repeated promise to take them all on a conducted tour of the geological gems to be found in Kensington's streets. Arnott was swaying on his feet, the unfamiliar spate of sociability finally spent. Judith made urgent gestures behind his back and, wordlessly, she and Gus steered the ex-inspector into the spare room. Arnott slumped on Pixie's studio couch in an exhalation like a mighty steam engine finally coming to rest. Judy fetched a duvet and draped it over the snoring old boozer and closed the door with relief.

"Bless you, Gus. Sorry to drag you in on all that. Here, don't forget your tin of tomatoes." She darted into the kitchen and produced a can from the shelf. "There you go."

"I meant it about the walk," he persisted. "If it wouldn't bore you, that is?" This air of hesitation was so totally at variance with the style of invitation she was used to from Laurence Erskine that Judith found herself acting ridiculously skittish.

"Sounds great. But let's leave Arnott out of it, shall we? There's only so much I can take."

They shook hands on it and Judith closed the door with mixed feelings, almost sorry to see him go. But she was dead beat, certainly too tired to clear up the living room before she turned in. At least tomorrow was a bank holiday, a chance to have a lie-in. Then, remembering Arnott spark out in the spare room, bitterly concluded it would have been far simpler to have hired a professional carrier to collect the damned sofa. But then she wouldn't have invited Magnus Fielding in to help dislodge the old boy . . . Not Fate exactly but Judith was a great believer in one thing leading to another.

She lay in bed trying to read, her eyes flickering away from the book, casting about for some explanation of a nebulous anxiety. She felt keyed up, on edge, unable to relax. It was ridiculous. For the same rent she had exchanged a loft conversion subdivided by flimsy partitioning for a real flat. A flat with a real bathroom. A flat with panelled wooden doors instead of the plywood ones upstairs. And this was a real bedroom, not an area requisitioned from storage space. Moving house – if only down one floor – was often cited as a major upheaval and seeing her former eyrie totally transformed *had* been a shock. But she had swapped accommodation before, swinging from one end of the metropolis to the other without so much as a backward glance. Why this crazy disorientation? Perhaps such persistent disquiet was nothing to do with the new flat. Perhaps she was missing Laurence more than she cared to admit.

She surveyed the room in detail, taking in the fitted cupboards either side of the chimneybreast, a huge uncurtained window overlooking the garden, an original fireplace with its pretty de Morgan tiles, the picture rail circling the walls. What could be nicer? Twin flexes hanging from the ceiling culminated in switches which dangled by the bedhead, one controlling the light over her head and the other an electric bell, presumably to enable the lady of the house to summon her maid. Judith giggled at the mental picture of Dave rushing upstairs in a white pinny bringing her morning tea.

She dropped her book on the floor and switched off the light, the window glowing amber from street lighting near the park. Exhaustion suddenly claimed her and she crashed out immediately, oblivious to Arnott's stertorous rumblings, his terrible snoring relentless as a steam hammer.

Judy dreamed of lying in a cave peopled by troglodytes applying their little pickaxes to a glittering vein of ore in a mineshaft which sheared downwards towards a black pool on which raindrops pattered in a relentless tattoo. Even in her dream Judith was aware of the illogicality of all this but was unable to quell acute anxiety about the rising level of water at the bottom of this pit and the fact that she herself was slithering towards it. She jerked awake, bathed in sweat.

Touching her cheek with a clammy hand, she discovered the imagined raindrops were real. A steady drip-drip was splashing on her face. She snapped on the dangling switch, revealing a spreading rusty stain above her head, water dripping from the light bulb in an evil rivulet. Hastily, she doused the light, dire warnings about water and electricity flashing like neon signs, and lay in the darkness shaking with fearful apprehension. She must get help. Bloody Ellie had obviously left a tap running. Stumbling out of bed, she felt her way to the door in the unfamiliar room as if picking her way across a minefield, too scared to try the lights again.

Once outside the bedroom, panic was swiftly superceded by rage. Barefoot, she launched herself upstairs to beat on Ellie's door, screaming a verbatim reprise of Arnott's abusive recitative describing the stupid woman's shortcomings.

CHAPTER THREE

There was no answer to her frantic fusillade, not a sound from within and no light showing under the ill-fitting door. What time was it? For water to flood the ceiling, Ellie's tap must have been running for hours. Had she stayed out all night for God's sake? Were the footsteps Judy had heard when she went to fetch the second bottle of wine those of the two of them going out? Exasperated, she shook her head in furious disbelief and flew down to the basement to borrow the spare keys from Dave.

Sod's law, Dave Barnes had absconded too. That meant there was only Gus. Would he agree to help break down the door? If Ellie didn't come back all night Judith's whole flat could be ruined. She bounded back upstairs and rang the bell on a dingy door on the first floor landing. It rang on and on, the sound piercing the silent house like a fire alarm. Even the Osimas must have been woken by the racket. Had Gus vanished off the face of the earth as well? Was there something they had omitted to tell her? The millenium? The last trump had sounded? Chemical warfare had broken out in the EEC? Was Judith Pullen the only one still here?

Now unquestionably frantic she took the next flight at full tilt, grabbed a torch from her mac hanging behind the door and burst in on Arnott still out cold in the spare room. He woke with a start and reared up, shielding his eyes from the torch beam, his grey hair whispy and dishevelled.

"What the bloody hell—?" he expostulated, throwing off the duvet and leaping out of bed. He was fully dressed and for a split-second Judith could see the funny side of it, she and Gus Fielding shoving the old drunk on the sofa for the night without even taking off his shoes. This flash of amusement fizzled out like a duff skyrocket in a bucket of water and she stuttered out the reason for the emergency.

Arnott took the torch and trundled upstairs breathing fire and brimstone. Anyone would think it was *his* nice new ceiling that was ruined. Judith half-hoped Ellie really was out, not just keeping her head down, pretending to know nothing of the disaster. Arnott didn't even bother to knock, handing her the torch as he applied his massive shoulder to the door with a sickening thud. Two more shoves did it, the hinges splitting clear away from the door jamb. Arnott marched in. He unerringly located the switch and they both stood blinking, the room still littered like a jumble sale.

Ellie was definitely out. Judy checked the bedroom while Arnott surveyed the kitchen area which, like hers, was part of the living room. No dripping tap, no burst pipes, nothing.

Judith pushed open the bathroom door and yanked at the light pull. Her bare feet got the message. The floor was awash, the water lapping in a gentle overflow, swilling under the cracked linoleum and soaking a candlewick bath mat. She flung back the half-open shower door and let out a scream of pure terror. Arnott burst in.

Ellie sat propped against the wall, her knees splayed. The shallow basin of the shower cubicle was full to the brim, the showerhead spraying even more water, the plughole blocked by her petticoat which had been drawn into the drain exposing french knickers, the peach coloured satin adhering to her hips like a second skin. The loose panties revealed suspenders supporting sheer black hose and an expanse of thigh white as Carrara marble, a glimpse of brown tufts at the crotch. Ellie's hair lay plastered to her head, the long wet strands now dark, the seemingly drowned figure slumped against the tiles like a woman literally tired to death of living.

Arnott pushed Judy aside. She wept, leaning against the door, the sodden linoleum numbing her bare feet, unable to drag her eyes away. Using his handkerchief Arnott turned off the shower and bent down to examine the body, touching nothing. Both arms hung loosely, the palms of her hands open as if in mute appeal, the water lapping her stockinged feet. An empty gin bottle lay on the lino and shards of thick glass from a broken tumbler, almost invisible under the floodwater, were

20

caught up in the wet folds of her silk slip. One sizeable chunk, ominous as a stiletto blade, lay in her lap.

He knelt in the wet peering at the girl's face. Her throat had been cut, the wound gaping like fish gills, squeaky clean, the considerable loss of blood having been washed away by the flow from the shower head. Arnott was satisfied. He had seen this sort of thing before. The poor kid had simply bled to death. He hauled himself to his feet and stood back.

She was a goner all right. Only the single spurt of blood across the tiles betrayed the violence of her suicide, the pretty underwear faintly marked with a rusty line where the bloodstained water had risen, then gradually rinsed, under the shower. Arnott backed out, pulling Judy with him into the living room. He fixed her brimming eyes with a hard stare.

The normal reaction of a policewoman had entirely deserted her. He would expect Pullen to stand back, not to interfere with anything at the scene. Fair enough, that's how she'd been trained. But this extreme shock reaction was a facer. There wasn't any professional move at all. And it wasn't the instinctive horror of finding a friend in such circumstances either. She hadn't rushed to help the poor cow and neither had she cooly appraised the scene with the natural curiosity of a trained observer. After all, it wasn't every day a member of the Force is the first to discover a body in her own house. Perhaps he had misunderstood. Perhaps the poor bitch had been a pal of hers, not just someone living under the same roof.

He firmly took her by the shoulder.

"Get yourself downstairs, lass, and call the police. I'll stay here. Pour yourself a stiff drink and wait in your own place. I'll deal with this." He gripped her shaking hands in a clumsy gesture of reassurance, then pushed her outside, warning her to leave the lights off downstairs till he'd had a chance to check the old wiring.

Arnott was totally sober, perfectly in control of the emergency, his steadfastness bringing the spinning spectacle to rest. Feeling the ground solid under her feet at last Judy fled downstairs, beaming the torch ahead of her, glad to be released from that terrible paralysis of shock and, shamefaced, aware of being gloriously, miraculously alive.

Arnott stood in Ellie's bathroom, the strip lighting dazzling as a laboratory, and took in all the details. The hand basin was stained with grimy tidemarks and grubby towels draped from a wooden rack had syphoned up water from the floor. A reddish romper suit affair, the sort he remembered seeing advertised in his late wife Peg's mail order catalogue, was tossed on a wicker chair, the sleeves dipping onto the lino, sopping wet.

His eyes under shaggy grizzled brows slid back to the girl under the shower. It was a shipwreck, a woman drowned by despair. He shook his head, depressed by the sheer bloody waste of it. And for what? A broken promise? Easter alone? Why put on nice undies, sit yourself under a shower and watch your lifesblood go down the drain? Why so neat and tidy? Judging from the state of the place Ellie Juniper had been no housewife. Fancy putting on them silky knickers an' all! Why bother? It reminded him of his old mum's horror of being run over in dirty drawers. He sighed, nonplussed. But then Arnott never could understand women.

The police arrived like an invasion force, the patrol car screaming to a halt outside. Judy croaked hoarsely into her entryphone and opened the front door on the entry button release. She sat bolt upright in the dark waiting for the boots on the stairs, overcome by the typhoon which had snatched her up, pulling her into Ellie's vortex of misery. The policemen pounded up, seeming to have taken over the whole house. Not that there were many of them, probably only two or three at a guess, but the influx of strange voices and heavy feet overhead substantiated the reality of death in the house.

She shivered, shrinking back into the cushions, staring at the dawn defining the uncurtained window, the outlines of furniture now softly illuminated in a room still strange to her. Judy forced herself to relive the appalling discovery and her thighs began to tremble. She gripped her knees, trying to control rising panic. It was no good. She would leave it all to Arnott. Let him explain everything. The flash of guilty self-congratulation at the joy of just being alive had evaporated as swiftly as it had come.

She sat in the semi-darkness shaking from head to foot like someone who had narrowly escaped a fatal accident. The trouble was the attic rooms still felt like home. It was all too familiar. Ellie's bathroom was *her* bathroom. The girl under the shower could have been Judy Pullen. When she had pulled open the shower door the person sitting in the shallow water wasn't Ellie at all. It was some sort of doppelganger, her own alter-ego.

These alarming reflections were broken by a soft knock on the door. Judith dragged herself up like an exhausted swimmer and shuffled to the door, realising that she was bitterly cold, her feet and hands icy. It was a WPC, a plump-faced girl with a worried expression.

"Can I come in, love? Mr Arnott said we could all do with a nice cup of tea."

Judith stood aside, closing the door behind her, and the policewoman took matters in hand. She guided Judith into the kitchen and gently bullied her to find mugs and sugar while she filled the kettle, her inconsequential chatter filling the void like a warming breath. She eyed Judith's obvious state of shock with concern and snatched a pair of socks from laundry airing on a rack pushed against the radiator, pressing them into Judy's hands as if she was a robot incapable of action unless programmed.

The WPC was naturally curious. Ex-inspectors bracketed with clever young officers from the Serious Fraud Office were a unique cabaret act. She had quizzed the rest of the squad as soon as they spotted the odd set-up but the others were new to this manor like herself. Even so, the fabled accounts of the early retirement of Inspector Arnott the previous summer were folklore in the police canteen, Arnott's pungent one-liners still going the rounds like quotes from a favourite TV show. He had left in a cloud of smoke, determined to make a stand against the Superintendent's poor showing when it came to combatting growing interference from Special Branch on Arnott's final case – and specifically the interference of Inspector Laurence Erskine, a newly-minted smartarse not himself noted for tact. Rumour had it, this pretty sergeant sitting here shivering in front of the unlit gas fire, had later taken up with the Special Branch man Erskine, but then an odd duo like Arnott and Judy Pullen attracted rumours like fluff under the bed.

The WPC introduced herself: Rita Bigglesworth, "Biggles" to everyone at the station, and bustled about fetching things from the bedroom, switching on the gas fire, making herself useful. Judith obediently pulled on the socks, donning the towelling dressing gown which Biggles held out for her. Bundled into all this clothing and cradling a mug of tea, the blood began to flow again and gradually the trembling subsided.

Biggles regarded her charge with all the experience of years on the beat and judged it the right moment to slip back upstairs with a tray for the boys. They had to hang about for the Doc though an incident like this, a regular occurrence at Christmas and Easter, was hardly likely to take long. The sky had brightened, blooming in the dim interior. Biggles had been warned what to expect and had caught sight of the nasty, spreading stain on the bedroom ceiling when she'd gone in search of a dressing gown for the poor kid.

She took a good look at Arnott when she handed round the tea. She'd heard all the stories about that crusty old copper in the police canteen. Created quite a stir he had, put the Chief Super's hat on straight and no mistake. What was *he* doing sleeping in Sergeant Pullen's flat? It wasn't as if the old devil was even anything to look at . . .

Arnott – unaware of this conjecture – was firing on all cylinders, impressing the nervous patrolmen with his control of the situation. They eyed each other with growing amusement, letting the old boy run on, waiting for the official machinery to clank into operation. He was regaling them now with accounts of old cases, mostly from the period when "the bloody villains were real crooks, not the vicious buggers we get nowadays".

Biggles buzzed up and downstairs like a blowfly, checking which tenants were actually in the house, fetching things from the patrol car, keeping the investigation moving. They tried to get Arnott to join his girlfriend in the flat below but he wouldn't budge. Arnott was in his element, cocky as a bantam, strutting round the untidy rooms, throwing himself onto the flimsy sofa, lighting a succession of foul-smelling cigarettes.

"You blokes had a dekko at this pissheap? I took a very careful look round before you lot got here. That's when you really see what's what, nothing's the same once the gang moves in. These sloaney tarts are all the same, believe you me. I was called to a place down by the river, just off Cheyne Walk it was, lovely big flat-share rented by these four smarmy typists. Been turned over, hadn't it? Whole place like a bloody lucky dip, stuff all over the shop, a real bugger's-muddle. Me and Reg Connor try to get these birds to decide what'd gone and lo and behold, one of them, all dolled up and toffee nosed as you please, says nothing of hers'd been nicked. Hearing alarm bells, me and Reg insist on seeing her little nest and by 'eck I could see the poor sod's problem. 'E clearly thought someone 'ad got there first. You've never seen such a shit-hole. They live like pigs, them girls, never even make their beds till the blokes come round. You should have seen the—"

Biggles breezed in, followed by the police surgeon. Doctor Bathgate, being not only a man not at his best before breakfast but one who had seen more than his fill of young women topping themselves in bedsits all over Kensington, gave short shift to Arnott's summary of events. He brushed him aside, disgusted by Arnott's concertinaed trousers which looked as if they had been slept in, unimpressed by the ex-inspector's nefarious reputation.

He examined the body and formally pronounced the woman dead. Arnott greeted this with a snort of derision, having crossed swords with Bathgate before. The doctor addressed himself to the uniformed men, ignoring Arnott, and issued his instructions.

The overcrowded flat felt a lot better when he had gone. The men settled down for another wait, sending Biggles to phone back to the station. Arnott pushed off back to Judith wondering if the silly mare had pulled herself together, gloomily aware that his little brush with excitement had almost run its course.

Two things still bothered him: first, how had the cat got out? And second? The other thing flickered at the corner of his eye like a grain of sand. He worried at it as he put the kettle on the gas stove and made a fresh pot of tea, then thrust it aside, sure he would pounce on this little inconsistency just as soon as he'd stopped jabbing at it. Arnott had experienced this sort of irritation before and knew with absolute certainty he was never wrong about such things.

CHAPTER FOUR

When Inspector Coles heard that Arnott was on the scene he decided to play safe and have a look at Rectory Gardens, himself. Arnott was bad news. Even on the retirement list Arnott spelt trouble. Coles didn't need any loose ends tripping him up at the inquest and even a run-of-the-mill suicide could explode in your face if Arnott was anywhere near the blue touch paper.

He alerted Bernie Allen, the coroner's officer, he was on his way and they arrived within minutes of each other.

Coles made short work of examining the body and moved off into Ellie's living room, seating himself at the monstrous desk to study her papers. He played back the answering machine, irritably jabbing the mechanism backwards and forwards. There were just a few brief messages, one from someone called Sheila who said she was coming up from Bath for a few days and wanted to arrange lunch. Another was a vet's receptionist reminding Miss Juniper that Nelson was due for his boosters. There were also two no-shows: wordless gaps where the caller had declined to leave a message. The last recording was from a Doctor Janssen. Said he'd be calling early on Monday for the typescript. No details. Some work the Juniper woman had brought home? Perhaps she was moonlighting . . .

He started in on the accounts littering the surface of the desk. They all seemed in order. No nasty broadsides from the bank manager, no evidence of mortgage arrears or any pressing debts likely to tip her over the edge. He flicked through the word processor disks and tried them in her neat little portable. It was a natty piece of equipment no bigger than a portable typewriter, weighing only a few pounds and incorporating its own printer. The mini-screen glowed as he ran the stuff through. Nothing but medical guff: some sort of report on a conference in Paris; some notes about an incomprehensible orthopaedic procedure; patients' records – nobody Coles had ever heard of and nothing particularly confidential or embarrassing. Just ordinary people with bad backs. So what's new?

He searched the desk drawers and drew a blank. Apart from the girl's passport, most of the stuff was old correspondence and income tax returns. He tilted back on the stripped pine kitchen chair and rubbed his hands in an effort to warm up. The place was freezing. Also damp. Presumably the flood hadn't helped. He checked the radiators. They were all off. Was this Juniper woman some sort of masochist? Maybe she was saving up for a holiday, anxious not to run up a lot of bills. Coles hadn't removed his raincoat and gave the impression he was only passing through. His long face was sallow and lugubrious, signalling all too clearly that here was a man with more important things to do than poke about in a crappy garret. Coles supposed these places were called studio flats now, estate agents having coined new words for everything these days; even a mousetrap'd be called something flash – "Rodent-Lure" perhaps? Coles was a crossword addict – but just the quick puzzles in the *Evening Standard*. His education had never encompassed the classical references required by the quality press brain teasers.

He rose and slowly circled the room picking up books and CDs from the odd piles spread about the floor, getting the distinct impression that the poor cow had suffered from arrested development. The place looked as if it belonged to a teenager, all primary colours and basic bits of furniture. No pictures except a big pop poster pinned to the back of the flimsy plywood front door. The police surgeon had inferred she had been in her thirties but for a grown woman she must have led a sheltered life.

He took a turn round the bedroom, idly examining the clothes in the wardrobe, searching her handbag. It was stuffed with bits and pieces: house keys, a purse and a tatty map of the Underground, old bus tickets and bits of fluff. He threw it on the bed in disgust. The dressing table displayed a lot of make-up as if she'd been experimenting but his gut feeling about the whole case was a reflection of another suicide he'd investigated before Christmas. A kid in her teens, snowed under with homework, years younger than this one but the vibrations were the same.

Trouble was there was no note. The Coroner put a lot of weight on a suicide note. It tidied things up no end. Women *always* left a note. Had to have the last word, didn't they? Men didn't always oblige. But men generally tanked themselves up before they did it. Dutch courage. Coles brightened. That must be it. The Juniper woman was out of her skull on drugs or booze before she slashed her artery. He'd get the pathologist to check it out. He could do with a few pointers.

The coroner's officer was quietly going about his business, taking notes, unobtrusively picking his way through Ellie's things. Bernie Allen was a conscientious man in his fifties, a bit finicky but astute, missing nothing. He spoke little and privately held Coles in poor regard. The inspector was young and thrusting, ambitious and hot on all the new scientific methods. A dangerous combination in Bernie's view. Gave these young officers tunnel vision – if it didn't show up on a computer screen it didn't exist.

Bernie Allen enjoyed his job. It gave him a degree of independence and authority. The paperwork was no hardship, in fact he took pride in the painstaking assembly of the facts, delving into minutiae on which the Coroner might call.

The funny thing was Bernie Allen was one of the very few officials in the royal borough who actually *liked* Arnott. It probably stemmed from the knowledge that they were both misfits in a profession where rank hermetically sealed each strata from the next. Bernie Allen and Ralph Arnott were paid-up members of the Awkward Squad but each in their own style, Bernie polite but obdurate, Arnott blustering, short-tempered and prejudiced, both men equally determined to root out the truth.

When Arnott's wife had died of cancer the previous spring, Bernie had been one of the few to attend Peg's funeral. He had stood in the rain, silent as a professional mourner, restricting his condolences to a handshake. Bernie had never married and few on the Force were aware that he had shared most of his life with an aunt in Battersea. It was not the sort of lifestyle the blokes in the police canteen could understand and ignorance generally took the form of ribbing. Why would a grown man choose to go home to an old lady? Either he was gay or the old lady was rich. Either way it was a funny way to live. Bernie's aunt had passed away years ago. But he still missed her.

Arnott kept his counsel. As a coroner's officer Bernie Allen and Arnott often had occasion to meet professionally but neither had betrayed their personal friendship. They liked to play their cards close to the chest. The odd poker game they really did play took place at Mortlake after Peg had gone. That was about the size of it. Sometimes a few beers in The Frigate to finish the evening off but no fripperies like Christmas cards or such.

Leaving Bernie to sift through the dressing table in the bedroom, Inspector Coles decided it was time to interview Pullen. A serving member of the Force who was also an intimate of the decedent was an ideal witness. She should be able to throw some light on things. Might even agree to identify the body. This Sergeant Pullen he'd heard so much about could trot upstairs in two ticks and one more formality would be out of the way. No need to scour the country for a grieving relative. Coles dreaded grieving relatives, they took up too much police time. It would also cut his visits to the mortuary to a minimum. His abhorrence was not for reasons of delicacy. The charnel house was so damned unhygienic. He would rather check out an abattoir where at least the dead were clean and disease-free.

He had a quiet word with Biggles and asked one of the men to secure the door or, at least, nail back the hinges and keep the draught out. Biggles followed the inspector down to Judith's flat and stood quietly in the background as he went through the preliminaries. Coles was in luck. Arnott had commandeered Judy's bathroom and was in the process of sprucing himself up, purloining one of the disposable razors she used to shave her legs.

Judith hadn't moved for ages. She sat on the sofa, half dazed with disbelief, her mind churning. Shouldn't she have realised the state Ellie was in when she took Nelson back upstairs? If she had insisted Ellie joined them last night would the disaster have been averted? If. If. If. The roulette wheel spun again and again. But the numbers were always the same.

Coles became impatient with Judith's lack of response and Biggles intervened, urging her to help the inspector wrap up the case. Then they could *all* go home, he privately added. She was asked again to return upstairs and answer a few questions. Would she look around? See if anything struck her? Judith stared blankly at him like someone sleepwalking, trying to make sense of it all.

Arnott emerged, interrupting Coles's rephrased interrogation, and insisted on confirming the facts of the discovery himself. Coles thrust his hands in his raincoat pockets and tried to remain calm. Arnott was looking surprisingly refreshed, by no means hungover and smelling like roses. He had discarded the loopy woollen cardigan and the shirt underneath was clean as a whistle. He had found one of Laurence's rowing club ties in the pocket of a pair of chinos folded up in the airing cupboard and even the creased trousers had smoothed out.

"Look here, Coles, give her a break, will you? You can see she's upset. Wouldn't you be? Come and look at the bloody mess that silly cow upstairs made of Pullen's bedroom ceiling. Only just finished painting it, she 'ad. No wonder the poor lass is in shock."

Biggles stifled a gurgle of laughter and patted Judy's hand, unfamiliar with Arnott's labyrinthine methods. Coles gave up and followed him into the bedroom and they stared up at the ceiling. In daylight it was a nightmare. The plaster was now engorged, bowed like the belly of a drowned corpse which has been long adrift. The patch on the ceiling was not particularly bloody, more as if rusty water had burst from a tank in the loft. The water had dripped onto the bed forming an obscene reddish stain, unnerving even to hardened observers like Coles and Arnott.

Judith silently moved in behind them and stared up at the dangling light flex emerging from the swollen plaster. She coughed, then suddenly bolted. They could hear her retching in the bathroom, dry ugly sounds like a child with a bilious attack. Biggles anxiously peered at her through the doorway, glancing apologetically at Coles as if it was all her fault. Arnott's morning face had clouded over. The two men retreated into the living room and stood awkwardly by the window staring down at the traffic coming to life at last in Rectory Gardens.

There was a rap on the door. Coles hurried to open it and impatiently nodded at the constable on the landing.

"A gentleman's waiting in the hall. He rang the bell for the flat upstairs and Sergeant King spoke to him on the entryphone and went down. A Doctor Janssen. Says the Juniper woman's expecting him. Has some typing for him he said. The sergeant told him to wait. Thought you'd want to break the news yourself, sir." He passed over a business card and, reading the address, Coles brightened.

Coles was glad to postpone the complications of trying to interview Judith Pullen. If this doctor had employed the dead girl he might get some sensible answers at last. The man could give a medical opinion of Juniper's state of mind at least. Could even identify the body and they would all be spared any tears or hysterics. A nice clean-up all round. Bugger the suicide note.

"Get him upstairs," he snapped and beat a retreat.

Coles greeted Doctor Janssen on the top landing, urging him inside before briefly introducing himself, making no comment on the smashed door frame or the shambolic state of the Juniper pad. For all he knew it always looked like this. He fingered the man's business card, studying the expensive engraving and, without raising his head, remarked, "Funny time to call on a secretary early on a Bank Holiday, wouldn't you say? Lucky to find these girls out of bed this hour in my experience." He chuckled, testing the man's puzzled reaction. Coles was a firm believer in catching a witness on the hop, even fancy doctors from Harley Street. The man seemed perplexed but not unduly worried.

"Is there a problem, Inspector?"

The accent was mid-Atlantic, but far from obvious, perhaps a Canadian who had practised in London for some time; younger than Coles's idea of a successful consultant but the fact that he was not English might have some bearing on it. Talk about a smooth manner! Coles, in fact, was never ill and gleaned all his preconceptions of medical men from television, mostly American soaps. He repeated his original question without enlightening Janssen about the suicide.

31

"I've been on call over Easter. I left a message for Ellie on her answerphone saying I would call this morning. She's expecting me – a typed report – er – some notes –" The words faded. "There's been an accident?"

Coles explained the way matters stood, making the death of the man's secretary sound an everyday occurrence, a matter with which men of their calling were obviously familiar.

Doctor Janssen was taken aback by this bald statement but imagined it was all part of the Englishman's stiff upper lip routine. He answered Coles's questions unhesitatingly, adding his own observations about Ellie's health. "She hasn't been at all well in recent months. Had to take days off. But I was reluctant to let her go because she tried so hard to make up for lost time. Worked at home when she could and was always more than happy to fit in with emergencies at holiday times and so on. Doctors are like policemen, Inspector, always on duty. We make rotten employers." He smiled.

"What was wrong with her?"

"Ellie wasn't my patient. My colleague and I were somewhat puzzled but the girl was rather young for her age and I got the impression she had been somewhat sheltered by a domineering parent. Mrs Quick – our senior receptionist – thought it was probably some feminine ailment Ellie was too shy to mention. Her absences were never more than an afternoon off, a day or two at the most. I suggest you consult her NHS doctor."

"Were there any other relatives, apart from this parent you mention?"

"I couldn't say. We got the impression there was only Ellie and her mother and the mother died a few months ago. My wife and I had become very fond of the girl, Inspector, and after Mrs Juniper died Ellie seemed to have few ties in London. Helen will be most upset to hear all this."

The man was frank and answered Coles's enquiries in a clipped businesslike manner, cooperative in every way. He explained that he was off duty for the rest of the week and on his way to join his wife in the country. He wore a sports jacket with a white T-shirt under a denim shirt and his thick hair, greying at the temples, was cut *en brosse* as the French say. He smelt of very expensive soap, the sort one can only buy in Jermyn Street. On closer examination Coles guessed the man was probably about forty or forty-five but muscular and obviously kept himself in good shape. Probably one of those jogging freaks Coles sourly concluded, patting the incipient beer gut which strained his shirt buttons.

He persuaded Janssen to formally identify the body, not knowing where his next reliable witness would spring from. Pity Judy Pullen turned out to be such a wet nelly. Just as well the Super got rid of her. People like that should never join the Force. Fancy fainting at a splash of blood on the ceiling? At least a doctor could take viewing the corpse in his stride without throwing up.

Coles led Janssen to the bathroom and flung open the door, nearly catapulting Bernie Allen into the shower cubicle.

"Sorry, mate. Didn't know you were still here."

Coles propelled Janssen forward, his face setting in grim lines as he confronted the macabre reality of the corpse stiffening under the shower. Bernie was anxious to instruct the mortuary van and patiently listened to the inspector's hushed explanation of the doctor's presence. Bernie reluctantly agreed, his lizard eyes flickering over the tall man blocking the doorway, his immaculate weekend attire putting the two officers sartorially in the shade without a shadow of a doubt.

Doctor Janssen played his part with despatch, formally identifying Elinor Juniper while Bernie totted up more details for the Coroner.

As soon as Janssen departed, Coles drove back to the station leaving his sergeant to interview any tenants who innocently flew back to the nest. The Spanish waiter had somehow slipped in unnoticed but had, on holy oath, been working till four and spent the rest of the night with the Domino barman. Dave Barnes put in an appearance about ten o'clock, his eyes totally obscured by RayBans. He accepted the news stoically, staring into the attic rooms which already looked anonymous like the stage-set for a '60s kitchen sink drama. He insisted on repairing the door himself, returning with his toolbox and planing off the split door jamb. He fixed it up like a real chippie. In fact, the door shut better than before. He also called up an electrician to check Judith's wiring. Nobody thought to thank him. Bernie Allen spoke to the tenants but gave up all effort to wring any

33

information from the Osimas. It really did seem that Sergeant Pullen had been the last person to speak to the deceased.

Arnott turned up like a bad penny, of course, but got no change out of Bernie, a stickler for the rules, Arnott being well aware his old crony was not at liberty to discuss matters. The only concession he wrung out of Bernie was a promise to run a detailed check over the dead girl's personal effects and trace one important item. The irritating inconsistency had worked itself to the surface and when he asked Bernie to be *absolutely* sure, he knew there would be no slip-ups. Bernie sighed, promised to let Arnott know, and made a painstaking note in his book. Yet one more detail to follow up. It was agreed between them by some sort of osmosis that, whether they liked it or not, Coles could not be faulted. Bernie conducted a sympathetic interview with Judith and left her feeling considerably relieved, as if she had been in the confessional box and was now absolved of any lingering guilt.

Bernie Allen was very good at his job. Even Coles would admit that. Elinor Juniper had died by her own hand. The flat had been secure, the mysterious visitor she claimed was expected had never arrived – if he had existed at all – and unless the post-mortem showed anything different, the Juniper case was as good as interred.

Arnott went back to Judy's flat and made a pile of toast, taking a chance on the electricity supply fusing. He tried to tempt her to eat, having an almost religious faith in the efficacy of food in the combat of misery. Judith mooned about sipping tea, wishing Arnott would go home, trying to shut her ears to the proliferating details of the investigation he insisted on sharing with her.

Finally exasperated, she threw him out, locking the door behind him, leaning against it with her face in her hands, feeling nausea rise again in her throat. She ought to get out, get right away from this house. But the two people she trusted most were both abroad, Laurence in Washington and Pixie still jazzing around Paris. She couldn't face sharing her trauma with anyone else, confessing the terrifying confusion that the body in the shower was in some strange way her own, that she had never moved out of the attic rooms.

Scraping sounds of feet on the stairs brought her heart in her mouth, the noise inevitably followed by a chorus of shouted advice as the mortuary men stumbled back down the steep attic stairs, negotiating the narrow landing with muttered oaths.

Ellie Juniper was leaving Rectory Gardens for the last time.

CHAPTER FIVE

Sleeping badly the previous night, combined with the traumatic early start, left Judith displaying all the classic symptoms of jet lag. It was 11.30 a.m. and she remained seriously under par.

However, shunting Arnott upstairs to join the continuing police presence was a move in the right direction, and she lay on the sofa listening to the drone of their voices from the flat above, the voices occasionally interrupted by the scrape and bump of mysterious furniture moving. What were they up to?

She considered going back to bed but the thought of lying under the gruesome, swollen ceiling made her shiver. After a further ten minutes shuffling her options, it seemed best to bite the bullet and strip the bed. Keeping her eyes strictly on the job in hand, she hurriedly bundled all the wet bedding into plastic sacks, grabbed some clothing from the wardrobe and slammed the door on the entire mess. Down in the basement area she stuffed everything in a dustbin, too shellshocked even to consider passing the stained sheets through a washing machine. Back upstairs, she opened all the windows and vacuumed the entire flat. After all this frantic activity, apart from a thudding head, she felt a lot better.

The living room was now bearable, all evidence of Arnott and Coles's temporary incursion flushed out and all the glasses and dirty mugs washed and tidied away. What next? There was still almost the whole of a bank holiday Monday stretching ahead. What a waste! She tried Pixie's number on the faint off chance she had flown home early but was greeted by the answerphone.

Turning on the radio, Judy tuned in to some musical slosh which only went to show how comforting intellectual junk food can be in a crisis. She peered into the fridge and surfaced with half a bottle of white wine left over from the Gus Fielding Hour and, cradling the radio and one of her very special hand-blown glasses normally reserved for her mother's rare visits, took herself and the Sancerre into the spare room.

Pixie's sofabed was surprisingly cosy. She settled down with her home comforts and was asleep even before she had refilled the glass, finding herself back in familiar territory: the dark bottomless pit of her nightmare. Fortunately, this time, the troglodytes had completed their shift and were presumably tucked up in their troggy bunkbeds. It was quite disappointing. She could have done with some company. Anything was better than lying sleepless, remembering Arnott poking away at the sanguineous plaster of her bedroom ceiling.

Judith must have dozed for hours. She woke refreshed and silenced the radio. The sounds from Ellie's flat had muted to a dull conversational hum and she guessed the police had covered all the humdrum procedure following a suicide. A wave of sadness swept over her as she reconsidered the ghastliness of it all. In an effort to escape, she decided to get some fresh air and tossing a towel and swimsuit into a duffel bag, she bolted.

Noiselessly letting herself out of the flat, Judy ran down to her Volkswagen parked at the kerb and accelerated away. There was no sign of Arnott's van and more residents' cars had homed in on Rectory Gardens. For March the sun was already quite brazen, rehearsing for June, and a breeze tossed tiny white clouds back and forth like a promotional ad for Wimbledon week. She found a parking slot in Chelsea Manor Street and slipped into the public baths where at least a shower held no nightmares for her. The pool was uncrowded and she swam up and down, relaxing in the warm turquoise water, deliberately emptying her mind. It was an old-fashioned building and a favourite bolt-hole in times of stress. Anonymous and mentally cleansing, the interior echoed only with children's voices and water sloshed about only in fun.

Afterwards she rang Pixie's number again but there was no reply. The Kings Road was thronging with shoppers, mostly young fashion freaks roaming in packs, exploring the leather shops and boutiques. Judy made a beeline for an Italian café which never seemed to close, serving pasta and omelettes round the clock. Even in winter its pavement tables attracted customers intent on watching the passing show and, inside, the dimness was accentuated by discreet booths where lovers whispered, dawdling over cappuccinos.

Judy suddenly felt ravenous and ordered pizza and salad. An elderly lady slipped into one of the booths, a chihuahua tucked inside her coat. The little dog peered out between the woollen folds, its ears erect, making no sound, the old woman clasping it to her fleshless bosom for warmth and comfort. Judith smiled, sipping her coffee, and compared the tiny animal with the gargantuan proportions of the late Mrs Juniper's cat. Poor Nelson, what would become of him now? Judy's sister despised the national veneration of dogs and cats and laughingly considered it proven that "English children are animal substitutes. For people with leases which don't permit pets, you know".

Judy glanced at her watch, unwilling to return to Rectory Gardens while the police were still sifting the attic rooms. It was now late afternoon and the shoppers were dispersing. She left the café and crossed the road to gaze at the shop windows, startled to discover Ellie's new pine furniture on sale at knock-down prices. Judith stared at the uncluttered Scandinavian designs and could see the appeal of it to a girl who had spent all her life in that stultifying atmosphere, hemmed in by her mother's antiques, all heavy pieces and likely to endure forever. But why had Ellie chosen to take the pedestal desk?

Judith struggled with the puzzle, all too well aware that she had lived under the Junipers' roof for more than two years and barely knew them. And now both women were dead. In an attempt to nullify the regret threatening to re-establish itself, she carefully considered all possible reasons why Ellie should save this one enormous item of furniture and abandon the rest – including some pretty Regency pieces – to the Osima family? To anyone who knew Ellie, the answer was obvious and Judy got round to it eventually. Ellie was chronically untidy and, at a guess, Mrs J. had been a hoarder of every scrap of paper, every bill and receipt, every family document since the Commander, bless his soul, had stepped ashore from his intrepid exploits off the Dardenelles. The monstrous heirloom was a portable muniment room. Ellie harboured no sentimental attachment to the bloody thing, she was just too idle to face sorting out all that paperwork. Whatever the inconvenience and despite a laudable desire to feather her nest in her own style, it was so much simpler for Ellie to move the damned desk upstairs than comb through all those bottomless drawers.

Judy slipped into a cinema and caught the early evening performance. It was a French film and not entirely comprehensible, the plot pivoting on a curious Gallic fixation about food which the director had mirrored in the hero's pornographic fancies – all very difficult to follow even with subtitles. However, the mental gymnastics kept Judy's anxieties at bay and, dizzy with conjecture, she emerged onto the street, surprised by the darkness, relieved to discover she had managed to dispose of the dregs of the most horrible Easter weekend of her whole life.

In fact, the day was not entirely over. As she was parking her car, Gus Fielding's ancient MG drew into a space. He waved and Judith waited, shivering, under the lamplight. He caught up and cheerfully commented on his swift journey back to London, falling into step beside her.

"You haven't heard then?"

"Heard what? I took off to Birmingham after I left you and Arnott last night. Couldn't face that tin of tomatoes after all."

"Ellie killed herself."

He stumbled, catching her arm. She shrugged him off and continued walking, her face set.

"Why the hell—?" he muttered, hurrying along beside her.

"I can't bear to talk about it! I found her – the police may still be in the house." Judith took a deep breath. "Ellie cut her throat."

He didn't reply and gently pushing her aside, inserted his key in the front door. She hurried in. The hall smelt of disinfectant.

"Come up for a drink," he insisted. "You look terrible,

Judith. We don't have to discuss it, of course we don't. You poor thing." He touched her arm and stood on the first floor landing barring her way. "It must have been horrible for you finding her like that."

"I d-don't think—" she murmured, straining to catch any sounds from upstairs.

"Tell you what. Why don't we push off right now? Get your coat and we'll take a walk. I'll bore you stiff showing you all the wonders in stonework you've passed like a blind beggar a million times. Then we'll go to a little fish restaurant I know. Nothing fancy. My treat. After a plate of scampi and chips you'll sleep like a baby."

What was it about men and food? It flashed through her mind that the underlying meaning of that French film was perhaps not so obscure after all.

"You won't want me to go all over it again? Ellie's suicide, I mean? I've really had it up to here, Gus, if you must know . . ." His offer was tempting; one of the sets of boots still banging about upstairs might even be Arnott's.

"Scout's honour."

"OK. Give me five minutes." Judith disappeared upstairs for a topcoat.

They departed like truants, closing the heavy front door without a sound. Dave was rehearsing in the basement, his uncurtained window shining through the area railings, the mournful sound of his saxophone dismal as a dirge.

Gus stepped out, setting a cracking pace, and Judy found herself subjected to a seamless commentary on every granite step and marble porch they passed. His enthusiasm was like a river in spate, carrying her along, allowing her mind no mossy resting place where recollections might re-form. He drowned her in a flood of references to igneous rocks, volcanic ashfall and travertine. The names of fossils trapped in the carboniferous limestone cropped up in Gus's conversation like public figures too well known to require any introduction. Brachiopods, zaphrentis, bryozoan fenestella, crinoids. Words tripped off his tongue without a stutter, his unstoppable monologue, once hitched to his own special subject, was untrammelled by the man's natural shyness, a vulnerability which Judy – and probably a lot of other women besides – found irresistible.

40

He dragged her to the Russian Church, enthusing about weathering features on something Judy thought he called serpents' tits. They were already jogging towards the Albert Memorial which Gus revered as the holy grail, "a positive cornucopia of geological marvels" he promised her. Judith was relieved to see it was shrouded in scaffolding, her mind already reeling with a timescale presented as if four hundred and sixty million years were but a breath.

She pattered along beside him saying little and understanding less but grateful for the sheer volume of information sweeping them along. It was like the contemplation of the stars, light years away, unimaginably distant, reducing the human predicament to a grain of sand. Who was Judy Pullen to question the irrefutable truth of the Ordovician period?

She started to giggle which brought him up short. Gus laughed and flung his arm around her shoulder, recognising that, yet again, he had overdone it, been carried along like a blissful skier unaware of the avalanche stirring under his feet. They picked up a taxi in Kensington Gore and he attempted to salvage his standing with this pretty copper with a fish and chip supper.

In her own mind, Judy later attempted to justify her alacrity to savour the Fielding experience – and the pleasures of a personal survey of The Geologist In His Own Habitat – by reason of the threat of falling plaster hanging over her own bed.

They talked about Ellie, of course. Cradled by the dark, reliving the terrible sequence of events seemed less painful. Gus said nothing, never once attempting to rationalise Judy's neurotic illusion of witnessing her own death under the shower. Sharing this crazy transposition of images did, in fact, help, and in the cold light of dawn, the horrid fixation had slipped aside like something glimpsed at the corner of one's eye. It was fading, almost gone.

Forced to brave her own bedroom to fetch a clean blouse from the chest of drawers before she could get dressed for work, Judith impulsively emptied everything into a couple of suitcases and resolved to move into the spare room and lock the door on the bloodstained ceiling for ever.

She'd had it with Rectory Gardens. She would move in with Pixie if necessary.

CHAPTER SIX

Judith dressed for work, emerging from her flat only to run full tilt into Mavis Clements. Mavis carried a tray, her capable hands steadying an empty coffee pot and a plate scattered with the remains of a sausage roll. Her eyes lit up with curiosity.

"I've just been up to take a little something to that policeman up there. They've left him in that freezing attic all on his own, sifting through poor Ellie's papers. There's only a little electric fire – the young man's positively numb with the cold. Is it true you found the body . . . ?"

Judy edged to the stairs anxious to get away, her head nodding like one of those ridiculous toy dogs people put on the back shelf of cars.

"Mind you, I'm not surprised, are you?" Mavis's avid glance skimmed Judith's mini skirted suit, missing nothing. She darted forward, clasping Judy's arm in a clear invitation to confide.

"Oh – er – I really didn't know Ellie very well, so there's nothing – you must excuse me, Mavis. I shall be late for work."

"My goodness, wasn't she a dark horse?" Mavis was not to be so easily shaken off and rooted herself squarely at the top of the staircase. "Once her dear mother passed away, that girl really came out of the closet as they say. Discos, clubbing, out all hours."

"Ellie wasn't a teenager, Mavis."

"Oh, I'm not saying Ellie sowing her wild oats was a bad thing at her age. Not that it's all that recent. A dark horse as I said before. You ask Dave. And it was Ellie who brought that Spanish waiter here you know. Right after Flavia's funeral. Oh no, my dear, Ellie was always a secretive little thing, by no means the young lady her mother brought her up to be.

42

Mind you, I thought she was settling down at last. She told me she was getting married."

Judith paused, caught on Mavis's hook.

"Really? Are you sure? She'd just spent all that money fitting out the flat, setting herself up with new furniture and stuff."

"Well, I can only repeat what Ellie told me only last week. Said she would be living abroad. I was quite shaken, I don't mind telling you. Did she intend selling up, do you think?"

"I must fly, Mavis, or I'll miss my—"

"Flavia used to complain about Ellie's little fantasies. But we'll never know now, shall we?"

"Perhaps there *was* someone. She was expecting a man that night."

Judith manoeuvred herself to the top step and hurried down, Mavis firmly stuck to her heels.

Mavis Clements had lived the longest in Rectory Gardens apart from the Junipers, of course, her occupancy of the first floor front giving her considerable standing in the tenants' league table. Hers was one of the larger flats with an enviable sunny window overlooking the street. From her vantage point Mavis missed nothing. Easter spent with her niece in Putney would rankle for years to come. Fancy, being away the very weekend dramatic events overtook the Juniper house! It was really *too* frustrating.

Her job in the library of the Royal Geographical Society gave her a sense of power, her dragnet approach to tardy returns causing palpitations to the academics who relied on her goodwill. Also, from Rectory Gardens she could walk to work in ten minutes, a great advantage now that public transport was so unreliable and an added bonus when she helped out at lecture evenings. Mavis Clements was a kind-hearted soul who enjoyed her work and had, until this tragedy, felt herself double blessed to live under the roof of real gentlefolk like the Junipers.

Judith's flight was suddenly impeded by the emergence of Nelson from behind the oak chest which occupied a considerable amount of space under a stained glass window at the turn of the staircase. Mrs Juniper had placed brass candlesticks and a huge copper urn filled with dried grasses on

43

the chest and the disposition of these dusty furnishings always struck Judith as being some sort of altar to which tenants must genuflect on their way out.

Judy laughed. "Ah, Nelson, you old rogue. Where *have* you been?"

"He scratched at my door last night after I'd gone to bed. Poor thing was ravenous. In all the excitement no-one seems to have given a thought to Nelson."

"He's been AWOL, Mavis. Nobody's caught sight of him since all this happened."

"I shall adopt him. Flavia would have wished that. Ellie never really cared for the creature, you know. She pretended to love cats but once her mama had passed on, Nelson had to scrounge where he could, poor mite."

The enormous feline wound itself between their legs, purring like a generator and looking far from undernourished.

"I really must go, Mavis. The trains are always packed out after a bank holiday and I'm late already."

"Won't you come in for a light supper after work, my dear? It would be lovely to have a girls-only evening and I hardly ever see you these days."

Judith drew back, stuttering her excuses. Spending the evening being grilled about Ellie Juniper would be the last straw. It flashed through her mind that Gus Fielding might have something planned . . . She found herself flushing under Mavis's scrutiny and wondered if there might be a place for the nosy librarian in the Special Branch with Laurence Erskine. The woman could pull a mole from any security system with one hand tied behind her back. She was wasted on the geographers and their missing library books.

"Actually, Mavis, I'm not sure if I shall be back this evening. My bedroom's in a dreadful state. I shall probably move in with my sister for a bit."

"But you can't! You can't possibly do that!" The older woman was stricken, grasping Judy's arm like a swimmer caught in a rip tide. "Mr Fielding's gone back to Birmingham – I saw his car leave before eight – and if *you* leave too that means I shall be left here alone with that alcoholic caretaker and the Spaniard. He's sex mad, you know, Judith. Those Mediterranean types are all the same. I'm warning you, Mikki

Ferrero is running some sort of immoral ring of some kind; you take my word for it. Oh no, Judith, you can't possibly abandon me to all these men."

"There's Mrs Osima."

"Good gracious, you can't count Mrs Osima. I've never heard her pass a single intelligible word and as for that husband of hers—!" Mavis's plump shoulders rose eloquently under her tweed jacket and she snatched up Nelson as if to protect herself.

Judith stood on the landing, confused by Mavis's abrupt disintegration and the news that Gus had again slipped away without a word.

"Are you sure, Mavis?"

"Sure what?"

"Has Gus Fielding really gone home?"

"Oh yes. He asked me to cancel his milk. I passed him on the landing when I was taking the tray up to that constable. But I know what you mean, Judith. Mr Fielding's the only gentleman left in this house. Flavia got Dave Barnes here by special arrangement and I do see that having a man like that on the premises to look after little odd jobs about the house is a blessing. But, really, he's hardly our sort, is he? And as for that sex-fiend from the Costa Brava, Flavia would never have entertained him as a tenant for an instant. I presume Ellie met him at one of those clubs she used to go to."

Mavis pleaded with Judith to stay, terrified that the Rectory Gardens ark she had carved out for herself was about to be inundated by yet more disasters.

"All right. I've got to pack in any case. I'll think about it. You were lucky to be away, Mavis. I can't tell you what a nightmare it's been here."

"Please stay, Judith. There's no knowing how long the policeman will be on duty upstairs. I'd feel so much safer with you in the house."

Judith broke away, anxious to reach the relative sanity of her office, perplexed by her own preoccupation with a bearded geologist who had all the attributes of a first-class Houdini. Here one minute, gone the next.

When she got to work she found a message from Arnott waiting for her. Mary Sumner, who shared her office, was all concern, having been filled in by Arnott about the tragedy at Rectory Gardens over Easter. Judith felt herself growing increasingly irritable, hemmed about by sensation seekers all suffering from the delusion that the death of Elinor Juniper was something she would be eager to discuss. She let Arnott stew and did not ring the Mortlake number until three o'clock.

"Took your time, didn't you, Pullen?"

His response did nothing to smooth her ruffled feathers.

"I've got a job to do, Arnott, even if you haven't," she snapped. This was below the belt and she could have bitten off her tongue as soon as she'd said it. Arnott was touchy about his early retirement, all too well aware that he was floundering about, marking time. Still, at least you knew exactly where you were with the old has-been; there were no grey areas and never any misunderstandings, his abrasive protectiveness being oddly comforting. He cared about her even if he'd choke before admitting it. Arnott made no bones about listing Judy's shortcomings but his insensitivity was a disguise, his gruff abuse the reaction of a battle-scarred bull terrier defending his own.

"Get off that high horse of yours, Pullen, and listen for a change. I've been back to that place of yours and that fluffy-faced bastard they've put on the filing wouldn't let me over the bloody doorstep. One of Coles's poncey boys seems to think shuffling through the corpse's belongings makes him Sherlock bleeding Holmes."

"Whatever did you go back for, Arnott? There's no mystery. Ellie just ran out of hope. Someone let her down, I think. Miss Clements thinks she had a fiancé in tow."

"Fat chance! I just want to get things straight. You'll have to speak out at the inquest, missy. No point in putting yourself up there to be shot at not knowing the facts. I asked the Boy Wonder if Coles had found a suicide note."

"Any joy?"

"Not a whisper. But I collared Bernie Allen later. We had a jar in The Queen's Head at dinner time. Wouldn't say nowt about the Juniper woman except he's turned up a next-of-kin. A cousin. Bloke called Basil Meek. Works as a steward on a cruise ship. Still sailing round the palm trees by all accounts. They're trying to get him flown back."

"No-one else? No fiancé?"

"No billets-doux and no pictures of any boyfriend. That much Bernie did admit. Strikes me the poor lass was having your Miss Marple on."

"Miss Clements, Arnott. Mavis Clements. I'm still bothered about those footsteps going up to Ellie's flat that night. I told the coroner's officer about it but no-one takes me seriously. It was when Gus Fielding was with us. I'd gone to the bathroom to get another bottle and I'm sure I heard someone on the stairs."

"Could have been her coming down. Hard to tell either way. Still, you might be right. P'raps she was on her way back up after nipping out to post a letter to her cousin – or that so-called fiancé of hers. Suicide note's sure to turn up later. Suicides always seem to think they owe somebody an explanation. Beats me. Still, it bears thinking about, Pullen. Bernie's got his work cut out trying to square it all up. The Juniper female seemed to be pretty flush by all accounts and a house full of lodgers bringing in enough rent to keep her in clover even if she got the push from that typing job. Got a funny feeling about that flat of hers though. The place was a like a bloody tomb. Wasn't that cold when you rented it, was it, Pullen?"

"Ellie had turned the radiators off. I didn't know her that well, Arnott. Maybe she had a mean streak and didn't want to waste money on fuel bills. Perhaps she thought being out at work all day and away at weekends it wasn't worth running the central heating."

"Where did she go weekends?"

"Haven't a clue. Dave told me she wasn't here much. Look here, Arnott, I'd give it a rest if I were you. If I hear anything new I'll call you. I *must* go, I'm due at a meeting."

"Well, here's something to chew over, Miss High and Mighty. When your skinflint mate Juniper cut her throat under the shower why didn't she run the hot tap? Was that shower of yours on some sort of geyser? A time switch? I soaked my jumper turning the water off and you could have floated ice cubes in it. If you're topping yourself, you'd have to be a real scrooge to spend your last half-hour saving on the gas bill."

Even to a Yorkshireman, parsimony on that scale took a lot of swallowing. He slammed down the receiver, pleased as Punch to give the cocky madam something to think about.

Judith was still thinking about it when the phone rang again. It was Veronica Messop, a solicitor friend she had once shared a flat with in Notting Hill Gate.

"Hi, Veronica! Surprise, surprise. Long time, no see. Who gave you my new office number?"

"Dave Barnes, the caretaker bloke at Rectory Gardens. I was round there this morning trying to gain access to Ellie Juniper's flat but he didn't have a key."

"Oh? Flat hunting? Bit quick off the mark, aren't you? The previous tenant only died five minutes ago," she said with a brittle laugh.

"None of your sarkiness, Judith. It was strictly business. Didn't you know I handled Flavia Juniper's estate? You were the one who recommended me to Ellie, remember."

"Ah, yes. It had completely gone out of my mind. Every-thing OK, wasn't it? Ellie *did* settle up with you before she slit her throat, I hope?"

The bitter tone was lost on Veronica Messop, a hefty girl never guilty of subtlety.

"On the nail. The old lady died intestate and having unscrambled it all for the daughter I nagged Ellie to put her own house in order. Make a will. Saves a lot of hassle. Be prepared and all that."

"I didn't know you and Ellie Juniper were girl guides, Veronica."

The sniff at the other end of the line was unamused. Jokes were obviously banned in business hours. Judy smiled, recall-ing the long-past frolics of the Notting Hill parties. "Well, what can I do for you, Ms Messop?" she added, a no-nonsense edge to her voice.

"It's this business of Ellie's next-of-kin. Basil Meek. Did you ever meet him at Rectory Gardens, Judith?"

"Never even heard of the man till this afternoon. A relation of Ellie's you say?"

"First cousin. There was nothing for him from Mrs Juniper, of course. Not that he sounded the sort of nephew to be proud of from what I heard. But he was kind to her after her mother died and I think she felt he'd had a bad press. She made him sole beneficiary."

"Lucky Basil."

"Quite! Having tidied things up only a few months ago, everything was left in apple pie order and this time round Mr Meek's struck lucky. No legal snags of any sort."

"When is he arriving?"

"That's the problem. He's not. He's asked me to go ahead with the funeral, no expense spared."

"Two Junipers down and he wins the jackpot. It could all have been left to Nelson."

"Nelson? Nelson who?" Veronica squawked, suddenly terribly afraid Judy knew something she didn't.

"Never mind. Just kidding. Surely it wouldn't put Basil Meek out, all things considered, to attend to the interment himself. A small price, I would have thought."

"Joining the Met was a rotten career move of yours, Judith. You used to be such a nice, sympathetic girl."

Judy recognised a superior stance all too often taken up by solicitors in their dealings with the police. Anyone would think they were on different sides. Perhaps, in Veronica Messop's book, they were.

"Look, Veronica, this business of Ellie's suicide may be just another legal chore to you but I found the body. And if you must know, it's knocked me sideways. Also my new flat's ruined. I've got to find somewhere else to live and—"

Veronica hastened to interrupt, fearing her mission doomed to failure despite appeals to Judy's good nature or even a rocky reliance on a personal friendship, which even in the Notting Hill days was more a matter of convenience. "Yes, of course. Absolutely appalling for you! Dave told me. It's very difficult to talk on the phone, Judith. Can't we meet for lunch? How about Wednesday the seventeenth? The inquest will be over by then and we can talk it over."

"Talk what over?"

"You very kindly helped Ellie organise her mother's funeral. You know the form. As Basil Meek can't fly back in time, he's

49

instructed me to ask Ellie's best friend to do the honours and I thought you might—"

"Best friend!" Judith exploded. Across the office Mary Summer raised her eyebrows, wondering if this was yet another contretemps connected with Judy's handsome Special Branch guy, Erskine. The man was generally at the root of Judy's rare bouts of temper. Judith turned aside and lowered her voice to a whisper.

"Deal me out, Veronica Messop, you scheming little summons server," she hissed. "And if Dave Barnes thinks I'm—"

"Please, Judith! It's all very simple. I've already arranged for the Barnes man to redecorate your *entire flat* if necessary. Basil Meek is even willing to pay for you to stay in a hotel while it's being painted. Hear me out. Lunch on the seventeenth? Bibendum, one o'clock?"

In her mind's eye Judith saw the bloodstained ceiling and mentally calculated the pros and cons of Veronica's proposal. It was Bibendum that swung it. There was about as much chance of Gus Fielding – or even Laurence – coming across with an offer like that as – well – as Gus's Ordovician Period rolling round for a second spin.

"OK Veronica. But no promises. You did say Bibendum, didn't you?"

CHAPTER SEVEN

Arnott went off to Rye to work on his boat. Getting the cold shoulder from Bernie Allen was a hard pill to swallow but he held no grudges. The coroner's officer had his job to do and even Arnott could see the man's point of view when it came to compiling evidence. Sudden death was to Arnott like the sound of distant cannonfire to an old war horse, and, for a moment there, he had scented blood. He shrugged off his disappointment, but unanswered questions still lodged awkwardly in his brain, fuelling his frustration.

From Arnott's point of view he was in a no-win situation, boxed in on all sides. Coles naturally wanted shot of him and Bernie Allen was put on the spot by his persistent queries about the Juniper case. Even Pullen seemed anxious to put the whole thing out of mind and was talking about doing a runner, taking herself off to Hampstead to stay with that sister of hers at least until the bedroom ceiling was repaired.

Judith threw herself into her work and, as luck would have it, found herself assigned to a four-man investigative team in Maidstone. The squad had been working on the case for months, painstakingly sifting balance sheets and tracing the movements of a former county councillor turned property developer who, now bankrupt, was spitefully pulling the whole house of cards about his ears, involving an ever-widening ring of fellow-travellers. As the new girl on the team, Judith had a lot of catching up to do and was well aware that her inexperience was a bone of contention. She booked into a small hotel on the other side of town, not wishing to become embroiled in their nightly piss-ups.

At the weekend she drove over to Ashford, spending a couple of days with her mother and warning her that the inquest on Elinor Juniper might get into the national press.

51

Not that it was at all likely. Ellie was a very small item in media terms and hardly newsworthy beyond the royal borough. Claire Pullen, being a loner barely interested in her own neighbours, let alone the suicide of a stranger in Kensington, would never notice even if her daugher's name *did* crop up. Claire was an art potter and had been a single parent a generation before that term was coined, never deeming it necessary to wedge herself into any conventional motherly slot and entirely absorbing herself in her studio work which, at last, was highly sought after.

The change of scene did Judith a power of good. It gave her a chance to distance herself from Rectory Gardens and the prevailing guilt that she had failed Ellie in some way, had ignored a cry for help. She dreaded the inquest. As an experienced officer, giving evidence was child's play and finding the body was clear cut. But the question the Coroner would be posing pivoted on Ellie's state of mind and, as the last person to speak to the suicide victim, her opinion struck a hollow note even to herself. Claire brushed this aside, unimpressed by such soul searching. If every man was an island, Claire Pullen was way out in the Pacific well beyond any shipping lanes.

Judy returned to London gratified that the fraud investigation had gone well and her inclusion on the team had elicited grudging approbation. There was a postcard from Laurence on the hall table and an affectionate message from him on her answering machine. Judith felt a twinge of conscience about her brief fandango with Gus Fielding but thrust it away, well aware that her relationship with her Special Branch Lothario was, at best, semi-detached and at present that was just the way she liked it.

She had managed to evade Mavis Clements on her return, arriving late afternoon; only the yellow eyes of Nelson watching from his vantage point on the wooden chest at the turn of the stairs. She quickly changed into a track suit and trainers, anxious to shake out the cramps of the car journey and stretch her legs. She jogged through side streets, making for her gym club. Bumping into Gus Fielding outside an Indian take-away off Fulham Road came as a bolt from the blue. She had filed away the geologist in her memory bank and had not expected to encounter him off-limits at the seedier end of town.

"Judy, where've you been? I've missed you." He clasped her in a bear hug right there on the street, his beard brushing her cheek, the rough feel of it sending a frisson clear through her carefully constructed emotional defences. He was hard to resist, a wide grin wrinkling the corners of blue-chip eyes, the rough texture of his Harris tweed jacket scratchy as moorland heather under her palms.

She laughed, pushing him away. "I've been working in Maidstone. And you?"

"Ditto. Not Maidstone. Hard at it in Battersea, as a matter of fact. A friend of mine asked me to keep an eye on his dog while he's on a field trip. I've been staying in their flat all week – it's bigger than that shoebox of mine and I have the use of his girlfriend's computer. Poppy's another geologist."

"How do you cope with the dog? Pooper-scooping like a regular Londoner I hope?"

"Peddler's trained himself to hide his do-do's in the bushes. It's only a scrappy little beast but too snappy with Keith's students to take with them. I just give it a run two or three times a day. Battersea Park's just opposite the flat. Poppy picked the thing up at the Dogs' Home. Can't think what appealed to her to be honest, it's a ratty animal. Reminds me of Arnott. Why not come back and see for yourself? Doesn't eat police sergeants, I promise."

He grabbed her arm, ignoring her protests and steered her to his MG at the kerb. "Here. Quick! Get in, I'm on a double yellow." It was impossible to argue and he bundled her into the passenger seat before the stupidity of all this surfaced. Did she really want to get involved with this barmy scientist?

He was right about the flat. It was part of a mansion block and the lofty rooms were an enormous improvement on his bedsit at Rectory Gardens. Peddler, some sort of terrier, hurled himself at them as they crossed the threshold, knocking the vindaloo out of Gus's hand and clear across the carpet. They giggled, watching the scruffy black and tan mongrel waffle Gus's supper.

"Well, that's that then. Let's take the mutt for a quick run and eat out."

They emerged onto Prince of Wales Drive and crossed the road to the park. An asphalt area was floodlit for a match, the perimeter crowded with noisy teenagers. Gus kept Peddler on a lead, cheerfully admitting that the feisty little beast was alarmingly aggressive and hell-bent on scattering the geese on the lake. Gus strolled along, his arm draped over Judy's shoulder, entirely at his ease. Perhaps that appealing shyness of his was some sort of "come-on". It certainly worked. That and a quirky sense of humour. He entertained her with vignettes of the scientific establishment peppered with hilarious mimicry of his academic colleagues. He was a man Arnott would call a "card".

"Aren't you a bit old to be a student?"

"I'm a late developer," he retorted, squeezing her arm. "This post-graduate stint has been hanging over me for years. I thought I'd better get on with it." He extended the leash to give Peddler a bit of leeway and the dog leapt into the bushes, flushing out some pigeons.

"Why London? I thought you lived in Birmingham?"

"Only place willing to put up with me. I drive up once or twice a week, stay a few days, put in a bit of work and get my ticket punched. I spend a lot of time in Dublin. My granny left me a house there. Wonderful city, lovely people. I'd live there all the time if I could swing it. Fancy a trip? We both deserve a break. I've been hard at it all week editing a manuscript. I've got a tame publisher on the hook – a potential blockbuster on sedimentology – Jackie Collins eat your heart out! But they want me to get my PhD before publication. To add a few brownie points to the biog."

"What about the 'biog'?" Judy persisted.

"Me? Thirty-three and lovely with it."

She laughed, affectionately punching his arm. "But don't you have a 'proper job'? How do you manage?"

"Oh, this and that and as a research graduate I get a bit of funding, plus, of course—"

He broke off, suddenly yanked into a stack of chestnut paling rolled neatly at the side of the path, Peddler darting about, yapping and baring his teeth at an inoffensive labrador, both shaping up for a scrap. Gus reeled him in like a fighting fish and they agreed to race back to the flat before a full-scale war broke out. Peddler shook himself and flew ahead, anticipating more vindaloo.

They fell into the flat behind the terrier and shut the door, breathless and giggly. Peddler charged into the bedroom and leapt onto the bed, licking his muddy flanks in satisfaction. Judy regarded the pawmarks with dismay, Gus's eyes rolling upwards like a holy martyr in a Spanish altarpiece before turning his back on the problem and pulling Judy to him. His mouth nuzzled her ear, and he murmured something nice in an undertone too faint to decipher. For all Judy knew he was reciting his own personal mantra: Travertine, Precambrian ophicalcite, xenoliths, basalt and gneiss. *Amen.*

Peddler having requisitioned the bed, they took the sofa. Gus Fielding may have failed as a seismologist but he could certainly make the earth move for Judy Pullen.

Later, they decided on omelettes and Gus made himself useful in the kitchen. Judith roamed about the living room examining the rock samples dotted about like abstract sculptures, watching the light fade over the treetops in the park. She sifted through Gus's incomprehensible print-outs on the desk and was about to try one of the CDs scattered over the coffee table when the phone rang. Judith picked it up. A woman's voice answered.

"Hello, Poppy. You back already? It's Cora Fielding here. Is my husband still there by any chance? Gus said he'd be at your place till the weekend. There's a letter here from his publisher – it might be urgent and I've been trying to get in touch all day. How was your—"

Judy quietly replaced the receiver and stood perfectly still. It was as if she had been turned to stone. Gus would have the right word for it. An ammonite or something. A fossilised outline of a soft-bellied creature that had lived and breathed. Had been happy. Oh, light years away it seemed.

She grabbed her bag and walked out, closing the door, ignoring Gus's shout, oblivious to the clamour of the little black and tan monster barking its bloody little head off.

CHAPTER EIGHT

Arnott put on his best suit and a clean white shirt to attend the Juniper inquest although he knew his testimony would not be called upon. Coles insisted it was unnecessary for Judy Pullen's account to be repeated by the ex-inspector.

He arrived in good time only to be confronted with a printed notice: "The Coroner's Court is temporarily relocated in the former magistrate's court while refurbishment takes place." No-one had thought to warn him. The new place was a mile and a half away and by the time Arnott arrived, red-faced and cursing, proceedings were well under way. Coles had already completed his evidence, admitting that despite an exhaustive search, no suicide note had surfaced.

Arnott burst into the courtroom like the wrath of God and was quickly ushered to a seat. Judith was now giving evidence, describing how she had found the body, keeping her remarks strictly factual, revealing nothing of the personal trauma of her discovery. She wore a primrose-coloured shirt and navy suit, her pale hair pinned back with tortoiseshell combs, her lips bloodless as she carefully recounted the sequence of events. She glanced at Arnott, taken aback by his sudden appearance, smiled, then continued without a pause. Arnott relaxed, relieved to see the silly tart had regained her composure. They had not spoken since his phone call to her office when Arnott had been left in no doubt that his continued dabblings were unwelcome. He had retired hurt to a yard near Rye and filled in his empty days doing up the boat, a nice little centre-board gaffer, clinker mahogany and, like himself, past its prime.

He slumped in his seat concentrating on the Coroner's questions. Yes, Judith agreed, she had spent a short time with Miss Juniper on the evening she died and, yes, she admitted Ellie had given the impression of being excited but seemed by no means depressed.

"She was expecting a friend, she told me."

The Coroner, a heavy-featured man, had an air of indifference, a weary attendance on the details of the death of yet another young woman whose demise was all too familiar in his courtroom. The impression was a false one. Doctor Baillie was an astute observer, well served by the meticulous preparations of his coroner's officer, Bernie Allen.

Coroner: Miss Juniper was in normal spirits, not inebriated in any way?

Judith: Er, no. I don't think so. She had been playing her violin just before I knocked at her door – not very well but certainly well enough to discount her being drunk. She might have had a gin or two but, at the time, I got no impression she was intoxicated.

Coroner: Did she tell you *whom* she was expecting?

Judith: No. But we were not on intimate terms, sir. Ellie *said* she was expecting someone and I got the impression she had a date but perhaps it was merely an excuse not to join me and my friend in my flat.

Coroner: A politeness?

Judith: Quite probably.

After a further flurry of questions about their last encounter, the Coroner called the next witness. The pathologist came to the stand. Dr Russell was a senior man, well versed in the vagaries of sudden death, his direct gaze unflinching and somewhat steely. He covered the basic facts and went on to the details of his report. The post-mortem showed that the deceased had alcohol in her bloodstream and he assessed the intake to be in the region of half a bottle of spirits.

Coroner: This would make the woman unsteady on her feet?

Russell: I would say so. There was an abrasion to her forehead caused by a fall against a flat surface. Possibly in the shower. Nylon stockings on wet tiles would be treacherous.

The Coroner then asked Russell for his opinion on the cause of death and the pathologist launched into the somewhat obvious conclusion which was nevertheless required for the record. Arnott snorted, impatient with this foxtrot being played out in the crowded courtroom, the Coroner and the pathologist completing the complicated choreography as accurately as ballroom dancers toeing the official line.

"Like Victor Sylvester's bloody step-by-step diagrams. Teach yourself in twelve easy lessons," Arnott muttered all too audibly. He had sat in on too many such proceedings and wondered why he had made such an effort to attend this time. Because of Pullen he supposed. Didn't want to see the girl made a monkey of. But there was more to it than that . . . Arnott realised, too late, that he had lost his opportunity to air his own misgivings about Ellie Juniper. Being alone on the boat had not settled his mind. Quite the reverse. And the snags deserved mulling over at the very least. He tried to catch Bernie Allen's eye but the coroner's officer was glued to his notes like a conductor determined to keep the orchestra strictly to the score.

Arnott dragged his attention back to the pathologist. He was pedantically describing the cuts to the victim's neck, typical of those of a suicide, the initial tentative wounds culminating in the fatal severance of the trachea from the left. Russell confirmed that the injuries had, in his opinion, been inflicted by a jagged piece of glass, quoting forensic evidence to support this and other details, not all of the blood having been entirely rinsed away under the flow of water, he said. He added more stomach-churning facts, his voice droning on, occasionally interrupted by the Coroner's questions.

Coroner: Would you say that the deceased was a reasonably healthy person?

Russell: The body was infected with HIV – Human Immunodeficiency Virus – which can damage the body's defence system leaving it open to infection.

That brought Arnott up short! He leaned forward, riveted by this dramatic turn of events, dying for a fag.

Coroner: Did the deceased suffer from AIDS?

Russell: People who have been infected with HIV do not *all* have AIDS. It is possible to present a perfectly healthy aspect and not even know oneself to be infected. But medical opinion at present is that at least 25% of these people will develop AIDS within seven years.

Coroner: Are you saying that this young woman may have been ignorant of this risk?

Russell: There may be a long period after infection with HIV when a person may be entirely free from symptoms. Although the infection may be latent for years, HIV multiplies in the lymph nodes and other organs of the immune system – the adenoid glands, tonsils, the spleen. The signs of virus multiplication in the lymph nodes of people infected with HIV can be measured.

Coroner: And her doctor might not be aware of this condition?

Russell: If her NHS doctor was not consulted she may have taken a test privately or even abroad. Many people are anxious to keep this information quiet – employers have been known to be unsympathetic. But without evidence of any anxiety about her health or any proof that the infection had been diagnosed there is no clear answer. But this patient would undoubtedly have been in indifferent health and would have been concerned about it.

Coroner: Could you give a professional opinion regarding the duration of her infection.

Russell: No. But at a rough guess I would say this young woman had been suffering from the virus for some years. The infection was well established in the lymph nodes.

Arnott listened to the rest of the evidence with scant attention, his mind racing ahead, processing this new information. If the Juniper woman knew she had a terminal illness it would explain everything.

Her own, NHS doctor had not been consulted for nearly three years it seemed and the Coroner had his work cut out keeping the man to the point. Determined to nullify any latent criticism of his professional conduct he elaborated on his frequent attendance on the late Mrs Juniper, stressing her daughter's stoical acceptance of her mother's illness and subsequent death, protesting most emphatically that Ms Juniper was never treated by him for alcoholism or drug dependency, let alone AIDS. She had made no suicide threats to him or been reported by a relative as ever having done so. Oh no, most certainly not. The woman had not even required tranquillizers after her mother's death and there was never any mention of depression. The Coroner swiftly reassured the doctor that, in his experience, a person who made a successful suicide attempt frequently – contrary to popular opinion – gave no indication of any mental distress.

Matters were swiftly brought to a conclusion. The Coroner had no hesitation in saying Elinor Juniper took her life while the balance of her mind was disturbed owing to ill health.

The room emptied and Arnott hung about in the corridor, hoping to waylay Bernie Allen. The man finally emerged, the vestibule now deserted. Arnott pounced. Bernie glanced at his watch and agreed to a lunchtime drink, well satisfied that even Ralph Arnott could pick no holes in the evidence presented in the Juniper case.

They adjourned to a pub tucked well away behind the High Street where the dim, unpleasantly musty interior attracted few customers. Arnott bounced up to the bar, eager to get in the first round. He had a special favour to ask Bernie.

Next morning Judy Pullen sat over her breakfast coffee and newspaper and, bypassing the latest dismal unemployment figures, turned to Constanzia's Star Guide.

"Because Saturn has been passing through your opposite sign of Aquarius since the beginning of the year you are experiencing some kind of personal crisis. Therefore your main purpose must be to face up to whatever disturbs you and determine to enjoy yourself at all costs. Now is the time to act entirely in your own interests, ignore the clamour of colleagues and partners and HAVE FUN!"

That perked her up. In fact, today was the day Veronica Messop had invited her to lunch at Bibendum. How's that for a fun quota, Constanzia? After the previous day's inquest she could do with a treat, the bombshell disclosure of Ellie Juniper's illness casting an entirely different light on things. In fact, were she entirely honest with herself, the news had been a blessed release, the persistent anxiety that she had been insensitive to Ellie's state of mind now lifted. Good heavens, the possibility of incubating full-blown AIDS would be enough to tip anyone over the edge. Nothing Judy Pullen could offer would have made the slightest difference.

The radio bleeped a time signal and the weatherman forecast a warm spring day. Judith rinsed her mug and plate under the tap and hurried into the spare room to fetch her raincoat. Who took any notice of meteorologists anyhow? Or geologists! Weathermen were no more reliable than Constanzia and her astrological promises. Perhaps Constanzia did have a point though. Why not promote one's own interests for once? At least Veronica Messop held out the alluring prospect of paying for the bedroom ceiling to be put right. In fact, Judith had become quite used to sleeping on the sofabed. It wasn't at all bad, providing you had it all to yourself, of course. She pushed aside the bleak reminder of her romp on the sofa in Battersea and narrowly focused on Constanzia's injunction to HAVE FUN.

She set off for work and put in an immediate request for a long lunch hour. "Now is the time to act entirely in your own interests", Constanzia had demanded. And why not? The revelation that Gus Fielding had led her up the garden path had been a body blow – not his duplicity as such, but her own naivety in assuming so much. Ah, well.

She approached the old Michelin building in Fulham Road with a spring in her step, enchanted by the lovely faience tiling with its jolly scenes of old motor cars set into that architectural wonder. The flower stall by the entrance was lively with daffodils and catkins dancing in the breeze which swirled around the converted showroom area fronting the store. She flew inside, eager to see what miracles had been achieved upstairs in the restaurant.

The Junipers' young solicitor was already seated, a good table near the windows, confirming her status with the head waiter with whom she seemed to be on surprisingly congenial terms. Judith waved, wryly recalling the vituperative exchanges over the meagre supplies in their shared refrigerator in those not-so-distant Notting Hill days.

Veronica Messop had obviously done well for herself since then. Always a "well-built lass" as Arnott would have phrased it, but now the edges were firmer, the hair smoother, the polished nails beautifully manicured. Veronica rose and they air-brushed kisses, Judy breathing in the delicious aromas of freshly chopped herbs and expensive wine, the clink of cutlery music to her ears. Sunshine slanted through the windows,

61

dancing on the silver and glass, accentuating the jaded winter complexions of the *bon viveurs*.

Judith relaxed in her seat, pushing back a strand of hair from her cheek and grinning. Veronica had discussed the menu with Rico and was giving it her entire attention, her eyes greedily darting down the selection of beguiling choices. Judith let her pick for them both. Veronica was obviously more than competent and Constanzia's instruction to assert her own interests could afford to wait its turn.

Judy had her priorities firmly in place and top of the list was that blasted bedroom ceiling.

CHAPTER NINE

Judy worked till seven that evening in an attempt to shift at least *some* of the paperwork stacked in her in-tray. She attacked the proliferation of forms and memos with growing panic, not unconvinced that her well-publicised smart lunch in Chelsea had encouraged her new colleagues to load up the free-loader in her absence. It was her own fault. She should never have mentioned Bibendum to Mary Sumner. As the latest recruit to the Serious Fraud Office and being blonde and pretty with it, she attracted initiation rites as in any other organisation.

Since choosing a transfer, following the rumpus over Arnott's last case, Judith's initial trepidation about joining the Serious Fraud Office had lulled. In fact, the work proved fascinating, the minutiae of evidence piling up like the slow accumulation of an ant heap. It was no surprise to her that there was a faction within her department cheering on the investigation into the necessity of jury trials in complicated fraud cases. It was difficult enough to unravel the complex evidence even with specialized knowledge and Judy's heart went out to the inexperienced juror faced with a long and complicated trial. The difficulty with which she herself continually wrestled – possibly rooted in her CID training – was drawing the line between criminal conduct and breaches of regulation.

In Mary Sumner's absence she had, however, made a few quick calls to arrange Ellie Juniper's funeral. That had been the unavoidable toll Veronica had imposed on the road to Judy getting her ceiling made over and, having guided Ellie through the ordeal of burying her mother only six months before, Judy had to admit that Shiner's Funeral Service had taken the sting out of it. The director, an obsequious nerd called Mr Sweeting, had handled the whole thing with barely a twitch to the reins of the bereaved. It would be a doddle.

But having agreement to this, Veronica had pounced again. Before the dessert trolley had even trundled across to their table, the Junipers' solicitor demanded more, passing a typewritten signed letter across the tablecloth. Judith read it open-mouthed. It authorised Detective Sergeant Judith Pullen full permission to dispose of the possessions of the late Elinor Juniper. Judy sighed. One had to hand it to the woman. It was crystal clear why Veronica Messop paid the piper and was able to call the tune. Godzilla was a pushover compared with this one. Judith sat stunned, all too well aware that getting the flat redecorated was probably no bargain after all. Veronica's voice smoothly overran any objections.

"Honestly, Judith, it really isn't *much* to ask! It will take a matter of minutes to shunt all of Ellie's clothes into a couple of suitcases and bung the lot down to Oxfam. The furniture stays – Basil Meek may re-let the flat in due course. Here are the keys," she said, placing them on top of the letter of authority. "Don't lose them. They're the only set."

"What happened to Dave's spares?"

"I tackled him about that. He swears Ellie locked herself out one night, said she'd left her keys in the office and used his. Never gave them back apparently. Dave said he kept asking her but got nowhere. Mind you, it may have been a ploy to keep her affairs private. Can't say I'd relish the idea of that weirdo having access to all my rent books and papers while I was at work. But I'll check with this Mrs Quick, the doctor's secretary. Ask her to empty Ellie's desk at the office and put aside anything interesting. Incidentally, there's a valuable word processor in the flat which should be returned to the doctor's surgery. I'll try to arrange something."

"Why involve me, for heaven's sake? What happened to the executors?"

"Just take it from me there's no-one else," Veronica briskly retorted. "Would I go to all this trouble if there was?"

So much for old time's sake, Judy reflected.

"What about this Basil Meek?"

"He's stuck on a cruise. I phoned the shipping line when the girl died and they sent a cable. Trouble was he was missing at that point. No-one knew his whereabouts for over a fortnight. I managed to persuade the Personnel Officer to spill the beans and this is strictly confidential, Judith. Meek had been involved in a fight with another member of the crew and had been put off at Miami before Easter. Both men were given a severe reprimand and placed on suspension. When the next cruise sailed Meek was provisionally reinstated – I gather he's a senior steward and had an unblemished record prior to this fracas and his employers gave him another chance. I imagine having been kicking his heels for weeks he was terrified of losing his job and could hardly refuse their offer. Frankly, I can see the logic of it. No point in throwing away your livelihood to return to the UK just for a funeral, is there?"

"What was the fight about?"

Veronica's mouth pursed and Judith caught a glimpse of the woman her old flatmate would become; solid, obdurate and very, very successful.

"How the hell would I know?" she snapped. "Look here, Judith, it really would be sensible to help out on this, quite apart from an understandable wish anyone with a shred of decency would have to see the poor woman laid to rest in a civilised fashion. Basil Meek sounds a perfectly reasonable landlord but he's not got money to burn. If you can organise all this as a *friend* it would be much nicer all round. The Junipers had no family apart from this campy steward and—"

"Aha! So you *do* know what this fight on board was about!" Judy crowed.

"OK. Strictly between ourselves, it was a scrap between two gays. Not totally unheard of in such circles, I believe, but as I was saying, Basil Meek cannot take leave until this current cruise docks."

"Why not just postpone the funeral till he gets here?"

"He's instructed me to get it all settled as soon as possible, that's why." Veronica took a breath and reined in her exasperation – she was beginning to wish now she had never set eyes on the penniless Juniper tribe. "Look, I thought you'd be willing to help out. His offer to accommodate you in an hotel while Dave repaints the flat is extremely generous, Judith, and, believe me, being cooperative with this would save a lot more time than playing footsie with the insurance company. Added to which, he's buying our lunch."

Veronica glanced at her watch and called for the bill. "I've got to dash. Take the keys and think it over when you've had a chance to look at Ellie's things. There isn't much there, honestly. I had a quick shufti with Dave Barnes and there's hardly room to swing a cat. If Basil Meek got rid of that horrible Victorian desk of hers the place wouldn't seem nearly so claustrophobic."

"But it's a lovely flat! I lived there for nearly two years myself. I *liked* it."

"Oh, did you? Yes, of course. I'd forgotten . . . Well, then," she added briskly, patting Judy's hand, "give me a ring in the morning. I feel we do owe something to Ellie Juniper, don't you?"

They left together, Veronica hailing a taxi. Judith had already made her decision before she had walked the hundred yards from the tube station back to her office. Veronica had put her finger on the deciding factor: the memory of Ellie Juniper slumped in that shower cubicle still haunted her. The poor wretch deserved a sympathetic appraisal of her personal things. If Judy refused to play ball Veronica would have no hesitation in putting in a house clearance man to comb through everything. It seemed the least she could do for the girl who had taken her place in the attic rooms. Who else was there?

Someone else did spring to mind: Mavis Clements. She had known the Junipers, mother and daughter, for years. It was only the fact that Judith had been the person to recommend Veronica Messop's services to Ellie that she had been leapt upon at all. All things considered, Mavis Clements would have been the obvious choice, she even knew Mrs Juniper's cronies on the church garden committee, the ladies who had turned out in force to attend the mother's burial.

Judith knocked on Mavis's door on her way in from work that evening, determined to enlist some sort of support in this bizarre obligation which had been forced upon her. The door opened, Mavis almost entirely blocking the lamplight streaming from her cosy sitting room. Nelson was at her feet, his flag of a tail weaving between Mavis's sturdy calves.

"Oh, Judith. How lovely to see you, do come in. I was just

watching *Panorama*. My goodness, juvenile delinquency these days is quite horrendous. It makes the inner cities sound like ghettos, a mirror image of the seamier parts of New York."

Judith stepped inside, glad to see Mavis's apartment was sealed from the terrors of urban living by damson coloured velvet curtains. Judy had never called on this neighbour before – had avoided her, in fact – and the warmth of the welcome made her feel slightly guilty. The woman must be missing the Junipers more than anyone else in the house, the foundation of her existence in Rectory Gardens having shifted alarmingly in the past few months, a woman alone existing on a small salary with the strong possibility of her home being sold over her head. In any event, the reign of the Junipers was at an end.

She was offered a glass of sherry which was welcome. The proposal Judy had in mind was a delicate one which might affect Mavis Clements more than she had envisaged. Perhaps it would have been better to leave well alone. But it was too late now. After a few initial pleasantries, Judith jumped in at the deep end and explained the responsibility with which she had been charged.

"I've been in touch with Shiner's and fixed a tentative date for Ellie's funeral. Thursday week. At two o'clock."

"Shiner's do a wonderful job, Judith. You couldn't have chosen more wisely."

"As the Junipers' closest friend, Mavis, I was wondering if you could help? You see, I'm not sure if an announcement in the press would be appropriate. I don't want to attract nosey parkers. You know how ghoulish people can be and when the details of the inquest become public . . ."

"Of course, of course, my dear. I quite understand. We must be very discreet with this. I presume Mr Sweeting will arrange a service at St Saviour's similiar to Flavia's?"

"Much simpler. Ellie wasn't much of a churchgoer, was she? Not recently anyway. But Mr Sweeting seems *au fait* with details of the family plot and to be perfectly honest, Mavis, I'd rather leave all that to him."

"Absolutely, my dear. Would you like me to telephone a few close friends?"

"Would you, Mavis? I'd be terribly grateful. Mrs Juniper's garden committee would like to know about it but

67

I've absolutely no idea if there is anyone else we should contact."

"There's this cousin, the sailor."

"Basil Meek can't get leave. That's why the solicitor asked me to arrange everything. He will get back as soon as possible but wants it all dealt with without further delay. Did Ellie have any close friends, do you know? The solicitor says there's not been a single letter of condolence. Isn't that odd?"

"Ellie was a strange girl, Judith. Caused her poor mother a good deal of anxiety. Very secretive, always was. Living here so long it was impossible for me to ignore the rackety life Ellie was leading."

Mavis leaned forward, her thick legs splayed under the pleated skirt, her permed head bobbing knowingly, inviting Judy's curiosity.

"Ellie was gadding about town in a very unladylike fashion long before Flavia had her stroke. Man mad, my dear!" Her voice lowered as she pronounced heinous scandals. "I do believe she had an affair with that dreadful caretaker in the basement."

"Dave?"

Mavis's head bobbed ever more furiously and she continued, now well into her stride. "Not only him either. Ellie was always running up to that Spaniard's bedsit, you know. Fancy that, a common waiter! Set her cap at that nice Mr Fielding when he came here but he's married, you know. A charming man. Saw through Ellie's little stratagem right away."

Judith shifted awkwardly in her seat and steered Mavis back to the matter in hand. "There's no shortage of money for this funeral, Mavis. The cousin, Mr Meek, has instructed the solicitor to pay whatever's required which is pretty generous. He's only a ship's steward, you know, has very little money by all accounts."

"Inheriting this house must have been a windfall then! Though it does need a lot spent on it. Maintenance has been neglected, especially since Ellie took over."

"He may wish to sell, of course. The income from the flats is less than it should be. My rent is cheaper than anything I could find elsewhere in Kensington and Veronica mentioned that two tenants live rent free."

"Really? You *do* surprise me. Well, well, well. Dave Barnes would be one, of course, but he's hardly a normal tenant, is he? I bet Ellie let that Mikki Ferrero stay here for nothing. I can't begin to imagine what Flavia would have said about *that!*"

Judith rose, exhausted by the murkiness of the Juniper pond. "Well, I'll leave you to your telly, Mavis. But if you're free on the twenty-seventh, I'll confirm the date with Mr Sweeting."

Mavis nodded eagerly, for all the world as if Judith was issuing an invitation to a masked ball.

"And if there's anyone else you feel should be informed – I'll tell Ellie's employer, the doctor, as a matter of courtesy, of course – please pass the word around. It would be nice to give Ellie a dignified farewell, wouldn't it?"

She escaped, glad that was over at least, pleased now to have involved Mavis Clements, who seemed gratified to be included in all this. Later, lying in the bath relaxing in the hot scented water, Judy mulled over the day's events. It was all vaguely depressing, pleasures anticipated at breakfast relentlessly sliding downhill, the fun quota Constanzia's Star Guide had forecast running out of steam. After making some coffee she did an unexpected thing: she telephoned Arnott.

"Well, missy, this is a turn-up for the book. What can I do for you? No more furniture humping – my sciatica's been playing me up ever since that last lot."

"Nothing like that. Actually, I've decided not to move out after all, not for the present anyhow. The new owner's redecorating for me. The whole flat if I like."

"You'll regret it, Pullen, you mark my words. That bedroom of yours'll never smell right no matter how many coats of paint you slap on. Once the weather warms up you'll get swarms of bloody blowflies buzzing round the place, you see if you don't."

Judy grimaced, realising, too late, Arnott was the last source of encouragement if you were feeling low. She hurried on to describe her meeting with Veronica Messop and the agreement that had been made. His whistle of disapproval was more piercing than a whole carillon of alarm bells.

"The funeral is at two o'clock on Thursday 27th. Will you come? Mavis Clements is going to try to rustle up some supporters but I suspect it'll be a thin turn-out."

He agreed, too readily Judith thought, and she wondered if he had an ulterior motive. The cunning old dog was never *that* acquiescent.

"One thing cropped up at that inquest, Pullen. When you went into the bathroom that night and found the poor gel in the shower, you told the Coroner you switched the light on. You sure?"

"I pulled the light cord. That's right. I'm certain of it. *Then* I pulled the shower door fully open."

"So the bathroom was in complete darkness when you opened the door?"

"I suppose it was."

"Well, the blind was down, I saw that for meself right enough and the window's at the back of the house, no light from the street outside."

"The blind was always down, Arnott. It was a Venetian blind if you remember. When I lived there it stayed in place always – I didn't want any peeping toms. Not that anyone could look in without binoculars or something, the window's small and way up under the eaves but I felt more comfortable with the blind down and I imagine Ellie did too."

"So the poor little bitch takes her bottle of gin in the bathroom, turns on the water, sits in the shower, half closes the door and has a few last snorts before breaking the glass to cut her wrist. Then she changes her mind and decides to slit her throat instead. All in the dark?"

"Well, now you mention it, she must have done."

"Bit odd, ain't it?"

"Perhaps she couldn't stand the sight of blood."

"Well, if it was me I'd like to be able to see what I was doing. Lucky she had her contact lenses in."

"Did she? Well, with water pouring on her head her glasses would have been impossible to see through anyway, wouldn't they?"

"She'd need bloody windscreen wipers."

Judy had to smile. It was a pretty sick response but all the time she had worked with Arnott his dubious jokes had been her only lifeline. Presumably, after years dealing with accident victims, stabbings, rape and gang warfare Arnott's black humour had grown upon him like a bullet-proof vest, immured him against the sensitivity which had ultimately driven Judith Pullen into the bloodless arms of the fraud squad.

"You'll come then, to the funeral, I mean? It's at St Saviour's. I'll have to go straight from work, take the afternoon off."

"Right, lass. Count on Uncle Ralph. I'll be there. Black tie do, is it?"

He chortled, putting the phone down on her.

CHAPTER TEN

Arnott was waiting at the church door when Judith hurried up at ten to two on the afternoon of Ellie Juniper's funeral. It was a miserable day, cold and drizzling continuously, the daffodils flanking the path bedraggled, lying at angles in the mud like broken spears on a battlefield.

Judith shook out her umbrella and left it in the porch, glad to see Arnott was in a cheerful mood. The occasion was gloomy enough without having to withstand pithy remarks from that quarter. They went inside. St Saviour's was empty and, for no obvious reason, they lowered their voices as they strolled along a side aisle discussing the arrangements.

"Mavis has been a brick. She more or less took over the discussions with Shiner's, chose everything, phoned the Juniper crowd and so on. I've really had very little to do."

"Where is Miss Marple then?"

"I keep telling you. It's Clements, Arnott. Don't try any funny business with Mavis, for heaven's sake, she has no sense of humour, none at all."

"Hold up, Pullen. Look 'ere." Arnott grabbed her arm, pointing to a plaque high up in the wall commemorating the service and devotion of George Fitzallen Juniper, Magistrate and Church Warden, 1846–1910.

"I suppose it's another one of them. Ellie was the last."

They shuffled on, Judith glancing at her watch, wondering where Mavis and the other mourners had got to. Flowers arranged on a pedestal in front of the pulpit struck an unusual note; a waterfall of lilies dotted about with yellow freesias. It was like a jumbo bridal bouquet, heavy with scented blooms, ivy leaves trailing to the floor. The perfume was breathtaking, wafting round the draughty aisles like the very breath of spring. Judith wondered if Mavis had organised this, too, and was struck by the thought that without this floral masterpiece the setting for Ellie's funeral would have seemed horribly spartan.

The vicar suddenly emerged from the vestry and hurried over, mouthing sympathies and ushering them to the front pew. Mavis clumped up the aisle, queenly in purple, her frizzy hair jammed under a beret on which a silver thistle was pinned like a regimental badge. She pushed in beside Arnott, whispering unintelligibly across him to Judith just as the organ burst into life.

"Is there no-one else?" Judith hissed.

The purple beret shook, Mavis's bleak look speaking volumes. The music swelled, disguising an undignified scuffle in the porch as Shiner's men manoeuvred the coffin between them and shouldered their burden to its place at the front. Judith stared fixedly at the strange pedestal arrangement, unable to shake off the impression that someone somewhere had produced these flowers especially for Ellie and that the bridal bouquet effect was grimly appropriate. Ellie was certainly here on time; only the bridegroom was missing.

Afterwards they stood in the rain while the coffin was interred and Judith was glad Arnott was there to lean on. He stood between the two women, stiff as a soldier as the last of the Junipers was laid to rest. Mavis sniffed into her hanky and dabbed her eyes while the vicar intoned the final liturgy. There were just three wreaths: one from Mavis, blue irises from Judith and an extremely expensive tribute from Ellie's former employer.

Arnott offered to drive them all back to Rectory Gardens in his ramshackle van and, the obsequies completed, Mavis Clements became positively skittish. She had prepared a funeral tea and was disappointed that her effusive invitation could not budge the vicar from pressing parish duties.

Back home, Judith put her key in the front door and Arnott and Mavis went ahead up the stairs, Nelson thumping down from his observation post on the oak chest to join the cortège. The house was as quiet as the grave, even the Osima's pram missing from the hall, the steady drip-drip from a blocked gutter over the porch making Judith shiver. She trailed upstairs behind them, gloomily aware that over a week had passed and still she had not plucked up courage to sort out Ellie's things. She would tackle it tonight without fail. Really she would.

Squaring her shoulders, she entered Mavis's sitting room, anxious to get the ghastly finalities out of the way. Mavis had removed her royal purple and was even more majestic in a maroon dress and pearls. Arnott was at his most affable, revealing that other side of his Mr Punch persona, delighting Mavis with his genuine appreciation of the ham sandwiches and home-made Dundee cake. Mavis offered sherry, setting a saucer of milk in the hearth for Nelson who ignored this, his yellow eyes firmly focused on the ham. It reminded Judy of Veronica's unswerving concentration on the menu at Bibendum and she cheered up, sipping the Tio Pepe and feeling the tension relax.

Arnott and Mavis were already dissecting the late Mrs Juniper's garden committee.

"I telephoned every one of them, Judith, and they all made excuses. I thought at least the vicar's wife might have put in an appearance considering all the sterling work Flavia undertook for St Saviour's over the years. But, oh dear me, no. Not a single soul among them willing to be associated with Elinor Juniper."

"They passed by on the other side," Arnott intoned.

Judith quickly looked up, suspecting a crack in the serious demeanour but Arnott was playing it perfectly straight. Judy prayed it would last and hoped Mavis would go easy on the sherry.

"Actually I'm not being entirely fair," Mavis admitted. "The ladies made a collection for all those lilies – a tribute to the last of the Junipers they said. Olive Masson arranged them and sent a little note of condolence for me to keep for Basil Meek. Very strange design though, wouldn't you say? One of those modern arrangements one hears about. Continental, I expect."

Arnott nodded sagely as if he were totally cognisant of all this floral chit-chat and Judith stifled a giggle. Mavis passed the sandwiches and went out of the room to make some tea. Judith put her plate on a dinky wine table by her chair and leaned forward to speak confidentially to Arnott in Mavis's absence. Nelson judged his distance and in one deft move swept Judy's ham sandwich to the floor and streaked into the bedroom with it, disappearing under Mavis's bed.

She returned with the teapot, delighted to find Arnott and young Judith consumed with laughter. Mavis's Irish forebears had instilled a sincere belief that funerals were also a reminder that, conversely, "In the midst of death we are in life."

Judith tried to retrieve the dignity of the occasion, unaware that a Clements was the last to regard a burial as an occasion for long faces, and struggled to pick up the thread of the conversation. Something about flowers . . . ah, yes!

"The wreath from Doctor Janssen was impressive."

"Did you read the card, Judith? Written by Helen Janssen herself, I'm sure of it. A lovely person. Did you never meet her? She used to drive Ellie home from work occasionally, especially after Flavia was bedridden. The Janssens have a flat over his consulting rooms, you know. Ellie must have worked flexitime. She kept very irregular hours and often came back early. The library gives me Wednesday afternoons off and I was surprised to find Flavia entertaining this pretty young woman at her bedside more than once."

"Mrs Juniper and the doctor's wife? They knew each other?"

"Oh indeed. Helen Janssen got on remarkably well with the old lady. Better than Ellie but then daughters are under a special strain, are they not? And, of course, Flavia could be charming to strangers and perfectly horrid to kith and kin. She couldn't stand that nephew of hers."

"Basil Meek?" Arnott said, scoffing the last of the sandwiches.

"Flavia never said anything directly, you understand, but I could well see why she made no provision for him in her will. Her sister's only son, too."

"But Mrs Juniper didn't make a will, Mavis. She died intestate. That's why I introduced Ellie to my solicitor friend. Ellie was totally at sea, poor love, had never even paid a phone bill before."

"It wouldn't have hurt Basil to come home and give Ellie a bit of support then, would it? He didn't even attend his aunt's funeral, you know. Not that it was a quiet affair like this afternoon. Oh, dear me no. All the garden committee

75

turned out in force for the service and two representatives from the Admiralty came."

"I expect Basil was abroad at the time. He would have been here today if he could have possibly managed it, Mavis. His work you know . . ." Judith finished lamely, feeling a certain obligation to the man who had promised to redecorate her flat.

"Quite possibly. Yes, you're perfectly right, my dear. I am being ungenerous. Who are we to judge? After all Basil was extremely kind to Ellie after her mother's death. He arranged for his cousin to have a free cruise in the Bahamas. She only had to pay her air fare to America and afterwards she took extra leave and toured the southern states. Had a wonderful time. She had to sell Flavia's rings to pay for it but it was awfully decent of the doctor to give her an extra month's holiday, wasn't it?"

"This young lass had a way with the gentlemen, it seems to me," Arnott dryly put in.

"Oh, Ellie could be very charming, Mr Arnott. Too fond of men if you ask me. Just think, there was not a single female friend at her funeral. Very strange, I would say."

"Perhaps Mrs Juniper demanded more of Ellie's free time than an ordinary parent – left her little leisure to develop personal friendships."

Mavis's laughter pealed out, her large horsy teeth flecked with ham.

"My dear, Ellie was never *in*. Even when poor Flavia was bedridden after the stroke, it was only myself and that Dave Barnes who took care of her little necessities. There was a district nurse, of course, but the poor soul needed more companionship than a nurse and an alcoholic caretaker. That's where Helen Janssen was so good. She brought photograph albums of their travels and Flavia and she spent hours talking about these foreign places they both knew. Flavia travelled a good deal before the war, you know, knew all the Outposts of the Empire as she used to call them. Oh yes, the doctor's wife was a real tonic to her, popped in at weekends occasionally when Ellie was off on one of her jaunts."

Arnott cut himself a second piece of fruit cake and said, "Where did she go?"

"Who knows? Ellie was very keen on horses at one stage and went off for riding weekends in Wales but lately she had a dance craze. Out all hours. Flavia was very worried about it, never knew who Ellie's friends were, she said. Never brought anyone home to meet her mother."

"But you said Ellie had a fiancé."

Mavis poured more tea and thought for a moment. "She mentioned it only once. Just after Christmas as I recall. We bumped into each other in the hall. Ellie was off out and looked very 'sparkly' if you know what I mean. Said she was going to a party. I enquired about her escort, why he hadn't called for her but, of course, I'm out of date with modern etiquette and Ellie thought this remark of mine dreadfully old-hat. Said she was meeting him there and they were flying to Paris next day. 'With my fiancé,' she said, meaningfully if you understand me – as if to say 'And you can put that in your pipe and smoke it, Mavis Clements.' I congratulated her, of course, and asked about the wedding but she cut me short and intimated the marriage would take place abroad. But I never saw any engagement ring and no name was ever mentioned. I took it with a pinch of salt."

Judith exchanged a smile with Arnott, each recognising that the Tio Pepe had released a trickle of pent-up malice in their hostess. "You didn't believe in this fiancé of hers then?"

"Well, no-one ever saw him, did they? And there were no letters. I collect foreign stamps for my niece's little boy. Everyone in the house knows to keep their envelopes from abroad for me. I blame her mother. Flavia was presented at court, you know, set her expectations for Ellie ridiculously high. It made the girl fanciful. Flavia lived in the past, of course. The Junipers were well known in Kensington for generations. Extraordinary to think that a family like that finished up with only the one descendant, poor little Ellie. Extinct now."

"As bloody dinosaurs," Arnott muttered.

Judith poked him in the ribs and rose to make her farewell. Arnott shuffled to the door, promising to call again, offering to drive Mavis down to Rye once the weather improved and show her the boat. Mavis blossomed, flushed with anticipation, her piggy eyes bright with expectation. She fetched their coats and stood in the midst of the funeral feast, still chattering on about the afternoon's debacle as if it had been a packed-out memorial service at St Martin-in-the-Fields. She closed the door on her visitors and joined Nelson for a little nap on the bed.

Arnott stood in the hall buttoning his overcoat, eyeing Dave Barnes's efforts with the vacuum cleaner at the far end of the vestibule under the stairs, well out of earshot.

"One thing you'd know about, Pullen. I got Bernie Allen to get me a copy of the pathologist's report and it says the Juniper girl was wearing false eyelashes. Strikes me as bloody difficult putting on them fiddle-arsed things if you was short sighted."

"If you're used to them you could do it with your eyes shut. It's a knack, Arnott, like putting on eye liner. Anyway, she had contact lenses, you said."

"Fair do's. But why go to all that trouble, putting on your best bib and tucker, getting all tarted up just to blow out the candle?"

"An impulse. Supposing Ellie *was* expecting someone. Got ready for her date and he doesn't show. Could have happened before, some men are real pigs," she said with feeling, edging Arnott to the front door. "He could have phoned and cancelled at the last minute or just not turned up. In despair Ellie decides to chuck it all in. Perhaps this bloke had found out about her HIV infection. Who knows? It might have finally dawned on her that she was on a hiding to nothing with this guy. She'd had a few drinks, remember, that would have had a depressing effect."

"Bit late to go out though, ain't it? Well after nine when you came back down after telling her to cut out the fiddle practice."

"If she was going out to a club that night it was *early*! You're antediluvian, Arnott. It wasn't the palais-de-danse she was off to. These smart clubs hardly get warmed up before midnight."

He gave up. She was right. He *was* out of his bloody depth these days. He looked out. It was still pissing down outside.

Judith closed the door and turned to go upstairs. Dave Barnes had moved on while she had been barneying with

Arnott and was now hoovering the stairs. He cheerfully confirmed he would replaster her ceiling if she gave him a date, saying he had already screwed an advance from the solicitor and happily anticipated an open-ended expense sheet. Dave Barnes was in for a shock: obviously he had never worked for Veronica Messop before. His cupidity got under her skin and Judy's temper flared.

"You're a heartless bastard, Dave Barnes. Why didn't you come to the funeral this afternoon? I left a note on the hall table for *everyone* to see. There were only three of us! And one of them was Arnott."

"And he was only there for the beer."

"Oh, shut up. You make me sick. You were treated very well by the Junipers and you don't even get off your backside to shuffle round the corner to the church for half-an-hour. And you had an *affair* with the girl!"

"And don't I know it." His reply was quiet, and cold as death. "When I heard about her filthy infection, don't think it didn't scare me shitless. That bitch *knew* she was trading dynamite."

"You too?" Judith whispered.

"No thanks to that secretive little cow as it happens. I'm in the clear. Got tested straight after the inquest, never been so panicked in my whole fucking life. We had a little something going for a while a couple of years ago but it was just a bit of fun – she was a real chip off the old block, set her sights a good deal higher than a jazz musician. No skin off my nose: Ellie was quite a dazzler between the sheets. Christ knows where she picked up the tricks. Not from any library books for sure. I tipped the poor Spaniard the wink an' all."

"Mikki?"

"Sure. Don't run away with the idea Ellie Juniper was picky. Probably had a twirl with Osima, too, given the chance. Why not? We all got the old heave-ho after a few weeks. Insatiable cow. Must have lived off oysters or something."

Judith backed away, startled by his hatred.

"That's what you say. But she *was* expecting someone that night."

"Well, it wasn't me. I was working, remember? And as it happens I was there early that Sunday. We were rehearsing a new singer. Are you trying to hang that bird's craziness on *me*, Judy?"

"No, of course not," she muttered, now not at all sure what she had meant. It was all mixed up with that paltry little turn-out at the graveside and not helped by Arnott's needling about the suicide. Why wouldn't the interfering old devil let the girl rest in peace? Why rake everything over all the time, create suspicions in her mind, sleepless nights, more nightmares about bloodstained water dripping on her head?

"You should be careful what you say, Judy Pullen. Mikki has an alibi too, so don't go accusing him of throwing her over that night. He was working, same as I was. If you're looking for a scapegoat why not go for that scientist bloke? He's always creeping about on the stairs. Wouldn't surprise me if he'd got his leg over with poor bloody Mavis. Do anything for a free drink that guy."

"Free drink! Coming from you that's rich. You were conning old Mrs Juniper for free drinks on her deathbed!"

Dave turned away, suddenly bored with the conversation, and started rewinding the vacuum cleaner cord, saying, "Ah, yes, the poor old girl and her pink gins. Drank like a fish, you know, and I never saw her in the least bit tipsy. Her blood could have pickled onions, 85% pure alcohol. Funny that, the mother into booze and the daughter into drugs."

"You liar!"

"You're right. That was unfair. Ellie's sexual stamina was totally unadulterated. She was a natural at screwing, needed no props. Into every kinky move *but* drink. Teetotal as a Sally Army tambourine shaker. Unbelievable."

"You are *so* wrong about Ellie, Dave Barnes. She didn't do drugs – the doctor at the inquest said so – but she *did* drink. Ellie sunk half a bottle of gin before slashing her throat."

Dave shrugged. "Beginner's luck."

CHAPTER ELEVEN

Judy raced upstairs, livid with Dave Barnes, sick of the whole sordid business. She slammed the door and flung off her suit, stung by her own stupidity in letting Veronica bribe her into getting involved. It wasn't as if Ellie had been a real friend; they had barely exchanged more than a few brief conversations in three years! Finding the body was the cruncher, of course. That was what bound her. Discovering the corpse of a perfect stranger would have been bad enough but a dead girl in the flat she herself had only recently vacated imposed a peculiar affinity, the brush with death too close to bear.

The funeral should have put an end to it. "Laid to rest." Wasn't that the whole point? It was *over*. Finished. Ellie Juniper was dead and buried. Judith angrily pulled on jeans and a sweater and banged about the flat, venting her temper on the previous night's washing up: a casserole now stiff with petrified lumps of cold stew.

Her anger slowly blew itself out and she felt better for the outburst. It had taken the lid off banked-down feelings of guilt and self-pity, leaving her calmer, able to face up to the final hurdle: clearing the attic rooms. She plunged under the sink for some dustbin liners and rubber gloves before her courage failed, prodding herself with the fact that the next day, Friday, was the morning the council refuse lorry came round. If she cleared out Ellie's stuff with all the other rubbish, her last connection with the Junipers would be carted away before breakfast. She would be free! Judy slipped the keys in her pocket, grabbed an empty cardboard box, shoved the bin liners inside and ran upstairs.

Unlocking the door of her old flat, she drew a deep breath and plunged in. It had been secured since the police left and the place smelt damp as a cellar. The loft conversion had been carried out by one of Mrs Juniper's odd-job men and had not been done with any great style. In fairness that had been its charm, the quirkiness of a layout full of surprises and the view over the chimneypots like a page from one of those arty coffee table books.

The door off the top landing opened into a tiny vestibule with the bedroom to the left and bathroom to the right. Straight ahead another door led to the sitting room and this capsule-like space acted as a sound buffer to the comings and goings on the stairs. Judith passed quickly through, averting her eyes from the closed bathroom door, and entered the living area, snapping on the overhead light.

It was a long garret with sloping rafters, the uncurtained windows now black, one end of the room disappearing behind a kitchen counter surmounted by hanging cupboards, beyond which a galley had been constructed by partitioning the room which was now the bathroom.

She wandered into the kitchen and checked the drawers which contained little but a pair of scissors, a polaroid camera devoid of film and three tin openers. It was all surprisingly neat, even the fridge was empty. No alcohol. Not even a bottle of tonic or angostura for the pink gins. She packed the remaining cans of beans and curried chicken in a carrier bag and added an unopened packet of tea. Dave Barnes was a ready repository for handouts. The rest she tipped into the cardboard box and methodically emptied all the cupboards, washing the china and cutlery and leaving it to drain. A first-aid box contained nothing but a dusty pack of lint and a few plasters; no aspirins or tablets of any kind. She wiped over the oven, obviously unused since she had cleaned it herself only a few weeks before. The dead girl had evidently not been much of a cook, even the coffee jar was empty. But perhaps the young constable had seen to that. Obviously, the poor chap could hardly rely on Mavis's ministrations, especially if he had no titbits of information to trade for the sausage rolls.

A matchfolder by the stove caught her eye; Judy was always running out of matches. She scanned the cover. The Domino Club. Presumably donated by the Spanish waiter. She seemed to remember Dave mentioning the name when Mikki first moved in. Judy had been impressed, the Domino being

82

an exclusive disco venue, membership strictly monitored, a fun palace for the well-heeled boppers of Belgravia. She studied the small print. It listed an annexe near Windsor, a place which, despite the management's strong-arm privacy policy, sometimes featured in the gossip columns, the tabloids' readers avid for news of any aristocratic shenanigans way out in the sticks. Membership of the London club gave access to the Berkshire venue but, in fact, the preferences of the membership were clearly divided, few patronising both premises. The Domino Country Club was less frantic, designed more for serious sports enthusiasts, attracting a regular following at weekends from the polo set.

Judith pocketed the matchfolder and knotted the first bag of rubbish. Then she turned to the sitting room. The massive desk presented the most obvious magpie's nest and she started with the bottom drawer, the way Arnott always asserted proper housebreakers tackled a robbery. Half an hour later she had the entire contents neatly sorted and secured with rubber bands. She had an aversion to destroying family documents of any sort and decided to leave all the paperwork to Veronica. After all she was getting a fat fee from Basil Meek, wasn't she?

Apart from some medical files it was mostly computer disks, income tax returns and letters, some dating back to old Mrs Juniper's wartime correspondence, too intimate to bear the scrutiny of strangers. The rent books and bank accounts were missing – presumably claimed by the solicitor. Judy stacked the remaining papers on top of the windowseat and dusted out the empty drawers, laying the medical typescripts and files on top of the word processor ready for collection, laying aside two library books which she could return next week. Or maybe Mavis would oblige? The titles were intriguing, one *Diseases of the Horse* and the other an illustrated guide book of Washington DC. They were both spectacularly overdue. On second thoughts, she had better take them back herself, even a suicide would receive scant sympathy from Mavis faced with such tardiness.

She stacked the few books on the landing and collected up the cassettes dotted about the room. They were mostly popular classics: Mendelssohn's violin concerto, some Bach, extracts from *A Month in the Country*; standard concert fare. That was the awful thing about all this, Judy reflected. Ellie Juniper was so bloody normal. It could have happened to anyone, anyone at all if this very ordinary person could decide life was not worth the candle. She ejected a tape from the battered boogie box and discovered it to be untitled, a private recording probably taken from the radio. Or maybe something Dave had lent her – a demo tape for Tears? She put it on and got the fright of her life, the sheer volume of noise knocking her back. The anonymous band belted out a hard rock number, the lyrics buried in an unholy racket. Definitely not Tears. Judy hastily switched off and placed the cassette with the others. She had recognised Ellie's choice straight away. It was the jangle of noise set in motion after Arnott's rude response to her violin playing. Judy smiled. Served the silly old bugger right.

She moved into the bedroom, donning rubber gloves. The bed had already been stripped, presumably by Coles's men turning the place upside down for Ellie's suicide note. She swiftly bundled all the bedding into bags, including the pillows, and wondered if Basil Meek would feel queasy about re-using the mattress. Feeling her old despair creeping back, Judy hurried to get the job over and started emptying the dressing table.

There was a lot of lingerie, some distinctly school outfitter stock but leavened with lacy silk camiknickers and a whole gamut of suspender belts and black stockings. The few bits of jewellery were all inexpensive: jokey plastic brooches and cheap earrings. Nothing more exciting than a digital watch and certainly nothing which could possibly have been handed down in the family. The last drawer was stuffed with old photographs spilling from a shoebox which she put aside to add to Veronica's stacks of memorabilia.

She paused to glance through the snapshots, always a sucker for such things, intrigued by old albums on sale in secondhand bookshops, fascinated by the yellowing portraits of people long dead, now fair game to bargain hunters and collectors of Victorian bric-a-brac. The shoe box contained all sorts, a lot of pre-war shots of picnics – the Junipers were clearly rambling enthusiasts. Some were coloured, the most recent as far as Judy could guess, a picture of Mrs Juniper in the back garden of Rectory Gardens, Nelson large as life at her feet. There were very few of Ellie beyond the age of twenty; no wonder the local press had published that terrible picture with the peek-a-boo hairstyle.

The wardrobe was mercifully uncluttered. In the course of this clearance operation Judith had come to view the deceased with fresh insight. Ellie had obviously struggled to encapsulate her belongings after commanding much more space in what was now the Osimas' flat, but had been something of a hoarder. Not much in the way of books but bundles of old sheet music, some still stamped with her school crest.

The violin was wrapped in a fringed shawl on the top shelf of the wardrobe. *That* had given her a nasty turn. She put it on the dressing table with the shoe box collection. Perhaps Basil Meek would keep the violin as a souvenir but somehow she doubted it.

She laid all Ellie's clothes on the bed, quickly sorting them into two piles, one lot swiftly bundled into plastic bin liners and the other comprising just three items. Judy went back to the kitchen to fetch the scissors and a roll of parcel string to secure the bags. She glanced at her watch. It was already after nine and she wasn't nearly finished. She felt famished, wishing now she had taken advantage of Mavis's funeral tea, but not daring to give up on the job even for a ten-minute break. Once she abandoned this gruesome task her resolve would evaporate. And she hadn't even glanced in at the bathroom yet.

The scissors were totally useless, blunt or something, making her feel inept. She gave up and tied the bags with the flimsy plastic strips supplied. It would have to do. She was already feeling nauseous from the stale smell which pervaded the piles of unwashed clothing.

Three special items remained: one an unworn organza blouse still bearing the label of a couture house and its mind-blowing price tag: the second a wonderful Gucci leather jacket: the third a pair of black multi-studded and zipped designer jeans, also apparently unworn, the pockets empty. Judy gained all her high fashion know-how from the glossies at the hairdressers, the purchasing power required even to enter the boutiques which sold items such as these well beyond a police sergeant. She sat on the bed, wondering what to do. "Basil Meek's not made of money, Judith," Veronica had insisted. And here she was consigning everything to the dustbin. She decided to put Ellie's designer gear to one side, maybe able to raise something towards Basil's legal bills by disposing of these three pieces of "in-wear" through a dress agency.

But how on earth did Ellie pay for them? Was there a credit card demand in the pipeline? Had she been a shoplifter? Or was Ellie Juniper some sort of blackmailer? A high class hooker on the side? Curbing escalating whirls of conjecture, one even more intriguing question remained: where had she *worn* such glamorous threads? Certainly not to work. Apart from heaps of tatty disco wear Ellie's clothes were standard chain store items. Except for the thigh-length red suede boots, that was.

These had been lying all askew at the bottom of the wardrobe and before adding them to the shoes in the bin bags Judy had removed the stretchers and felt about inside. An old trick learned on the beat in Soho. The Dick Whittington boots harboured a single WP disk, untitled, mysterious as an anonymous letter. Judy tucked it into her jeans and lugged the bags to the landing. She stacked a radio and the box of photographs on the desk with the camera and went back to the bedroom for a final look.

She got on her knees to lift the frilled valance and peered under the bed. Nothing but the usual fur balls and bits of fluff, presumably Nelson's contribution. She was almost through when a white square caught her eye, well back under the wardrobe. She drew a sharp breath, horribly aware that she might be about to discover the one thing the police had missed: the suicide note. It must have blown underneath when the men were banging about in their flat-footed way. She tried to push the wardrobe away from the wall but only reactivated the twinges of an old skiing accident, making her gasp with pain. She eventually fished it out with a wire coathanger and sighed with disappointment. It was just another polaroid print from the shoebox, Ellie and a thick-set young man with a cleft chin, smiling at the camera, posed in front of a manor house. The mythical fiancé? She wandered through to the living room, staring at the picture, smiling to herself, recalling Mavis and her virulent disbelief in the existence of any prospective bridegroom. She slid it under the flap of the word processor and got back to the job in hand.

She swallowed hard and made a rush at the bathroom before her nerve failed. The door had been kept shut and no-one had thought to turn on the radiators. The air hit her like a fetid face flannel, the mustiness almost palpable in the confined space. The towels were still strewn on the rail, the damp patches now black with mildew, Ellie's jumpsuit slimy. She bundled everything into a plastic bag, closing her mind to the horror of it, her hands shaking.

She lugged the bags to the basement, stacking them by the dustbins. It took two journeys and her back throbbed with the half-forgotten pain of that old back injury. Dave was obviously out. Ditto Mikki Ferrero. Mavis's TV was churning away behind her door but enlisting poor old Mavis seemed a mean trick. After all it was *her* ceiling Basil Meek was paying for. The Osimas' pram was back in the hall but Judy had never seen the man shouldering so much as a carrier bag. Wherever *he* came from the women of the tribe did all the donkey work. Here, too, she grimly agreed, toiling up to the attic for the last time.

Pausing on the top landing, she suddenly stiffened, soundless in her trainers. Someone was in Ellie's flat. She pushed open the door and waited in the tiny vestibule behind the closed sitting room entrance, hearing a muttered oath as whoever was inside stumbled over a pile of books. Judith burst in, all guns blazing, ready for a fight.

The man, his back to the door, was crouched over the scattered books, restacking them. He swung round, the flash of his spectacles catching the light. It was Gus Fielding.

She stood in the doorway as mad as hell, seeing Gus Fielding in an entirely new guise. Gone were the tweeds and comfortable cords. The bloke towering behind Ellie's desk in that low-ceilinged room was Executive Man personified, a picture straight out of the FT's fashion pages for men. He smiled, whipping off the wire-rimmed specs and stowing them in the breast pocket of the Savile Row suit.

"Judy!" he said, smiling, moving round the desk to greet

her, arms open wide. She backed off, holding up her hands in mute protest, exasperation bubbling inside like undigested vindaloo. Bloody Gus Fielding turning up like this, grinning away as if nothing had happened. What a nerve!

"What are you doing up here?" she said testily, eyeing the newly-minted geologist with interest.

"I've just got back from Malmo," he replied, still affable, far from disconcerted by her frigid tone. "I suddenly got called away for a job interview. There was no chance to call you after—"

Judy cut in. "There's no need to explain."

He touched her arm. "I thought you knew I was married – you see, I—" He faltered, the old hesitancy coming up roses, dark brown eyes deeply concerned.

"Of course I bloody didn't. Nobody thought to mention it. Least of all you, you snake, you two-timing rat, you – you – arsehole!"

He moved in close, his beard smelling of sandalwood, her resolve melting. She pushed away, distancing herself from temptation, slipping behind the mountain of a desk, its drawers now empty, the surface covered with all the stuff she had reserved to return to Janssen's consulting rooms.

"I said, what are you doing here?" she repeated.

He lit a cigarette, the flash of a Rolex glinting under his cuff. "I just got back from the airport, heard you lumping the bags down the stairs and came up to say hello."

"Need another tin of tomatoes?" she sneered, wishing now she had taken up smoking again, longing for something to calm her thudding pulse.

"Judy, don't be bitter, love," he said, taking another step round the desk. She held up a hand and waited for his answer. He took a drag at the cigarette before starting to speak.

"Naturally, I needed to speak to you about that business in Battersea. I didn't get the chance to explain. This job interview cropped up out of the blue and I had to grab the chance. My stint at the university finishes this summer. My wife's been very generous but—" He shrugged, inviting her understanding. She didn't take up the offer.

His voice rumbled on, perfectly sincere and utterly reasonable.

Judy was suddenly tired of the whole charade. "Don't go on. I've heard all this sort of thing before."

"Let's pop out for a drink then? All forgiven?"

She levelled with him, her anger dissipated. "Look, Gus, the fault was partly mine. Everyone else in this house knew you were married. It was a misunderstanding. Let's forget it, shall we?"

He stubbed out his cigarette and the old vulnerability briefly surfaced, his eyes clouded with disappointment.

"Friends?" he said, offering his hand.

"OK. Friends." She smiled, and, regarding the filthy state of her own, held up both palms in a gesture of surrender. He laughed and they relaxed, shuffling between the piles of books to hug briefly, all chums again. He gazed round the empty room, Ellie's presence now seeming quite evaporated, the ghost laid.

"I could have done with some help lugging those bags down to the basement, you dog."

He grinned, patting an immaculate lapel. "Sorry. I need notice for that sort of thing. Think yourself lucky catching sight of a prospective university lecturer in full plumage. A rare sighting. It doesn't happen often, I promise you. Actually, now I'm here I *could* do with something. The tape in my answering machine got all snagged up. Could I pinch Ellie's? I'm expecting a call."

"From your wife?"

"Hey, I thought we had a pact?"

Judy smirked. "Couldn't resist it."

"Seriously, darling, I've got to buzz up to Scotland on a field trip in the morning and I'm expecting a message from my contact in Georgetown. Please, Judy, be a pal."

He indicated Ellie's machine, the spaniel's eyes warm as honey. Judith snapped a cellophane-wrapped blank tape from the pile on the desk.

"Here, have this. I'm taking all this office stuff to the consulting rooms in the morning. The doctor won't miss one tape. Be my guest."

He pocketed it and moved to the door, eyeing the cleared rooms with distaste. "Who put you onto this filthy job? Bloody Mavis, I suppose."

"It's a long story, Gus, and I need to get some sleep. It's been one of those days."

"Then you *do* need a drink," he said, squeezing her elbow.

"I do but I must finish up here tonight. I couldn't face a second evening's charring. Let's take a raincheck on it, shall we? When you get back from your field trip."

She steered him to the door and closed it firmly, glad that piece of humiliation had been dealt with. It *had* been partly her own fault, that episode with Fielding. She had been all too eager to be taken out of herself, too easily charmed by all that geological enthusiasm. Judy was a sucker for enthusiasts. That was the trouble. That was what had snared her with Laurence Erskine, him and his naked ambition to climb to the top of the Special Branch tree. Ah well, everyone has their little weaknesses . . .

Her energy had seeped away with the anger. Now, she felt only exhaustion with the whole damned thing. She slumped at Ellie's desk looking round at the empty room and tears pricked her eyelids. Pulling a handkerchief from her pocket, the disk she had found hidden in Ellie's red boots clattered onto the floorboards. Gazing at this piece of technical magic, curiosity flared up, and the tears remained unshed. She plugged in the wizard little machine Doctor Janssen had loaned his secretary and played about with the menu display until the disk gave up its secrets. But it was merely a list of names and addresses with little symbols by each name and dates, all recent, tagging several entries. It could be a list of patients, something Ellie intended to take back to work after the weekend, had put inside her boot to make sure she didn't forget. But would she wear red suede thigh boots to the Harley Street consulting rooms? Judy shook her head, determined not to fall into Arnott's train of thought, questioning every move the poor woman made, querying her every intention. Must Ellie Juniper haunt her for all time?

She stacked the disk with the medical files and slipped everything including the library books, into a carrier bag. She would return them to Doctor Janssen herself. The files were probably confidential. Perhaps Ellie should never have brought them home in the first place.

Sitting idly at Mrs Juniper's old desk she tried the answering machine, steeling herself to hear the dead girl's voice cheerfully inviting her caller to leave a message. She tried to run back the tape. It was a basic machine, probably secondhand, nowhere near the class of the amazing little word processor. The signal flickered on and off at random and the tape kept jamming. She played about with it for a bit, getting bits of messages, then it would conk out for no apparent reason or rewind itself. Coles had probably broken the thing when he was checking everything out. As if anyone would leave a suicide message on an answering machine! Mind you, there was always a first time. Judy gave up. Basil Meek would be wise to toss the wretched piece of machinery in the dustbin with the rest. She removed the tape and looked round for the junk bag but they were all tied up, ready for the refuse collection. She put it in her pocket to take down to add to her own rubbish and limped to the door, her back aching like a twanging power line.

She took a last look round before locking up, tired to death, weary with the sheer brutality of life in general.

CHAPTER TWELVE

Judith overslept. Crashing out after that mammoth clearance operation upstairs, she must have forgotten to set the alarm. She flapped about like a grounded fledgling, repacking her briefcase, stacking the files she had promised herself to return to the consulting rooms that day. It had been weeks since Ellie typed them and could hardly be important or Janssen would have made a fuss, insisting Veronica Messop release his typescripts at least. But Judith was determined to get shot of Ellie's stuff before the weekend, purge her flat of the entire mess. She knew herself to be veering towards paranoia over this, the anxiety to rid herself of this undertaking overshadowing everything else. Once she had discharged this responsibility she had stupidly agreed to, she could get on with her life and forget all about Ellie Juniper.

Apart from the medical files there was the blasted word processor. If that didn't go back today she would probably have to take time off and wait in for it to be collected. It was by far the most valuable item in Ellie's flat, eminently nickable, and Judy was far from happy about security arrangements in Rectory Gardens. It *was* her responsibility to empty Ellie's flat; she had accepted that typewritten letter of authority from Veronica, hadn't she? Did that make her liable if there was a break-in? Dave Barnes was no deterrent and didn't even have the spare keys for the attic rooms. She could hardly expect him to keep his eye on it. She worried about all this as she flew about the flat dressing for work, slamming her dirty washing in a laundry bag ready for her regular Friday night session at the laundrette. She emerged from the bedroom only to be confronted with the designer gear which had been unceremoniously stashed in a supermarket carrier and left by the door the night before.

She started to panic. Time was marching on and there were all these damned parcels to deal with. If she didn't take her washing with her as usual she would have to come back to the flat tonight to collect it. An unconventional upbringing by Claire Pullen had left scars, imposed a character defect Judith would die rather than admit to. She was a martyr to orderliness. If any prearranged plans were threatened, she first became apprehensive then downright panicky. Perhaps that was why she liked fraud investigation. No chaos. Fraud was concerned with certainties, the logicality of balance sheets immutable.

She decided to make a clean sweep, take the whole lot with her and look forward to a weekend free of this awful responsibility. she could drive to work, drop off the doctor's files and the WP at lunchtime and get rid of the designer clothes at the dress agency round the corner from her office. Then she would be able to call at the laundrette after work as usual and be back on schedule at last. Brightening considerably she hurried upstairs to pick up the doctor's machine. The snapshot of Ellie and her "young man" stared up at her and she slipped it in her jacket pocket to show to Mavis some time. That would keep her guessing. Then she picked up the WP and balanced it on the stack of books on the landing to lock Ellie's door behind her, please God, for the very last time.

It took two trips to pack everything in. Fortunately, the Volkswagen was parked only a few yards up the street. Finally, she snatched up the supermarket carrier and clattered downstairs only to run full tilt into Mavis emerging from her own flat like a galleon setting sail for the Spanish Main. The carrier split and Ellie's expensive purchases tumbled onto the landing.

"Oh, shit. Oops! Sorry, Mavis. I'm late and now the damned bag's bust."

"Come in. I've got something stronger you could use."

Judy scrambled to recover the clothing, Mavis's eyes bird-like with curiosity. Come to think of it, wasn't a "mavis" some sort of thrush? Judy pushed this useless nugget of information aside and bundled into the flat in Mavis's wake. Nelson sidled from the kitchen looking hopeful, testing his claws on the carpet. Mavis gently footed him aside and hurried into the kitchen to ransack one of the drawers.

"Here," she carolled, "just the thing." She held up a large piece of brown paper and some string. Judy's heart sank. "Don't let me delay you, Mavis. Any old carrier bag will do. It's only Ellie's bits. I'm taking them to a dress agency."

"Very nice too." Mavis reverently touched the organza blouse, her lips moist. Judy dumped her briefcase on the floor and jammed the three items into some sort of parcel. Mavis fetched some scissors and held the knots while Judith finished it off, cutting the string and testing its strength. A work of art!

"Wonderful, Mavis. I would never have managed if this lot had burst open in the street. You're a saviour. I tried to tie it up last night but Ellie's scissors were blunt."

"Those orange-handled things? I bought those for her birthday last year. Sheffield steel, sharp as a razor. But, no wonder you couldn't cope. They're for left-handers. I got them for her at a shop in Brewer Street. Specialises in everything for sinistrists."

"Is that a problem?"

They emerged on the street, Mavis intent on making her point.

"Oh, indeed. Poor Ellie struggled and struggled over it. It made her feel so clumsy, you see. Then I discovered this marvellous shop. I've purchased several wee gifts for her there over the years. Flavia could be very unkind, you know. Constantly undermining the poor girl's self-esteem. Insisted Ellie was making a fuss about nothing, could perfectly well use her right hand if she chose to."

"Could she?"

"She tried but never quite managed it. It's congenital, of course. That violin of hers, for instance. Had to leave the ensemble – kept poking the other players in the eye with her bow."

Mavis roared with laughter and, once launched on one of her boring topics, wouldn't leave it alone, banging on about sinistral swordsmen and polo players, religious taboos regarding the use of the left hand, even diabolical connotations.

"Can I offer you a lift, Mavis? I'm taking the car this morning."

"Thank you, dear, but no. I'm only round the corner. So

94

nice to be able to walk to the library. I do so *hate* the underground."

"I *must* go. I'm awfully late." Judy stowed the word processor on the passenger seat, the pain in her back flaring as she manoeuvred the parcels. Mavis stood firm, calculating the extent of all this clearance, bristling with curiosity. Judith kept mum, determined not to get involved in any more explanations or she would be at the kerbside for another twenty minutes.

She claimed another long lunch hour and drove to Harley Street, leaving a note on the windscreen for the traffic warden, claiming delivery of important medical supplies. The consulting rooms were located in a house which sported a whole row of brass plates. He shared with a Mr Thompson, a surgeon rather past his peak but who had, in his time, pioneered orthopaedic work which was now standard procedure.

Judith had made a few enquiries about Ellie's employer and received mixed reports. Doctor Janssen was an American in his early forties who had practised in London for three or four years, specialising in back pain, an enormously lucrative field. His chief attraction was a range of corsets and support hose for men which were made to measure to Janssen's own design at a small factory outlet in Manchester. Judy's informant was sceptical about the efficacy of Doctor Janssen's treatments which bordered on those of a chiropractor. But his patients were loyal and the corsets had gained a certain notoriety when a VIP accused of cross-dressing ably defended himself by citing medical necessity. The sales figures for Janssen's corsets trebled.

Judy entered the reception area and was immediately fallen upon by a grey-haired lady of formidable presence who stepped smartly from behind a curving counter of limed oak to greet her. Before she could utter a word, the woman drew her behind the desk and pointed at a computer terminal. She explained the crisis, the fingers grasping Judy's arm tense as talons.

"You *do* understand these machines, don't you? I'm on my own here at lunchtime and I've lost Mrs Banks' entire records. And she's due at two o'clock! The doctor's at lunch," she whispered, her anguish all too plain, "and I hate to disturb him. It's not the first time, you see . . . Things were so much easier when everything was in black and white. Touch the wrong key and whoops – all gone into thin air!"

Judy sat at the console and played about with the keyboard. Displays whirled onto the screen, now lit up and twinkling like a Wurlitzer. After a rapid exchange of information, the missing case notes flashed up and the receptionist's hand struck Judith's shoulder like an accolade, her gratitude embarrassingly effusive. She scrambled up, stumbling over the little WP piled up with Janssen's files that she had placed on the floor.

"Oh, Miss Preston, thank you so much. You are just what we need. Doctor Janssen could have fixed it for me but I hate bothering that poor man, he has a greater caseload than any other consultant would dream of taking on. And, just now, understaffed as we are, I'm having to do *everything*. Temps have been hopeless. When can you start?"

"Start?"

"We need a replacement straight away. We were very impressed with your CV and," she lowered her voice, "I'm Mrs Quick, of course. We spoke on the phone. I feel sure the advertised salary could be improved upon."

"Could it?"

"Oh, indeed. Up to £13,000, easily. We are quite desperate for someone who can really cope with all this." She waved at the battery of screens visible through the half-open door of the rear office. "Our last girl was useless. Unreliable, though, of course, one must not speak ill of the dead." Mrs Quick hastened to cover her indiscretion. "An accident at home," she explained, nodding reassuringly. "If you could begin next week, Miss Preston, you could get the files reorganised before Doctor Janssen leaves."

"He's leaving?"

"Oh, yes. A sabbatical. But, of course the New Zealander you will be working for will take over next month, a very experienced consultant, Doctor Harris from the Mayo Clinic. You'll like him, I'm sure. Quite young, I'm told."

Judith wondered if she was wasting her time with the Met. Obviously this Mrs Quick was quite desperate for staff. And £13,000 for a typist? Flexitime with the option of working from home? If Ellie Juniper could hold down a job like that any fool could do it.

"Look, Mrs Quick. I'm afraid there's been a misunderstanding. My name's Pullen. Judith Pullen. I just popped in to return some of Doctor Janssen's papers. I live in Rectory Gardens and—"

"You're not Miss Preston? The girl who answered the advertisement?"

"I'm afraid not. You, see I didn't have time to explain. As soon as I came in—"

The inner door opened and a tall man filled the entry. He was in his shirt-sleeves and held a half-eaten ham roll in his hand.

"Oh, Doctor Janssen," Mrs Quick stammered. "There's been some confusion. I was expecting a Miss Preston at one, a replacement for – er—"

"Please excuse us, Ms—?"

"Pullen. Judith Pullen." She was getting rather fed up with this. Were these people from another planet? "I was asked to sort out Miss Juniper's flat." She passed her business card across the desk to the doctor.

"My lunch," he said, wrapping the sandwich in a paper napkin and tossing it in the waste paper basket. "Please excuse us. Do you need some information about her work here?"

Judith put her errand in a nutshell and proffered the files. Mrs Quick subsided in her chair and looked dazed, the doctor listening patiently, ferociously attentive. Judith could guess why the man was so popular. He leafed through the typescripts, offering her a seat, a cup of coffee, anything at all, profuse in his gratitude. His crew cut needed trimming and his tie was askew, the hands shuffling the typescript tanned, with long fingers.

"I've been waiting weeks for these lecture notes. I'm off on a conference this weekend. You're an angel from heaven, Sergeant Pullen."

"You see Ellie took a little work home," Mrs Quick explained, "And we have had difficulties extracting anything. An Inspector Coles insisted it would all be dealt with in due course but you know how bureaucratic these people can be."

The doctor winced, wishing Mrs Quick were swifter on the

uptake. Did she not realise this pretty blonde was with the police?

Judith scrabbled in her bag and extracted the disk she had recovered from Ellie's fancy thigh boots.

"And there's this," she said, leaning forward to place it on the desk. The sharp movement activated some sort of torture mechanism in her back and the spasm of pain momentarily took her breath away. Janssen was round the desk in an instant, all concern. Judith straightened, white-faced, and minimised her difficulty as best she could. No, she needed no treatment. No, not even later, after work. And bringing Ellie's files back was the least she could do. These stilted phrases sounded in her ear like words from the screenplay of some phoney TV soap and she backed to the door, hardly hearing Mrs Quick's repeated thanks.

Judith limped downstairs, and climbed into the car, wondering what all the fuss was about. Were Ellie's typescripts really so valuable? Or was the light that dawned in the doctor's eye when she produced the disk like a rabbit out of a hat the reason for what could only be described as a crazy set-up. If people beat a path to these consulting rooms and begged Janssen to take their money, wasn't it time they got someone who at least could handle the computer?

As if on cue, a smart cookie in a mini skirt and stilettos teetered up to the door and rang the doctor's bell. Their prayers had been answered. Miss Preston had descended from Paradise to pour light on the display terminals.

Mrs Quick telephoned her at her office later that afternoon and after a courteous preamble explained that the WP disk was not, in fact, part of the doctor's filing system.

"Oh dear. I'd better collect it then."

"I've already sent it over. By bike messenger. We use these boys for urgent medical deliveries and I thought it might be important."

"Did you run it through?"

"Ah well, I must confess I put one of the job applicants through her paces, just to test her ability to use the equipment here. The disk belongs to an organisation called Domino. Ellie's name appears right at the end. She was obviously a member of this group. I've sent a print-out with the package.

I didn't bother Doctor Janssen with all this, he's really only interested in getting his lecture notes back, I'm sure. He's off tonight. A medical conference in Venice, goodness knows how the poor man finds time for all these things."

"I forgot to ask you about Ellie's things in her desk. Did Ms Messop contact you?"

"I spoke to the solicitor on the telephone several times. I was trying to get the inspector to release the doctor's lecture notes and she promised to look into it. Miss Messop suggested I throw Ellie's personal items away as there was nothing worth keeping. Only some make-up and an umbrella."

"No diary?"

"Nothing like that!"

"Any keys?"

"Miss Messop did ask me to make a thorough search but there was absolutely nothing else, I promise you."

They chatted on for a few minutes like old collaborators, two worthy foot soldiers in the battle to save the dear doctor any possible inconvenience. Ellie, too, in her time, Judy assumed. My goodness, there were probably platoons of them out there. He was certainly very attractive. Wonderful what a job in the private sector could do for a medical man.

She stopped off at a smart dress agency near Walton Street on her way home and found the place full to bursting, women everywhere, scrabbling through rails of expensive cast-offs. The place had been recommended by her assistant, Mary Sumner, who insisted it was much more voguish than the agency Judy originally had in mind.

"We stay open late on Fridays," the salesgirl explained. "Evening wear's in great demand this time of year and we get a lot of panic buying before the weekend."

Judy watched the girl cut the string on Mavis's armour-plated parcel and stood back, waiting for her reaction.

"Oh, my. This is *really* beautiful," she crooned, stroking the ruffles of the organza blouse. "And this jacket will simply walk off the rails. Leather always sells."

She examined the zipped jeans, picking over the studded design with vermillion-tipped fingers. "Tomalski," she said, pointing to the label.

Judith shrugged.

"Wonderful designer. Very, *very* chic. But I'm afraid it must be dry cleaned."

"But they've hardly been worn."

"Our policy, I'm afraid. There's a smashing place just next door. You can bring them back next week. They'll go like a flash but we like to play safe with trousers."

Judith nodded, accepting a receipt for the other items, amazed at the resale estimate the agency suggested.

The dry cleaners was about to shut up shop and the bored assistant snatched the Tomalski jeans with ill-grace. She rifled through the pockets, discovering zipped crannies Judith had assumed merely to be decorative, wordless in her contempt for the tat which crossed her counter. She herself was dressed sensibly in a nylon overall and her irritability suggested she would be more than happy with a face mask and surgeon's gloves as well. Judy could see her point. Having sorted Ellie's clothing she was a little squeamish herself. This poor soul handled soiled items day in and day out, locked in the gagging atmosphere of cleaning fluid fumes.

"Here," she snapped, passing over yet another item Judy had overlooked in her cursory pocket search. It was a membership card issued by Domino and made out to Elinor Juniper. Judy thrust it in her bag and watched the woman write out the ticket, fascinated by her awkward grasp of the ballpoint, her hand curved above the receipt book as she wrote. The penny dropped. The woman was left-handed. She was obliged to hold the pen in an entirely different way from right-handers. Judith had never bothered to consider this before and Mavis's diatribe that morning came flooding back. She could well imagine old Mrs Juniper trying to force her child to conform, to write gracefully, not in this clumsy cack-handed fashion.

Later, as she sat in the laundrette watching the washing churn, the worm of suspicion grew, snaking about in her mind, impossible to ignore. She *must* speak to Arnott. He would know.

She phoned him from the pay phone in the laundrette.

"Come over, lass. I've got a nice wing of skate to sink your teeth into. Lovely bit of fish. Straight off the market this morning."

CHAPTER THIRTEEN

Before driving to Mortlake Judith did a round of all the off-licences within walking distance of Rectory Gardens. Ellie didn't drive, had never owned a car to Judy's knowledge, and a bottle of gin purchased late on Easter Sunday had probably been bought locally.

She bought a half-bottle of Islay malt at her first call and produced the polaroid of Ellie and the mystery man to show the chap behind the counter. Did he know this customer? Or the man? He was cooperative enough, especially when Judith flashed her warrant card, even offering to check his till receipts in case any purchase had been made with a credit card. Juniper was an uncommon name. He hazarded a guess, grinning. Another political scandal?

She moved on to the other outlets in the vicinity and drew a total blank. No-one even recognised the name. The last shop was empty and the man serving happy to play Sherlock Holmes.

"Could have got her gin in a pub or a supermarket, miss."

"Possibly. But this lady was something of a secret drinker. My guess it was a last-minute buy – Easter Sunday night – and there are no all-night supermarkets near here, are there? Not within walking distance anyway. And as this woman pretended she didn't drink, I don't suppose she would be a regular at a pub near home."

He studied the photograph, adjusting his bifocals, giving it his full attention. The girl in the owlish glasses was nothing special, hardly the sort to knock your eye out if she came through the door. He shrugged, passing it back over the counter, and reached behind him for the second bottle of whisky on Judy's shopping list. Dave had offered to start on her ceiling on Monday and she had promised to keep an emergency bottle of Bell's in the cupboard in case he fell off the wagon.

Come to think of it, Dave was the one who had vehemently asserted Ellie was teetotal, and he was a notorious cadger. Maybe she put this story of abstinence about to protect herself from Dave Barnes popping in all hours for a free drink. But it would be a difficult front to maintain. The most likely explanation lay in Dave's original response: Ellie, as an alcoholic, was just a beginner. She gave up and pushed on to Mortlake. The Islay malt was a sort of peace offering to Arnott for having been so dismissive of his suspicions about Ellie Juniper. The woman was an enigma.

Arnott lived near the river, not far from Chiswick Bridge, the only yellow brick house in a street of Victorian one-offs, a speculator's mish-mash of small dwellings. His wife had died the year before and he was always talking about selling up and moving back to Yorkshire but never did anything about it. Buying the boat was his only concession to retirement and he kidded himself he could live on board when he finally got it shipshape. Not that it seemed at all likely. It was too small to use as a houseboat and, though loath to admit it, his years with the Met had made Arnott more at home pounding city streets.

He opened the door and drew Judy into his stuffy kitchen, the table littered with instruction sheets from a model kit. He was trying to insert a little sailing ship in a bottle, his stubby fingers trembling with the effort of folding the delicate rigging. She stood by amazed, not daring to show her disbelief.

"Not your usual sort of thing this, is it, Arnott?"

"Bloody fiddle-faddle. That silly bugger Bernie Allen put me onto it."

"The coroner's officer?"

"Said I needed something to keep my mind busy. My bloody brain box nearly short-circuited trying to suss out these sodding wires." He gestured wildly and the flat-sided bottle skidded onto the floor, smashing into smithereens.

Judy leapt backwards, waiting for the explosion, but his reaction was more of relief than rage.

"Only one good thing ever comes out of a bottle," he said,

sweeping up the broken glass. Judy produced the single malt and Arnott's skies were blue, clear to the horizon.

"Clever lass!" he crowed, stowing the model tea clipper in a drawer. "Don't say nowt more till I've done the fish. Park yourself down there and pour yourself a stiff one."

"Not now, Arnott. After we've eaten. I've got to drive home."

She watched his speckled hands deal with two wings of skate, slamming them under the grill, liberally buttered, his breath laboured as he fussed over what Judy guessed to be yet another entirely new accomplishment. Cooking for himself was something of a conjuring trick for Arnott; cooking "for company" called for real magic. Judith perched on the edge of the table sipping from a can of beer, gazing round at Peg's neat kitchen, at the microwave on the counter top.

"You ever used that microwave they gave you? It's good for fish. Quick too." The oven had been a retirement present from the personnel at Arnott's last HQ.

He tapped his big nose. "You wait till you've tasted this little lot before you start offering any advice, Pullen. Good as Harry Ramsden's, this caff. Here, open up these chips while I watch the skate," he said, passing a pair of scissors and some oven chips.

She snipped the plastic bag and emptied the chips into the dish Arnott pushed across the table, feeling like the sorcerer's apprentice as usual.

"It was Ellie's scissors put me on to it, Arnott. If it hadn't been for Mavis I would never have guessed."

"Not now, missy, wait till grub's up. We'll chew over all this Juniper lark later. I've got a nice little apple tart for afters."

Judy's eyes widened. "You do pastry as well?"

"The nosey cow next door thinks I need fattening up. Keeps leaving plates on the back doorstep when I'm out," he replied with disgust.

The fish *was* good and the maligned neighbour's baking was tip-top. Arnott insisted on leaving all the crocks in the sink and they moved into the over-furnished living room where he had lit a fire. Peg's presence was still in evidence: lots of little knick-knacks dotted about and a dusty bowl of dried heather on the sideboard.

Arnott put coal on the fire and poured the whisky. "Now what's all this about scissors?"

Judith explained about the shop in Brewer Street. "Mavis discovered it. She bought these special scissors for Ellie. You see, Ellie was left-handed."

"So *that's* why you wanted to take a dekko at the pathologist's report on the q.t. . . . ." He whistled through his teeth.

She nodded, eyeing him with apprehension, waiting for the usual jeers, his normal reaction to any brainwave from his former sergeant.

"You sure, Pullen? Plenty of people can play it both ways. What about her fiddle? Was that from Miss Marple's cack-handers' shop an' all?"

"Of course not! I expect she just got hers adapted – I've never thought about it. But she couldn't play like a normal violinist in a string section, the bowing must have been awkward for the others – probably poked them in the eye. She had to leave her music group."

"Who says?"

"Mavis."

"Right old know-all, ain't she?"

"Mavis has lived in Rectory Gardens for years and years. Even before the Commander died. She must have been Mrs Juniper's original boarder, knew Ellie as a schoolgirl."

He scoured her face for any hint of a leg-pull but Judith's set features were desperately anxious, like a rock climber not daring to contemplate the crevasse opening up ahead.

"Right, lass."

Arnott lumbered out of his chair and trawled through a stack of files on top of the bureau, all mixed up with old newspapers and a few copies of sailing magazines.

They poured over the report in silence, the mantle clock ticking away like a time bomb. At last he drew back, making up one of his cigarettes, fuming the room with his special roll-up mixture, the dark brown smell strong as stewed teabags. Judith coughed, wondering if he grew the stuff himself in the back garden.

"You've hit the bloody bullseye and no mistake. You should have stayed with the CID, Pullen. Wasting your time with them pen-pushers. It's all here in black and white – fancy you remembering that one little word: the pathologist definitely said the trachea was cut from the left all right. All done in the dark an' all. If you believe *that* I'm a Dutchman."

"I'm quite sure, Arnott. I went into her bathroom and pulled the light cord. Then I pulled the shower door wide open."

"So not only did this woman slice her artery with the hand she couldn't even cut bog paper with but she gets up afterwards and puts out the light. If the floor hadn't been flooded we could have checked for any trail of blood on the lino."

The clock ticked on while they absorbed the implications of all this, Judith's eyes riveted on Arnott, waiting for him to confirm the truth of which she was now certain. It was a pity only Mavis had known about Ellie's left-handedness but, there again, from the police angle, suicides in bedsitterland weren't exactly rare and a victim who may have thought herself to be incubating AIDS invited presumptions which, even with the best investigation, shut one's mind to more sinister conjecture.

Judy wondered if she was subconsiously seeking a reprieve for *herself*? Willing Arnott to put his seal of approval on an explanation which not only disposed of the notion that Ellie Juniper – a perfectly normal girl – was capable of killing herself but that she, a trained observer, had failed to recognise someone on the verge of self-destruction? And if so, that left that other, darker question . . .

"I had my doubts right from the start," Arnott said at last. "Should have tackled Coles head on. Getting too bleeding polite in me old age." He didn't mention his other reason for holding off: a sentimental reluctance to bring further grief to a kid who had not only woken with the victim's blood dripping from her ceiling, but would have to live with the fact that a murder had taken place above her head in a flat she had only recently vacated.

Arnott regarded the girl with an unwavering eye. No doubt about it, this Juniper business had knocked her right off her perch. Arnott had been the last man to wish himself saddled with an eight-stone whispy female on his professional team and had given the lass a hard time of it. Never shielded her from a roasting and they had worked on cases every bit as violent as this throat-slashing suicide. But Pullen had always come up trumps – not so much as a flicker. Arnott was puzzled. Why had this case hit her so hard? It wasn't as if the Juniper female had been a particular mate of hers or even the first time his former DS had been faced with a cadaver.

He waited. The clock ticked in the silent room. At last, the words tumbled out.

"Do you think Ellie Juniper was killed by mistake, Arnott? Someone who thought it was me?"

There, it was out in the open at last.

Arnott ground out his fag end and laughed fit to bust. "You can swill that crackpot idea down the plughole, Pullen. What grudge merchants you got in the fraud squad? Poncing little confidence tricksters all you're likely to make enemies of. Not like on *my* patch. Vicious buggers them days, carve you up for a packet of Woodbines." He poured another whisky and beamed at Judith, reassuring as a toby jug. She relaxed.

"What shall we do then?"

"Lie low, my duck. I'll put my thinking cap on and have another word with Bernie Allen. No need to bust a gut. Coroners' verdicts *can* eventually get chucked out, and the poor little tart's not going to get up and wave a flag just because we alter the small print, is she?"

Judy leapt up, her anger flaring. "But this killer could strike again! It could even be someone living in my house."

"Now 'old on, no good carrying on like a drama queen. Typical! Let's just check it out first, shall we? Half the lodgers in your 'ouse that night was working or off on the razzle or sommat. In the clear, any road. That jazz bloke, the caretaker – 'e's a rough diamond all right. Wouldn't put it past him to rub her out just for the meter money."

"Dave Barnes was at his club Easter Sunday. All night. I expect Inspector Coles verified that – he's not a complete moron."

"Sez you! Still, these blokes in the band get a blow at 'alf-time, don't they? Could've buzzed back 'ome, done her in and been back in Soho tooting his horn afore no-one notices he's gone missing."

"Dave's not the type, Arnott. Honestly, he's pretty harmless. You think any man with a ponytail's a freak of some sort. Why should he hate Ellie?"

"P'raps she give him a dose of salts."

"HIV? I tackled him about that. He did have an affair with her but that was ages ago and after the inquest he panicked and got himself tested. He made no secret of it and I'm sure what he said is true: Dave knew nothing about the HIV till after she was dead. Anyway, he says there were others."

"What others?"

"The Spanish waiter, the one who shares my landing. Mikki Ferrero in number five."

"Him? I know that one. Not enough nous to rub out a cockroach. Clever, you know, setting her up like a suicide. Calculated if you ask me. The killer's not in the same class as that dago."

"How would you know?"

Arnott's smirk was hidden as the hooked nose dipped over the tumbler of whisky, savouring the peaty aroma. He reluctantly admitted speaking to the Spaniard.

"When?"

"I was curious about the so-called security of that flat of yours. Supposed to be tight as a drum that night, no-one at home but you, me, Gus Fielding and the Nigerians. I went round there on the quiet, didn't I? I'd had a beer with Bernie Allen after the inquest and Bernie wouldn't wear my doubts about the evidence. Insisted I had a copy of the pathologist's report to put my 'at on straight. Didn't even have to ask. Too narked by me picking holes in the verdict to see his own bald patch. Practically pushed the report down my throat, silly sod."

"You really are a toad, Arnott. I thought Bernie was a pal of yours?"

"What are pals for if not to put you on the right road? he said with a rough edge to his voice. It still rankled, the assumption that a retired copper was no more than a toothless old guard dog, good for nothing but the knacker's yard.

"Anyhow after a rollicking from Bernie Allen bang after a dose of Coles at the inquest, my gut was playing me up. I bundled straight back to your place and rang one of the bells. As it happened I hit the Spaniard. His voice comes over the squawk box like Rudolph bloody Valentino and I says I've got some flowers to deliver to Miss Pullen. She ain't in, I says. Would he take delivery, I says. OK, he says, put it inside."

"Then he opens the front door on the remote." Judith looked solemn, not a bit amused by Arnott's comic turn.

"Clements and Juniper both have their names up by the row of bells at the front door. But even if they was all just numbers, any sly bugger could talk his way in. A note in a milk bottle would do it, latch on any one name and bob's your uncle, even a shout through the intercom saying parcel for number six or whatever would be open sesame. Greed and laziness unlock any number of doors and that's discounting the slippy sam who hovers on the doorstep pretending to push a buzzer and just follows the next one in. Your place's no different from anywhere else. Takes a mugging to frighten people into taking more care who they open up to."

"Beats breaking and entering," Judy glumly agreed. "Even so, each individual flat is locked. Getting inside the building's only first base."

"Well, when I waltzed into your place it was like a tomb. I could have slipped the locks of any one of them doors. Easy as winking. Few stay in them bedsits long enough to put in decent locks. Even a kid can work a bit of plastic these days. Boys of ten wire up cars in two shakes just for something to do. Take it from me, Pullen, it don't have to be someone in the house who cut up that bird. Anyone could get in, lie low, prowl about. I should have slipped your lock that afternoon and left a daffodil on your bed just to give you something to think about."

Judith winced.

Arnott continued, blind to the warning signals.

"Take my point? It's open house. No sign of the jazz player in the basement. I'm inside. What next? Why not do the Cook's tour while I've got the chance? Legged it up to the top floor to take another squint at the Juniper set-up on me own without Coles's man breathing down my neck. Then I heard a door bang and got out quick before the Spaniard woke his ideas up."

"And Mikki didn't come down?"

"Course he bloody didn't! Wasn't going to get out of bed for a bunch of tulips, was he?"

"He didn't say anything to me about any flowers."

"Thought you'd picked them up from the hall where he'd told

me to leave 'em. It's a well-known fact if a villain wants to nip inside a block of flats any one of a row of doorbells'll do it.

"Well, don't ever try a trick like that again. You'll end up inside! Here," she passed him a set of keys. "These are due back with the solicitor, Messop & James, off Cale Street; the address is in the book. If you want to take a peek at Ellie's flat, do it with my blessing and return the keys for me afterwards. Mavis will vouch for you if there's any trouble from Dave. I'm clearing out while he's decorating."

Arnott put Ellie's keys in the pocket of his scruffy cardigan and impatiently picked up the thread of his argument. "You see what I'm getting at, don't you, Pullen? Any fool could have got in. But I'd lay odds it was someone from outside went up to her flat that night, a man she knew and someone a lot brighter than the Spaniard. Need all your wits about you to pull something like that. What about Fielding?"

"Gus? Why him? You'll be accusing Mavis next!" Judy's eyes slid away, avoiding Arnott's. "Mind if I make some coffee? My head's spinning."

Arnott watched her go, unblinking as a pike. She waited for the kettle to boil, taking deep breaths, willing her nerve ends to stop vibrating. Gus Fielding? Did Arnott seriously consider a man like that could slit a girl's throat, watch her die and then calmly spend the rest of the evening laughing and drinking with the neighbours?

By the time she settled by the fireside again, she had things back under control.

"About Gus Fielding—" she began.

"No need to go into all that," he said gruffly. "Let's get on with it. We're into deep water with this, you know. Let's go back over it. Step by step. You'll have to fill me in, Pullen. So bloody pissed that night I couldn't put a pin in a donkey's backside."

Judy felt her way forward, dredging for the details of that terrible Sunday evening.

"OK. We'll start with the violin. I went up to apologise to Ellie and took Nelson with me. She opened the door and—"

"Was she wearing her party frock?"

"No, just the jumpsuit – that all-in-one red jersey thing – and slippersocks."

"Made up, was she?"

"Can't remember. Is all this important? For heaven's sake stop interrupting."

"What time was all this?"

"Shortly after nine. I can't say exactly."

"You went in and stayed how long?"

"Gosh, it's so long ago, Arnott . . . But not long. Ten or fifteen minutes I suppose. I got the impression she wanted me to go. Said she was expecting someone."

"A man."

Judith paused, sipping her coffee, picturing that last encounter.

"Now you come to mention it, she only said 'someone'. I just assumed it was a date."

"Why?"

"Oh, I don't know. An impression . . . She was keyed up. Perhaps I was wrong. Maybe she didn't want me to think no-one had asked her out over Easter."

"She offer you a drink?"

"No fear. If she'd already started on the gin she was keeping it for herself. That's another funny thing, Arnott. When I was clearing out the cupboards there were no mixers. No tonic or bitter lemon or anything. Not even angostura—"

"What's that?"

"Bitters. For pink gins. Mrs Juniper's favourite tipple."

"A real toper don't faff about with ice cubes and bits of lemon, Pullen. Drinks her gin neat or with a drop of water. Don't waste the flavour diluting it."

"Yuk! Neat gin! Do you think that was it? Anyway, Ellie looked pretty sober while I was with her but that was early on. When I got back downstairs we watched TV for a bit then I heard rock music from the top floor. I went out onto the landing and found Gus on his way up to Ellie's and I asked him in. Later, I went to the bathroom to fetch another bottle of wine. That's when I thought I heard someone on the stairs."

"What time was this?"

"Must have been about a quarter to ten. I assumed it was Ellie's date arriving and they were going out clubbing."

"She say she was going out?"

"Not exactly . . . Actually, no, she didn't. I'm not sure if

I thought that when she mentioned someone was calling for her or assumed it later. But I may have misled you. For all we know she wasn't going out at all. She may have been planning to entertain this bloke at home."

"Went to a lot of trouble, didn't she? False eyelashes, silver nail polish, fancy silk knickers?"

"Well, why not? If this was Mr Right why shouldn't she put on a bit of a show? There was no disco gear in evidence, just the same old jumpsuit tossed in the corner of the bathroom, if you remember. Do you think the steps I heard were Ellie's? On her way out? Popping out for a bottle of gin? Perhaps this man phoned her and said he was running late, how about an evening at home for a change?"

Arnott looked doubtful and Judy confessed she had already asked at the local off-licences to see if anyone knew Ellie Juniper.

"Staff change all the time at them places. Happen it was a part-timer working late on a Sunday. You'd have to make a full enquiry of it to check if she was a customer or not. When did Fielding push off?"

"After midnight."

"And the rock-around-the-clock was still banging away upstairs?"

"No. Oh no. But I can't remember when it stopped. Mind you, if she put the tape on when this man turned up he could have killed her and been over the other side of town before the music finished. It's not like the business of the bathroom light being switched off. The music could have covered the comings and goings of a whole football team over quite a time sequence."

"And the pathologist can't pin down the time of death exactly. The poor cow could have died before or *after* midnight, don't forget. And while we're chucking bricks about, Fielding could have been on his way downstairs when you collared him, not *up*. Or he could have slipped back upstairs well after he left us."

Judith jumped up, slopping her coffee, her hazel eyes sharp as nutbrittle.

"Why have you got it in for this guy, Arnott? You get on a line with something and bend steel rods to point your argument in one direction. Have some sense for a change. Who benefits if Ellie Juniper dies. *Not* Gus Fielding, who gets absolutely no bonus out of all this. *Not* Dave Barnes – he may well lose his home and his caretaking job if the house is sold. And *not* Mikki bloody Ferrero whose only misdemeanor is to let any Tom, Dick or Arnott through the front door! The only beneficiary in this sad, sorry mess is Basil Meek."

She broke off, two bright spots of colour flaring in her white face. She sat down heavily, dabbing at the coffee stain on her skirt.

Arnott said nothing, watching the girl with more than a flicker of interest. "You know sommat I don't?" he said.

"*That* wouldn't be difficult! Stop acting as if Gus Fielding's in a one horse race, Arnott, and take a fresh look at the facts. Basil Meek inherits zilch when the old lady died. He's over forty years old, still nothing more than a steward on a cruise liner and bored out of his mind with geriatric tourists doing the tropical islands. His aunt was a terrible snob, probably thought Basil the absolute end. He's gay by the way. Did I tell you that? Nevertheless, he pulls out all the stops to worm his way back into the family circle and attaches himself to his none-too-bright cousin Elinor. She falls for his 'Blood's thicker than water' spiel and accepts Basil's magnanimous offer of a free cruise to help her get over her mother's death."

"This all on the up and up, Pullen, or you making it up as you go along?"

"Cross my heart," she says, her eyes hard with determination to put the old bully in his place. "Ellie sells the family jewels and not only takes him up on this holiday but extends it touring the southern states."

"Where she picks up her HIV infection," Arnott insists. "These shipboard flings always end in tears."

"Now who's making it up as he goes along? Let's stick to what we know, shall we? The pathologist considered the infection to be of long standing and this cruise was little more than six months ago. Anyway, Ellie Juniper goes walkabout starting from Miami and probably gets as far as Washington before her leave runs out. I'm guessing about that last bit only on the strength of a library book."

Arnott attempted to interrupt but she silenced him with

a gesture straight out of the traffic warden's handbook and continued.

"Basil Meek persuades his lonely cousin in the course of this romantic cruise to reinstate him within the family."

"With that new will of hers?"

"Absolutely. But, dearie me, before the ink's dry, Ellie starts telling everyone she's got a beau and they're going to get married. Happy ever after, amen."

"Except that if she gets wed, the money bypasses Basil yet again?"

"Give that man the Doctor Watson Award!"

"Not much of a motive though, is it? A run-down boarding house."

Judith shrugged. "We're not all as ambitious as you, Arnott. If you were facing another twenty years paddling round the Caribbean being nice to blue-rinsed old widows, even Rectory Gardens would be alluring. Though I don't suppose the rents bring in much. I pay the minimum going rate and I daresay Mavis has special consideration, being the Junipers' original tenant. Dave retains the basement in exchange for his services and I gather another is also on a freebie. That only leaves Gus Fielding, Mikki and the Osimas to make up the difference. Hardly a gold-plated investment, I'd agree."

Arnott leaned back and roared with laughter, clutching his beer belly.

"There's a hole in your bucket, Miss Cleverclogs. Basil Meek was miles away when the poor little trollop bought it."

Judith sobered, suddenly sick of their little parlour game.

"So he says. But I have it on good authority Basil was put ashore and not only missed the Easter cruise but disappeared for over a fortnight. He was on suspension and likely to lose his job. He could have flown back to England on the quiet, tried to put Ellie off this boyfriend she was threatening to run away with and there was a row."

"The pathologist never explained the bump on her head," Arnott muttered.

"That was hardly a fractured skull, for God's sake. Probably wouldn't even knock her out."

"Don't you believe it, missy! Take only a tap if she was

already half-cut with half a bottle of gin inside her. Probably out cold!"

"And the killer takes his chance and stabs at her neck before she comes round, leaving not a drop of blood anywhere but in the shower cubicle! Funny place to stage a fight. Unless Basil isn't really gay, after all, and they were having water sports."

They look at each other in confusion.

"We're out on a limb with this one, Arnott. There's not a shred of evidence. No-one at the off-licences even recognised the man pictured with her either." She searched her bag and came up with the polaroid. "Fact remains she bought a bottle of gin somewhere close and I'm willing to bet she had no booze in the house when I was there."

"Too bloody mean to share it if you ask me. Careful with her brass. That crow's nest of hers was freezing. Saving up for another cruise most like."

"She didn't earn much as a typist, believe me, but that's another strange thing. Her wardrobe contained a few very, very expensive items. I wonder if she had a sugar-daddy on the side?"

"Wouldn't rate her any sort of bimbo meself," Arnott said, narrowing his eyes at the snapshot. "Have to blackmail a silly old sod like me before I coughed up. Here, look at this."

Arnott stabbed at the photograph with his ballpoint and before Judith could snatch it away, he had scribbed out the cleft chin.

"Hey, stop it, Arnott. I need that. I'm taking off while Dave replasters my ceiling. I thought I would flash it around. See if anyone knows this bloke. Mavis hasn't seen it yet."

She broke off, staring at the snapshot of the two of them standing in the sunshine in front of some sort of stately home, smiling at the camera. Classic hearts and roses.

"It is, ain't it?" Arnott insisted, filling in an inky beard. "Never forget a face even if I'm nine sheets to the wind."

Judith's mouth dropped. Arnott was grinning away like Mr Punch, absolutely full of himself.

"I'm right you know," he crowed, stabbing at the scribble which had transformed Ellie Juniper's anonymous fiancé. "It's bloody Fielding right enough."

CHAPTER FOURTEEN

She drove home in a daze, the possibility that Gus Fielding had been Ellie's lover tolling like a bell in her head. Had her own brief affair with the geologist infected her too? Could she set aside that persistent nightmare that the body upstairs had been something she herself had only narrowly escaped only to be haunted by that other bogie, the contemporary Black Death stalking sexual freedom? She must confront him with all this, demand to know if he *had* slept with the dead girl. But Gus was in Scotland, wasn't he? Wasn't that the reason he needed the tape from the answering machine upstairs?

Judith stiffened, sensing a strangeness about the flat, a fugitive male presence. Aftershave? Sandalwood? Was she becoming neurotic? She checked all the rooms but nothing was out of place, nothing missing. Perhaps Dave had been in to estimate for the ceiling repairs as he had said he would. She smiled as another thought surfaced: was it nothing more sinister than Dave's sweaty armpits?

She poured a stiff drink and sat in the newly-painted yellow sitting room, rigid with apprehension. After a second drink, a semblance of calm prevailed and she tried to put things on a sensible footing. Nothing was certain. Chances were Gus had no truck with Ellie Juniper. Mavis had insisted Ellie's overtures had been evaded, hadn't she? Would Gus be fool enough to seduce Mrs Juniper's daughter under her very nose? The old bat would have proved a formidable enemy if she had discovered a married man to be dabbling with Ellie, though Mrs J had certainly never guessed there had been anything going on between Ellie and her caretaker and Dave had clearly been exaggerating when he included Mikki Ferrero in all this, let alone Osima, for God's sake.

There was nothing she could do tonight. It was too late to

try to locate Gus, and Dave would be working at the jazz club. It must wait till morning. She dragged herself out of the chair and ran a bath, determined to relax and try to get some rest. Tomorrow she would tackle Dave about Gus Fielding, get everything into perspective, insist on some sensible answers.

The sun was already streaming through the window when she woke. Judy had slept better than she had dared to hope and a week's leave stretched enticingly ahead. She bounced into the kitchen and made coffee, switching on the inane antics of breakfast TV, her night sweats about Gus Fielding's love life shrunk to size. The faint hint of a male intruder still hung in the air and with a pang she remembered Laurence Erskine. She owed him a letter or at least return his calls. Truth was she felt uncomfortable with the turn events had taken and shied away from the decision whether or not to confide in the man who was the strongest thread in her life.

She turned off the TV and moved back to the spare room to get dressed. Judith avoided entering the bedroom while the stained ceiling remained and had got used to Pixie's sofabed. The room was pokey and her clothes tended to pile up on the desk but at least it was neutral ground. She wondered if she would ever be able to face up to that bedroom ceiling again, even after Dave had put it right. Rectory Gardens would never be the same. She really must set about finding another place to live even if her rent doubled.

Pulling on jeans and a T-shirt, she wandered back to the living room to check the messages on her answering machine, jabbing at it in vain. The tape was missing. She searched everywhere just to make sure she hadn't absentmindedly left it out. This was insane! But she already knew the answer. Someone *had* been here. Why had nothing been stolen? Were they only interested in her messages? She telephoned Arnott, full of foreboding, wondering if he had recorded any observations about the pathologist's report while she had been at work. He liked leaving niggling problems for her to solve, tease her a little. But why would anyone be interested in that? Surely Arnott would never have sneaked in as he had jokingly threatened and extracted a forfeit just to prove his point . . .

There was no reply. She guessed he had already taken off for Rye to work on the boat. Arnott couldn't stand weekends alone at Mortlake. He had admitted as much. Having the boat was really only an excuse to escape the loneliness of the neat little house with all its memories. No Peg. No career. No status. Only the unbearable sympathies of his well-meaning neighbour.

She sat staring at the machine, picturing that last encounter with Gus in Ellie's flat two nights ago. Had he guessed she might discover the photograph and hoped to recover it from those in the shoebox all too clearly waiting to be examined? So what? A resourceful man could easily explain it away: "Just taking the girl for a spin. Showing Ellie some geological dig somewhere." There was no clue when it had been taken or who the third person had been, the one who held the camera. When did he he grow the beard? Judith had never seen him cleanshaven but then she couldn't remember noticing him at all until recently. How long had this Lothario been living in the house?

Another idea surfaced, a more sinister conjecture. Had Gus Fielding's voice been on Ellie's tape? But why wait so long? If Gus *had* left a message for Ellie surely Inspector Coles would have checked it out. She drew the tell-tale cassette from the pocket of her jeans where she had almost forgotten about it. She was building all these suspicions on nothing but her own obsession with a man who was, after all, no more than a fleeting romance.

She inserted the tape in her own recorder and rewound it. It went on fast-rewinding for minutes which was surprising as the previous effort to play it back on Ellie's machine had produced only a smattering of messages. Obviously, Ellie's audible fan mail dispenser was seriously on the blink. Poor girl, no wonder her life was so muddled. She was only getting half the news. This tape was a record covering at least four or five months, all choking on a mechanical blip of some sort. Ellie's machine returned to the same point each time it was rewound, and, stored behind this tangle, lay glimpses of the dead girl's life.

Judith was hooked, playing the tape back and forth, recognising very few callers. One from Mavis was unmistakable – something about Nelson being sick in the broom cupboard. A receptionist coldly informing Miss Juniper that she had been billed for a no-show at the dentist's and would she please ring to re-book her appointment. An admonition about boosters, hopefully Nelson's. A reminder from Mrs Quick to bring in all the spare disks *without fail*.

Judy patiently heard it out. Nearer the end there were a flurry of eager enquiries about a tennis tournament Ellie was setting up and a jokey message from someone called Graham inviting her to an eggnog party in Wandsworth on Good Friday. Then a woman's voice suggesting she should call on Ellie to "discuss a final settlement. We are prepared to be generous. Name your own terms if you like." The tones were cool, English and unfazed. Would Ellie, the voice continued, please ring back and arrange a time? "There's no need to involve Stig; women are always better in practical matters, of course." A brittle laugh. End of message.

The voice seemed vaguely familiar. Judith ran it back again and again. Could this have been the "someone" Ellie had been expecting that Sunday night? Not a man at all . . . The arrangement sounded very businesslike; Stig – or perhaps she had misheard. Steve perhaps? – was presumably the bone these two were squabbling over. Judith's pulse quickened. She felt sure she had heard those flat tones before. In Battersea. There was only one woman it could possibly be: Cora Fielding.

It *was* true then. Gus – or "Stig" as he seemed to be affectionately known – a comfortably married man, finds himself inextricably trapped by Ellie Juniper threatening to expose the affair to his wife. Tired of being everyone's passing fancy, was Ellie playing her last desperate throw? If Gus was not prepared to leave his cosy set-up in Birmingham for her then the Fieldings must pay dearly for the humiliation.

She won either way. Either she got her man or she threatened to inform the university, thus blotting his career. How sensitive were universities to that sort of sexual wandering? Not much, Judith admitted. Even the most stuffy institutions were awash with lecherous lecturers these days. The students practically demanded it. No, there had to be a stronger reason. Was the ace up Ellie's sleeve her ability to denounce Magnus Fielding as a possible HIV carrier? A prospective AIDS victim even. That would put a cross against his name for *any* selection board.

But would Ellie need to go that far? Might she merely have threatened she would spill the full story to Cora . . . A woman willing to forgive adultery might have second thoughts if she knew the extent of the medical hazards that might entail. Ellie Juniper's secret virus endowed her with enormous power. She could expose Fielding to the academics. She could tell his wife. Or Gus could throw in the towel and run away with her. Ellie undoubtedly had sex appeal; Dave Barnes swore to it and he was probably no mean judge. But throw up everything to live on the rents from a third-rate rooming house? Logically, the man would do a deal, coax his wife to pay up, secure his career and their marriage and no-one, not even Cora, need ever find out about the HIV aspect of the blackmail.

The alternative – that Gus himself had killed Ellie just before driving home to Birmingham – was too terrible to contemplate: Judy winced at the idea that she could be *that* wrong about the man. Or could she? She shied away from this distinct possibility and tried the accomplice theory for size, the practical solution to Ellie's finances which would enable her to escape with the man of her choice *and* the pay-off from the Fieldings.

If Ellie had boasted about going abroad to live with this mythical "fiancé" maybe Gus was the pawn in all this, tricked into bankrolling the elopement? Did Ellie have an accomplice who recognised the potential of putting the bite on the wealthy Fieldings? How rich *was* Cora? Judith juggled with the possibilities but it was all too new, too much to take in all at once.

If she was right, Gus had driven home to Birmingham after midnight that Easter Sunday as he said and only later discovered that his persecutor had committed suicide that very night. Had Mr X, Ellie's accomplice – if there was one – taken fright at Ellie's criminal proposal to blackmail the Fieldings, and had they had a fight over it which ended fatally?

Once Gus had confessed to Cora about the threats, Judith could imagine the Fieldings' relief at finding themselves miraculously off the hook. Cora's realisation of her own possible embarrassment when the police discovered her recorded proposal to meet the victim would at first seem unimportant. But later, when she had absorbed the implications, would Cora beg Gus to retrieve the cassette, her only link with the dead girl? In fact, she need not have worried. Coles had probably heard the message, buried as it was amid dozens of other calls, and thought nothing of it. Or was Cora's message caught up in the blip that had stalled the tape in Ellie's machine?

It was difficult to tell. There were several more messages recorded after Cora's, the final one from Doctor Janssen warning he would be dropping in at Rectory Gardens early next morning to collect his typescripts. That was that then.

Judy slumped in the chair trying to determine the real content of the message. Was she reading too much into it? Had the police already checked it out? Had Coles even *heard* that bit or had it been snarled up in the faulty mechanism? The only way to find out would be to try the tape again in Ellie's crappy machine, check where it stalled. But she no longer had access to the flat upstairs: she had given Arnott the only set of keys.

Judith fumed, desperate to get away from London, to escape before Dave invaded the flat with his dustsheets and his BO. She had looked forward to a spree, to spending the weekend in a hotel at Basil Meek's expense and going on somewhere afterwards. He *had* offered after all. Why not take him up on it? Why hang about for Arnott to come back?

She decided to put the cassette in the post with a letter saying she was taking a week's holiday and would get in touch later. He would get it on Monday as soon as he got back from Rye. She could ask him to run it through on Ellie's machine and see what he made of the mysterious message. She tossed the tape in an envelope and scribbled a note before she was interrupted by the entry phone. It was the milkman wanting his money. Judy clattered downstairs to catch him on the doorstep, only just in time. He was already putting another black mark against "Pullen" in his book.

As she shelled out three weeks' delayed settlement, Dave dragged himself up the area steps to collect his litre of orange juice and two pints of milk. He sketched a lacklustre salute. He looked dreadful; grey faced, unshaven and heavy eyed, his hair hanging lank about the collar of a grubby rugger shirt.

"Hi," Judy said, all smiles. "Glad I caught you."

"Just rolled out of the sack," he muttered. "Something up?"

"Not really. Just to confirm about Monday. You said you'd make a start on the ceiling. Is it still on? I'm taking some leave so you can work late if you like. I've left a bottle of Bell's in the cupboard. Help yourself."

"OK. Thanks." He turned back to the steps, moving like a zombi.

"Hey, one thing, Dave! Did you drop in to check it out? The plastering, I mean—?" she queried, treading eggshells. Accusing Dave of anything was *not* a good idea, particularly when she was within striking distance of getting her bedroom back in shape. He paused.

"Oh, yeah. Yesterday. That Messop woman phoned. Told me to get my finger out. That bloke Meek's due back and wants to see results."

"Oh, er, that's all right then . . . Only I wondered—"

Dave continued as if he hadn't heard, his slow delivery rumbling on like a goods train in a siding. "Yeah, Friday. I was going up to your place to measure up and that Brummie stonebreaker, Fielding, struggles downstairs with all his frigging gear. Drills, surveyor's poles . . . I helped stow it in his car. Said he was off somewhere, taking core samples . . . ?"

"Scotland," Judith prompted.

"Well, anyway, he went back up for the second load and we was just shooting the breeze, and I said I was gonna fix the mess in your room. He followed me up, crazy to see the bloodstains, morbid jigger. His idea was Ellie got the push from her job that weekend. Her boss found out about the HIV and gave her her cards."

"Where did Gus get that information?"

He shrugged. "Search me. Sounds reasonable. Private patients don't expect the girl working in the surgery to be alive alive-o, eh?"

"The infection's not airborne!"

"They probably think they'd catch it off the seat of the waiting room lav if you asked 'em. Naked fear. AIDS is the twentieth century's leprosy. Why chance your arm with a Harley Street quack who employs loose women?"

"Loose women!" Judy exploded, realizing too late Dave was just winding her up. He grinned, slapping her arm, and started down to the basement. She hurried forward, still ticking.

"So Gus followed you into my bedroom."

"Wanted to have a quick butcher's. Didn't even go in. Just stood in the doorway while I made a recce of the damage."

"And you let him roam about my flat on his own?"

"No way. Hey, you think something's missing?"

121

"Er, no. But my place isn't the Chamber of Horrors, Dave. No more conducted tours, eh?"

He shrugged.

"Oh, and there was something else I wanted to ask you. Where did Mrs Juniper buy her gin?"

"Why? You having a party?" he said, brightening.

"No. I just wondered if she had a regular wine merchant. Or a stockpile somewhere. A cellar?"

He laughed. "Drank it too quick for that. Could hardly spin out the weekly delivery."

"Local?"

"Sort of. She ran a Harrods' account. Phoned through every Monday and they sent the lot over including food. No use the old lady relying on Ellie to bring home the rations. Dying of starvation she could live with, dying of thirst was something Mrs Juniper took no chances on. Ellie cancelled the order the week her mum died, the miserable cow."

He left Judith leaning over the railings, went inside and slammed his door. End of neighbourly chit-chat, she wryly concluded, jogging back upstairs to her own place.

There seemed no doubt about it. Gus Fielding had ejected the cassette when Dave's back was turned, hoping he might strike lucky and nab the right tape if Judy had, out of sheer curiosity, played Ellie's.

She made some scrambled eggs and a pot of coffee, attempting to bring some sanity to an increasingly odd situation. What was his game? Was there a chance Gus would come back a second time and rifle her room for the cassette? Was there something else hidden in all those messages? Something both she and the police had missed? Perhaps he thought she had stumbled on something implicating him in Ellie's death. The disk hidden in Ellie's suede boot? That membership list from the country club?

Was Fielding dangerous?

Judith jumped up. Arnott was right. She should clear out while she had the chance. She packed an overnight bag and grabbed her briefcase, only too glad to leave the investigation to Arnott. If Basil Meek was on his way back Arnott could question him, too, check out *his* alibi. And find out why Mikki lived rent-free while he was about it.

122

Judy was going to get out of the firing line and drive down to the Domino Country Club to empty Ellie's locker. Goodness knows who had paid the subscription let alone her entrance fee. It was her final obligation to Basil Meek. After this she would be free, her deal with Veronica Messop fulfilled, the last of Ellie Juniper's effects disposed of once and for all.

CHAPTER FIFTEEN

Bolting from London went straight to her head. The sun shone, woolly lambs gambolled, blossom was breaking out all over: the perfect backdrop to an attack of spring fever. Even the traffic was relatively thin, most of the freight lorries and all the weekenders having skipped Saturday afternoon on the M4. The exhilaration of escape even blew away Judy's underlying anxiety about those carefree romps with Gus Fielding. Boxed up in Rectory Gardens with its peculiar inhabitants had made her claustrophobic, exaggerating everything out of all proportion. It had got so she could hardly recognise herself any more.

She left the motorway to stop off at Bray for a late lunch in a wine bar on the far side of town and was in no rush to press on. It had been a late, cold spring; the blossom spoiled with unseasonal frosts. But now the sky, with its innocent little clouds basking in an expanse of baby blue, was pure Botticelli.

She drove on towards Staines, seeking out the by-roads, the scruffy Volkswagen finally trundling along an avenue overhung with willow trees, their trailing green ribbons on the point of breaking into leaf. The Country Club was well-signposted but hidden from the road by a high wall. Judith giggled, picturing the notorious venue as a hedonists' retreat, a sort of monastery in reverse. In fact, its reputation was probably all hype, fed to the press as a publicity exercise, the Domino's country annexe in truth being rather dull and filled with horsy men and women with braying voices.

The drive was long and densely planted on both sides with gloomy rhododendrons, excluding the spring magic which spangled everywhere else. The sight of the house came as a shock as Judith breezed round yet another twist in the approach road to find it laid out before her, surrounded by striped lawns. It was instantly recognisable. It was the house pictured in the background of the only snapshot of Gus and Ellie together, doing their impersonation of love in bloom. Well, why shouldn't Ellie invite him down? The Domino was an obvious bolt-hole away from the prying eyes in Rectory Gardens and the perfect situation for a Have-It-Away-Day.

Judith checked her hair in the rear-view mirror and gathered her briefcase and bag. She was glad now that before the swift exit from Kensington she had changed out of her jeans. The cherry pink trouser suit was sufficiently formal to sail through this, her final performance as Veronica Messop's "gopher". What *was* her status in all this? Unofficial executor, undercover investigator or just plain nosey parker? Judy disdained locking the car. What sort of crackpot in this bucolic sin bin would do her the favour of pinching it? Far off, the pop-bang of a clay shoot rivalled the birdsong and, as she walked towards the stone portico, she caught a glimpse of an archery class being put through its paces.

Inside, all was classical columns and stone urns, the octagonal vestibule lit by a series of high sash windows. An enormous copper bowl of forsythia almost obscured the receptionist who anxiously looked up from checking a print-out as Judith clattered across the chequer-board marble floor. The Georgian house had been tastefully extended at the rear to accommodate a swimming pool pavilion and gymnasium but on this glorious afternoon it was as quiet as a mausoleum, the activities of the members either frenetically engaged outside or hidden behind closed doors. The receptionist flashed a lobotomised smile.

Judith outlined her melancholy errand, producing Ellie's membership card like a passport and flashing her official ID for additional emphasis.

"I really need to see the manager," she insisted, capping the receptionist's smile with her own Fraud Squad version which was admittedly no warmer but expressed undeniable mission.

"Oh, well, I'm afraid Mr Brooke is in a meeting just now. Would you like to make an appointment? Call back later, on Monday perhaps? Mr Brooke is run off his feet at weekends and since Easter—"

The excuses floundered on Judith's clear obduracy.

"I am sure the manager would prefer to see me now rather

than call in at my office. My questions will take only a few moments and the contents of Miss Juniper's locker may have a bearing on her suicide."

The girl sighed and picked up the telephone. Judith tactfully withdrew and wandered round, studying the ancestral portraits which the former owners had leased to the Domino along with the house. The telephone receiver was replaced and Judith turned back.

"He's on his way down, Sergeant. Shan't keep you. May I offer you some coffee?"

Judith shook her head and ten minutes later wished she hadn't. Brooke took his time and she was bluntly checking her watch for the third time when he finally appeared: a smooth product of a Swiss hotel management course, healthily tanned and wearing a beautifully cut grey suit with a yellow rosebud in the buttonhole.

He extended a hand, shooting his cuff, all apologies, and ushered his unwelcome caller into his office with the air of a man pushing the bailiff into a broom cupboard. His private room overlooked the front lawn and he pulled up a chair for her, seating himself at a desk which seemed an exact replica of that monstrosity the Junipers had clung to.

"I heard about the tragic accident over Easter. Elinor Juniper was one of our most popular members. She will be sadly missed. I can't understand it at all," he said, genuinely nonplussed. "She was in the middle of organising our tennis tournament."

"I'm sure she had no intention of letting you down, Mr Brooke. Perhaps her backhand was giving her trouble," Judy snapped. "I think this may be yours." She passed over Mrs Quick's list of Domino members and waited.

"I've not the foggiest what this is but Jackie will know. I recognise the names, of course. They may have been entries for the tennis championship. What are these symbols by each name?" he asked, pointing at the sheet of paper.

"Absolutely no idea. I'll keep this list if you don't mind."

The manager leaned back, growing thoughtful. "She was setting it up with Helen Janssen. Such lively girls, always full of fun." He coughed, realising that the sympathetic tone had got washed out as if it had been exposed for too long to daylight.

"Did you say Janssen? The doctor's wife?"

"But of course. They were *great* friends. Helen Janssen loaned her the Volvo if she wasn't coming down herself."

"I had no idea. Ellie never mentioned having any personal relationship with the Janssens. I knew her myself, you see. We were neighbours."

He lowered his voice, waxing confidential. "Ellie Juniper often stayed with them, you know. Brought friends down too. All very hospitable – but then Americans are so 'open house', aren't they? The cottage is quite near here and if I remember rightly, Philip Janssen was her sponsor."

He spoke to the receptionist on the intercom and she appeared with a membership file.

Judy touched her arm as she turned to go. "Oh, er – Miss—?"

"Jacqueline," she sharply retorted, never having been much impressed by women police officers. Judith scrabbled in her bag and produced the vital snapshot.

"Perhaps you recognise Miss Juniper's friend, Jacqueline?"

"Of course. They often came down together. Mr Prentice is a first class doubles player."

"Prentice?"

"George Prentice," the manager put in, taking the photograph.

"Ignore the inked-in beard," Judy said. "He was cleanshaven when this was taken. Are you *sure* it's the same man?"

"It's definitely George," Brooke confirmed, treating both women to a wide smile. "Would know him anywhere. Marvellous service."

"Was he a member, too?"

"No, a guest. Came down a lot until recently. He always signed the book if you'd like to check it."

Judith shook her head and produced Veronica Messop's letter.

"This authorizes me to remove the contents of Miss Juniper's locker. Shall we? I don't want to take up much more of your valuable time on all this. It's merely a formality."

Brooke suddenly looked distinctly off-colour and read Veronica's letter twice.

"I have the solicitor's home number if you wish to confirm it," Judith said, laying her ID on the desk like a trump card.

"That won't be necessary. But I need to take a copy of this authorisation and will require a receipt for anything taken away."

"Naturally. Please keep the original. My enquiries are complete once the locker is cleared. I assume Miss Juniper left nothing anywhere else?"

Brooke took some keys from the safe and motioned both women to follow him through a second door which led to the sports complex. The ladies' locker room was deserted which was a bonus. As a precaution he whispered to Jacqueline and she stood sentry by the exit.

He opened the locker and pulled out a large sports bag. A tennis racquet in a tailored cover was propped in the corner and a pair of muddy jodhpurs hung from a hook at the back. On the shelf a hairdryer, a sponge bag and a black bikini were rolled up in a towelling robe. Judith made a careful search of the locker and Brooke stacked the sports bag and the other items on a table in the middle of the room. He stood back, looking grim. Heaven knew what a Pandora's Box this might turn out to be . . . You could never tell with women, especially singles like the Juniper bimbo, out on a manhunt.

Judith started with the sponge bag, which contained nothing unusual, and then ran professional fingers through the pockets of the racquet cover. No letters, photographs, not even a diary, just a half-eaten tube of mints and some small change. The riding breeches came in for the same meticulous treatment and, finally, there was the sports bag.

Ellie had stupidly stuffed a damp towel inside and when they unzipped it a strong whiff of mildew almost made Judy retch. Till they day she died, the smell of mouldy towels would bring Ellie Juniper instantly to mind. Judy hauled out a pair of trainers and a grubby bandanna plus a box of tennis balls. She shook it. There were no balls. The box contained nothing but a bulky plastic envelope. It was emptied onto the table.

The heap of banknotes brought a gasp from the receptionist like the release of a bubble in an air lock. Brooke's hands instantly closed on the money and he exchanged an unspoken agreement with Judith. The cash was counted. It was in a variety of currencies, and the sterling was of assorted denominations, but, whatever way you looked at it, it was one hell of a nest-egg. Jacqueline recorded the exact amounts as Brooke totted it up and the cache was bundled back into the envelope.

Judith wasn't exactly bowled over. She was getting used to Ellie's little secrets.

"Keep it in your safe for the present, Mr Brooke. We shall each have signed receipts which Jacqueline can type out for us. I'll dispose of the rest including all this other stuff." Judy indicated a half dozen folders identical to the ones containing medical typescripts already returned to Mrs Quick. Brooke leafed through the folders, just to make sure Judith was not syphoning off any more banknotes, and nodded.

They carried the contents of the locker back to his office and he ordered some tea while the girl typed up the relevant paperwork. Everything was painstakingly noted. After the signing, Judy said, "One more thing, Mr Brooke. Did Elinor Juniper have any *special* friends at the club?"

Jacqueline hung back, intrigued by the amazing turn of events.

"Apart from George Prentice? There were the Janssens, of course. The doctor was rarely free mid-week but Helen was a regular on the courts. Though not so much lately. She said they were packing up ready for a sabbatical. He was writing a book, I think. They were going to live abroad, somewhere like Spain or Portugal for a year, I forget which. Lucky people."

"Well, tennis isn't much fun in the rain and the weather's only just picked up, hasn't it? Perhaps Helen Janssen's a sun-lover."

"Oh, the Janssens played all year round. We have some covered courts. But since they took the cottage at Reapshaw they come here less often."

"Where's that?"

"Not more than eight or ten miles away. I haven't been a guest, of course, but the Janssens were generous hosts. Several of our members went to parties there."

"And George Prentice?"

"Heavens, yes. They were quite a foursome at one time.

The horses were the big attraction, though Helen mentioned last time I saw her that they had been sold a month or two ago."

"You don't have stables here?"

"Oh, no. Too much of a responsibility. No, the Janssens both ride. As did Ellie Juniper, of course. They stabled a pair of hunters at the cottage."

Jacqueline bobbed up, eager to put in her contribution.

"There was that other man, Mr Brooke. Don't you remember? He came down before Easter asking for Miss Juniper. Said he was her cousin?"

"Basil Meek was here?" Judith gasped.

"Was that the name, Jackie?"

"Can't remember. Small chap, a bit flash, wore suede shoes and a blazer."

Brooke winced. "Actually, I do recall now you mention it. Can't think how a visitor like that slipped my mind."

"Did Miss Juniper arrange to meet him here?"

"Dear me, no! She was quite annoyed, I remember. Got shot of him p.d.q. I was glad to see him drive off. Looked a dodgy customer if you ask me but she admitted he *was* her cousin. But then we can't choose our relations, can we?"

Brooke seemed to know nothing else and, as Jacqueline could throw no further light on the emergence of Basil Meek, the receptionist was curtly reminded about the tennis lesson rota which was already overdue. She turned on her heel, shutting the door with a flourish of pique.

Brooke looked startled and glanced at Judith, asking her to repeat her question.

"I asked if I might see Miss Juniper's application form? I'm curious to know when she joined."

Brooke unlocked a filing cabinet and handed over an entry form. Judith digested the details. It was perfectly clear. Philip Janssen had proposed her more than two years before and quoted his out-of-town address, and the seconder was someone called Clarissa Boulte from Barons Court. Presumably, this dream of an employer had no qualms about mixing business with pleasure or at best had no objection to sharing his playground with the hired help. Judith felt sure Mrs Quick enjoyed no such unprofessional camaraderie.

She jotted down the address of the Janssens' weekend bolt-hole and toyed with the idea of paying a visit to Borodino Lodge. The doctor said he was going to Venice for a conference, didn't he? Chances were his wife had gone along for the ride; a freebie at the Danielli would be hard to resist. Judith could take a peek while they were away. It was no more than half an hour's drive and all this talk about the Janssens had whetted her appetitite.

Jacqueline came in with a message from the chef about the dinner menu and the manager excused himself to hurry over to the kitchens. Judith wandered out to Reception and watched the girl run off copies of applications for lessons from the tennis pro. Her attitude towards Judy had softened since the excitement of uncovering the secrets of the Juniper locker and she wryly confessed to a certain boredom with her live-in job at the Domino Country Club where, it would appear, she was constantly on call. It occurred to Judy that perhaps Mrs Quick, Doctor Janssen's PA, was suffering a similar dose of overwork.

"May I use the phone?"

She put in a call to the surgery and was not altogether surprised when Mrs Quick answered. They batted a few pleasantries back and forth before Judith asked to be put through to the doctor.

"He's not in London this weekend, I'm afraid. Is your back still causing trouble?"

"Oh, no. It was something about Ellie I wanted to ask him. I remember you mentioning it now – how silly of me – there was a medical conference in Venice this weekend, wasn't there?"

"That's really why I'm here. The doctor rang me at home at lunchtime. He's had to back out. Poor man's caught a flu bug of some sort and is feeling awfully groggy so he decided to drive on to Verona and stay with friends for a few days. He asked me to ring his patients and cancel all his appointments next week. It's taken me all afternoon! It really is too bad, Miss Pullen, cancelling arrangements at such short notice. If Doctor Janssen were not the most diligent of men I'd suspect he was malingering," she said with a naughty giggle. "He didn't sound at all sick to me."

"Well, Italy in April must be awfully tempting. We'll give him the benefit of the doubt, shall we? Is his wife with him?"

"He didn't say. Is there anything I can do? Give him a message?"

"Oh, no. It's nothing which can't wait. Sorry to have bothered you, Mrs Quick. Enjoy what's left of the weekend. Bye for now."

She declined Brooke's offer to show her round and he accompanied her to the car, carrying the sports bag and helping stow the last of Ellie Juniper's effects in the boot. She tossed the office files on the passenger seat and shook hands, Brooke now supremely polite, relieved that a potentially unpleasant interview had been concluded without any damage. He had his own views about the late Elinor Juniper and it was a miracle that nothing ugly had crawled out of the locker. Apart from all that dosh, of course. Some sort of tax dodge he imagined. Even temps demanded cash in hand these days. Mind you, he should have searched the locker himself as soon as the news of the suicide broke. But everything had taken off at last and Easter had been the start of a really busy stretch. The complications of the death of a club member had slid to the bottom of his schedule and, as it happened, the nasty little bitch had left no dirt on the doorstep for once.

Judith drove away feeling slightly bemused. All that money in Ellie's locker! Thousands zipped up inside a sports bag getting steadily mouldy. Wait till Arnott heard about it.

The afternoon had faded and the little white clouds had grown into billowing grey ones, gathering against the sunset like dirty sheep huddling together out of the wind. It reminded her of the mildewed towel in the boot and she resolved to ditch Ellie's old clothes as soon as she found an unattended skip. No point in trailing them around with her for days. Veronica wouldn't thank her for jumble. Veronica wanted a clean sweep, and the proceeds from the sale of the designer gear would sweeten the account as far as Basil Meek was concerned. Judith had done more than enough on her side of the bargain.

It was nearly opening time and she really fancied a nice quiet drink in a nice quiet saloon bar with a big log fire and horse brasses winking along the old beams. In no hurry at all, she steered the rusting VW through darkening lanes, feeling as mellow as a jar of honey.

She passed a pub called the Slug and Lettuce set back from

the village street, its windows glowing. It looked just the sort of place to stay, decked out with all the accoutrements demanded of a tourists' calendar. But it was too early. She pushed on, thinking up pub menus, wishing Laurence were here to share the week stretching ahead. The road ran on into open countryside and it started to rain, the dark horizon merging with a plantation of pines like something from a Grimm's fairy tale. Judy decided to turn back and pull into the side of the road until the Slug and Lettuce opened its doors.

To pass the time she took her torch from the glove compartment and shuffled through the accumulation of paper in Ellie's folders. A lot of it was extracts from medical journals stapled to typewritten notes and flavoured with stomach-churning photographs of surgical procedures. It was all very similar to the work Ellie was typing for her boss and Judith grew bored, acknowledging that the life of a secretary was not a merry one . . . No wonder Ellie whooped it up given half a chance.

One of the files contained case histories and this was marginally more interesting, some dating back years and several not concerning back pain at all. A plastic folder held a whole sheaf of photocopied material from an American newspaper dated 1978, featuring a paramedic called Mark Trujina receiving a bravery award for saving people in an earthquake disaster. The photograph showed a thin-faced young man with a squint, shyly avoiding the eye of the cameraman. She re-read all the cuttings, trying to connect Trujina with the other case histories, but there was nothing to suggest he had suffered any back injury in the course of the heroic rescue. Why was Philip Janssen interested?

Judith stared at the picture, getting no clue. She searched for any unattached notes which would explain why this man would be of any interest to the doctor. Her mind swam about in a lazy doggy-paddle, circling the problem, waiting for some relevance to surface. All that kept recurring was the mysterious bundle of cash in Ellie's locker and, letting her imagination splash about, Judith wondered if the Janssens' generosity to his secretary was dictated by blackmail.

If Ellie had stumbled upon a skeleton in the cupboard she would be in an ideal position to milk her employer. There was no-one more vulnerable than a medical man. And any sort of scandal in Harley Street spelt professional suicide. If the Janssens were persuaded to foot the bill for Ellie's little luxuries in life the percentage might be bearable providing demands remained within reasonable limits. The cash, too, not to mention the rich rags and sports equipment, could be accommodated under the heading of business expenses.

But why, Judith probed, did her thoughts about Ellie Juniper continually veer back to this blackmail theory? First the Fieldings and now the Janssens. The idea had never even occurred to her before she started picking over the dead girl's belongings. But what else could explain it? A woman of diminishing resources, with no great income, living the life of Riley. Not only is she able to join the best clubs in London but has the clothes to deck out the lifestyle. It was not as if any other source of income was apparent and the rents from Rectory Gardens had not only remained static but, since the old lady had relinquished the reins, a second tenant was living rent-free. The nebulous "fiancé" remained invisible and her job was not particularly well paid. Blackmail seemed the only answer.

Having bumped into Philip Janssen on only one occasion, Judith was nevertheless certain that Ellie had no sexual hold over the man. He was too intelligent to fall into that sort of trap. And so, if Ellie was receiving a regular payout from Janssen, the threat must concern his career. She felt her pulse begin to race, a sure conviction taking shape. This man, Mark Trujina, was a ghost from the past which somehow or other Ellie had discovered. Perhaps on her little tour of the States the previous autumn?

The only possible alternative was that the squinty-eyed hero was something to do with Helen and *not* the good doctor. How about Ellie checking the matrimonial records and discovering Helen had been married before? Was, in fact, a bigamist? And if Judy had the wrong end of the stick thinking the voice on Ellie's answering machine was Cora Fielding's, the finger pointed at Helen Janssen. Perhaps she had jumped to the wrong conclusion; how certain was she that the woman's voice recorded on the tape was the same as the one she remembered hearing at Battersea? Suddenly she wasn't sure of anything any more. Had her own involvement with Gus muddled everything?

She tried to look at the facts dispassionately. The bottom line was Judy couldn't convince herself that Helen Janssen was involved with an ordinary guy like Trujina – he wasn't in the same league as the Harley Street back specialist even in the looks department.

Judy's money was on her original hunch: the Fieldings. She studied the snapshot of Ellie and her mystery man which had set her off on this goose-chase. It *was* Gus. Would he really use a pseudonym at the club? George bloody Prentice. He could have picked something with more of a ring to it, but playing safe sounded just like that geological tripehound.

It was a pity Arnott was incommunicado on his wooden hulk of a boat. He had a nose for such things, could tie her flights of fancy down to facts. Well, she would just have to soldier on on her own. Do a little private sleuthing. The prospect was alluring and she had all the time in the world to poke about in the Juniper dung-heap.

She locked the Trujina file in her briefcase and tossed all the other folders onto the back seat. Glancing at her watch, she realized time had flown. She deserved that drink. With luck the Slug and Lettuce did bed and breakfast. She started back to the village and passed a signpost. Reapshaw – 1 mile. All at once, she knew luck was on her side. She had stumbled, unaware, into the actual location of Janssen's weekend cottage. Judy wished now she had consulted Constanzia's Star Guide before setting out on this ghost-busting jaunt. It was positively spooky. Constanzia might have tipped her off.

She breezed into the Slug and Lettuce knowing she was on a winning streak. Nothing could stop her now. The pub was exactly the sort she had in mind, all gravy-brown ceilings and rush matting, the air smoky as a witches' coven. Judith perched on a bar stool and ordered a half of Carlsberg and a plate of steak and kidney pie.

The landlord was another Yorkshireman, the burr inescapable, the florid countenance reminding her of Arnott in a good mood. There were only a handful of punters in the saloon bar. It was too early for the Saturday night crowd and too late for serious drinkers. While she waited for her order, Judy chatted up the barmaid, a middle-aged East-Ender with extra-sensory perception. Maggie could spot a troublemaker the minute he crossed the threshold and out-bawl any lager lout. Nobody took any liberties with Maggie, not twice anyhow.

"On your own, luv?" she said, eyeing Judy's heightened colour.

"My boyfriend's in America. I'm hoping to look up an old school-friend tomorrow. She's staying round here somewhere. Borodino Lodge. Do you know it? It's in this village."

"That'll be on Mr Guy's estate. All his farms and cottages is named after battles: Salamanca, Trafalgar – search me why. His father set it up – thought he was being clever, I 'spect. Dead now. Mr Guy's not too clever these days, either. Must be over seventy. Mr Bradford Guy – he owns Baldwins, that chemists' chain."

"But that's the bloke who—"

Maggie touched her lips with a warning finger and whispered. "Yes, *him*!" She snorted with laughter, setting her dangly ear-rings a-wobble. "Got caught out in his fancy corset and had to get a sick note. Does your friend ride?"

"Helen? Used to – not any more. Do you know her? Helen Janssen. She and Philip must be quite well known in the village. He's American. They've been coming down here at weekends for some time."

"Oh, Helen! You should have said. It was Doctor Janssen who bailed *him* out, you know. They rent the Lodge on the cheap, so I've heard. Suits everyone. Nice couple, sociable pair. Not so much since Christmas – we used to supply the drinks for their parties and that – but she was always down more often than her hubby. Hated the city, she said. You *might* find her there but she's not so tied since the horses went. You ought to give her a tinkle first, save yourself a wasted journey. Can't say I've seen her for weeks now you mention it."

"Yes, well, I will. In the morning. Is this Borodino Lodge outside the village then?"

"Turn right and after about five hundred yards go through the big gates just past the garage. Can't miss it. The Lodge is poked away about a mile from the main entrance. Off on the left, up a track. Used to be another gate right by it straight off the road, but Mr Guy had it bricked up. To keep the baddies out, he said, force 'em to use the big gates to get in and out and he got a video camera mounted up there. Had no end of break-ins before he called in this security firm to tighten everything up. Not a bit of bother since. Only goes to show, don't it?"

"Perhaps there's nothing left worth pinching."

Maggie let out a raw chuckle and went to the kitchen to put some gunpowder under the idle sod heating up Judy's steak and kidney. She steered Judy to a corner table near the fire and admitted that they took no weekend visitors.

"Mrs Pollitt up at Grange Farm does a good B & B. Want me to give her a bell? Tell her you want a nice single till Monday?"

"Would you, Maggie? That'd be great. I've got a date tonight but I could pop round and leave a deposit first if you like. How about that?"

"I'll see what she says. Gets booked up weekends once the sun comes out but never say die. Beryl's a mate of mine, trusts me not to send any bedwetters."

The bar began to fill and later, over coffee, Judith got the thumbs up from Maggie. It was all fixed. No need to break a leg to confirm, the bed would be aired and waiting.

"Grange Farm's just up the road after the level crossing. Nice clean place, no scruffs. You'll be right as rain on your own there, ducks."

Judy left the Slug and Lettuce "fair stuffed" as Arnott would describe it and was in half a mind to postpone her snooping round the Janssens' weekend place until the morning. Even a bona fide police sergeant has qualms about creeping about a private estate uninvited and as the Janssens were not listed in the phone book Judith couldn't check before putting in an appearance. Not that a conversation with Helen Janssen would come amiss if the woman had foregone the Venice conference. Judith had heard so much about the Janssens that scotching her rampant imaginings by actually speaking to the woman would be no bad thing. Even so, a quiet pedal round first was her choice, just to get her bearings before barging in.

She drove off in the direction of the big house and, sure enough, it would have been hard to miss. Scrolled ironwork gates stood open under the Cyclops of the TV monitor. Judy swerved left almost immediately, following a rutted track through woodland. The estate seemed neglected, fallen branches everywhere and the undergrowth thick with holly and brambles. After a while she decided to walk the rest of the way and bumped the VW into a secluded clearing, its rusting chassis screened by a dense clump of rhodedendrons.

She changed into a pair of trainers and pulled on her raincoat, beaming the way ahead with the torch. The woods were alive with scrabbling animal noises and a hooting owl was in no mood for human disruption. She stumbled on, desperately trying to keep her approach as noiseless as possible.

' Judy was beginning to wish she had postponed this foray until daylight when the cottage loomed ahead, barely visible, hard up against the encircling estate wall. There were no lights anywhere. Judith let out a sigh and plunged on, less apprehensive now she knew herself to be alone.

Borodino Lodge was larger than she imagined a weekend cottage to be, its tiled roofs sloping steeply over the top windows, the front door hidden under a dark porch. A flower garden surrounded the house and in sunshine Judy guessed it to be a picture, banks of daffodils and primroses gleaming like splinters of gold in the narrow torchbeam. The place was obviously deserted, the ground floor rooms closely shuttered and a cellar window barred and wired over against vermin.

She skirted the cottage trying to guess the layout and came upon a series of outbuildings flanking a paddock. A Dutch barn had been commandeered to garage cars and shelter piles and piles of cut logs. Other farm buildings had stable doors and were redolent of horse and hay. It was as quiet as the grave, not even a gravel path to warn of trespassers.

She explored the barn first. A big Volvo estate was parked in isolation leaving room for at least another two vehicles. She crept up to the driver's side and shone her torch. The doors were locked and there was nothing on the seats to tickle her fancy.

Being off on her own was such a new experience Judith felt quite lightheaded. Normally she was under supervision, and fraud investigations were carried out within very strict guidelines. Working with Arnott had been entirely different – too exciting if anything, and his methods distinctly dodgy. But even with Arnott there were limits plus the gauntlet of his professional scepticism to run if she were to have her say. At last she was discovering things for herself and, what was more, she was feeling lucky. Laurence had a theory about his police work: being effective depended on two factors. Firstly, evidence and secondly, luck. And luck was the winner every time.

She was craning her neck to follow the beam of torchlight pinpointing the clutter on top of the dashboard when the roof fell in. The crushing blow to the back of her head sent her forehead crashing into the side window and Judith Pullen, lone detective, was out cold.

CHAPTER SIXTEEN

Arnott received the tape first post Monday morning. He read Judy's hurried account of the woman's anonymous message on the Juniper machine and studied the background notes she had scribbled down before taking off. He glowered. Pullen was like a bloody greyhound, out of the trap before you'd had a chance to read your race card.

He sat at the kitchen table filling the air with tobacco fumes, weighing the miniature piece of technology in his ham-like fist. He was never entirely happy with these newfangled gadgets and not encouraged by Pullen's insistence that the Juniper answering machine was likely to misfire; had probably already misfired on Coles, fuzzing the evidence. Arnott knew he would have to tread carefully here. Dragging in new evidence well after the case was wrapped up and the body buried wouldn't win him any medals. Especially if Coles had already investigated this little avenue of enquiry and the woman on the recording had a perfectly valid explanation. First, he must hear it himself and get a decent playback before jumping in with both feet.

He put on his only decent suit and set off to have a quiet word with Bernie Allen, not a man to get aerated every time a cold wind blew. Bernie was at his desk, patiently sifting the new files which had appeared over the weekend. He looked up and smiled as Arnott shambled in, glad to see a sensible bloke of the old school for a change. Bernie was unimpressed by Arnott's quick temper, his own phlegmatic approach going a long way to douse the old humbug's taciturnity before the first spark took hold. He had his own kettle and a supply of teabags on top of the filing cabinet and the two men were soon hunched together over steaming mugs while Arnott confidentially outlined his problem.

Bernie examined the cassette as if it was a letter bomb and

reluctantly fitted it into his own machine. They sat in Bernie's office and heard it out, patiently trawling through the dentist's and vet's messages and all the tennis tournament entries until they reached the female voice which had excited Arnott's former DS. Bernie nodded, sucking on his pipe, making no comment. Arnott eyed him with irritation, hardly expecting the man to jump up and shout "Eureka!", but even so . . .

Bernie ejected the tape and slowly re-read the file. Inspector Coles had made no reference to this possible assignation at the Juniper flat, he admitted that much. But that didn't mean anything. The woman on the tape merely requested a meeting, there was nothing to prove she had gone to the victim's flat on the night she died.

Arnott reclaimed the cassette and slipped it into his pocket, deciding, after all, to paddle his own canoe. Bernie was obviously not going to shake the tree if he didn't have to. Looking at the stack of new cases piled up in the in-tray, Arnott could see his point. He lumbered to his feet and turned to go.

"Here, 'ang on a mo, Ralph. Something came through this morning might interest you. A couple of ramblers found a stiff in a flooded quarry yesterday. Turns out he was another lodger in that Juniper house. Only identified him last night. Body's been submerged since Friday or Saturday they reckon."

"Foul play?"

"No suspicious circumstances. Straight-up accident apparently. A geologist called—"

"Fielding!" Arnott crowed, like a winner shouting "Bingo!".

"You heard."

"No. But I *knew* that bloke, Bernie. He was with me and Pullen that Sunday night the Juniper tart popped her clogs. Don't you remember? Said he pushed off back to Birmingham after midnight. His missus confirmed it. They had some sort of family do on the Bank Holiday. Where was this quarry you said?"

"Place called Sythetop, not far from Amersham. A well-known fossil place, so I'm told. The poor bloke was drilling out soil samples or rocks or something and there was a minor landslip. Must have been knocked out in the fall before he hit the water. Drowned, poor sod. They're still sorting it out. His wife identified the body last night. No mistake. Magnus

Fielding." He nodded sagely, drawing on his pipe, amused to see Arnott so cock-a-hoop with himself. Never known a man so glad to hear bad news.

Arnott went straight to Rectory Gardens and let himself in with Ellie Juniper's keys. Everyone was out at work or still asleep and he stumped up three flights puffing like a billy goat, grinning to himself as he passed Pullen's locked door, the silence underlining the fact that the jazzman was not busting a gut to get started on her ceiling like she seemed to think.

He entered the attic rooms with little enthusiasm, never happy on a trail that had obviously gone cold weeks before. The smell reminded him of a wet Monday in his ma's scullery with the washing hanging everywhere. Best thing would be to open up the windows and give the place an airing but he didn't plan on stopping, just play the tape then have a quiet look round on his own.

He roamed through the rooms acquainting himself with the odd layout, opening and shutting the doors and craning to see out of the windows. Like Pullen's flat there were no curtains. Would these young girls never learn? You put up curtains first when you moved in, not last.

A fire escape was bolted to the back of the building, finishing up on the slimy terrace outside the Osimas' French windows. It turned by a balcony on the first floor and snaked on past windows almost to the roof. The iron staircase was obviously a later addition, probably required by fire regulations when old Mrs Juniper started letting rooms. The garden was small and hardly used by the look of it, the tussocky patch of grass merely a convenience for the moggies.

Could they be dealing with a resident peeping tom who made a habit of creeping up the fire escape to get an eyeful? Judging by the dead girl's fancy undies she could have blown his fuse, especially if she was bopping about to that rock-and-roll racket. Folk living on their own often cheered themselves up having a bit of a jig. He'd shuffled round the kitchen himself when the brass band competitions were on the wireless.

He tried out the cassette and sympathised with poor bloody Coles. It took infinite patience to tease out the full recording and after ten minutes Arnott gave up, pulling the plug on the effing rubbish. Mind you, Pullen was right. Some woman had it in for Juniper by the sound of it and was coming round to settle the score. No mistake about it.

Pullen thought it was Cora Fielding but Arnott had his doubts. She could pick off Juniper any place, any time. Why stick her neck out barging up here? Unless there was a regular arrangement between the two women and the geologist's missus wasn't bothered about keeping his nose out of it . . . The message had been "*We* are prepared to be generous", hadn't it? Who was to say Mrs Fielding hadn't been reading Juniper's tea leaves that Easter Sunday night all the time Gus was hobnobbing with the neighbours downstairs, making sure they didn't crack on that there was a cats' fight brewing in the attic. Mind you the rock concert blasting away in the top flat covered any amount of spitting and there was no-one else in the house that night apart from the bongo players on the ground floor. Handy to have a look-out though, especially if they'd banked on Pullen being away for Easter. Gus Fielding was a cool customer and no mistake but to carry off a stunt like that with his wife, and then the pair of 'em drive back to Birmingham straight after? Arnott whistled through his teeth, mentally trying the facts for size, juxtaposing the evidence at his disposal like bits of sky in a jigsaw puzzle.

He made his way out, carefully closing off each room as he left until he found himself boxed up in the queer little vestibule with its four identical doors. For a split-second in the half-darkness he lost his bearings, trying to decide which one led onto the landing. One door went off to the right – to the bedroom? – and the other led to the bathroom so the way out must be the one with the pop poster taped to it.

He re-opened the door onto the living room to let some light on the scene and curiously peeled the bottom of the advertisement clear. The doors were DIY stock items made up of a cheap framework supporting flimsy plywood panelling. The poster had been stuck over an ugly indentation in the plywood as if a kick boxer had made his mark. Arnott adjusted his glasses and peered at the damage. A single hair clung to the splintered edges and there were smears which he bet his bottom dollar were blood. He replaced the poster as best he could, pressing back the sticky tape, harking back to his original doubts about the glancing blow to the victim's head which the pathologist considered trifling. But the dent in the door was important enough for *someone* to take the trouble to cover up, and from the look of the rest of the rooms the Juniper woman had never been house-proud. He would have to check with Pullen before he blew the whistle and pulled Coles back to see it. It might have been there before Pullen moved out though she never struck him as the sort to hide a bash in a door without even cleaning off the dirt first.

He locked up and made his way downstairs, his attention grabbed by an argument raging in the hall. The front entrance stood open onto the street, the Nigerian family shouting incomprehensibly at another black woman who translated for a worried young man with a briefcase, obviously some sort of social worker or income tax inspector. The bitter dispute was aggravated by another man Arnott had never seen before but who clearly felt justified in laying down the law.

Arnott watched from the stairs, standing under the beams of light which shone through the stained glass window onto the half-landing, colouring the carved chest on which the tomcat reclined, his yellow eyes taking in the hullabaloo with unwinking interest. Arnott got the drift of the quarrel and put a name to the bloke putting his spoke in. He was not a tall man and small boned but quick movements gave the impression of wiry strength, his legs firmly planted on the slippery marble tiles, alert and light on his feet like a judo fighter. It could only be Basil Meek.

The row escalated, Mrs Osima now weeping, the tears dripping on the head of the baby in her arms. Osima himself was mad as a bull, his eyes bloodshot with rage, spitting words at the gesticulating Basil Meek in a fusillade too rapid for the hapless interpreter to translate. Not that there was much to tell. The dispute was clear. The Osimas were being evicted, their bags packed on the doorstep, the pram on the pavement loaded up with baskets and bedding. The social worker finally threw in the sponge and pulled one side of the warring faction out. Basil Meek, quick as a flash, slammed the door, turning back only to find yet another stranger in his house.

"And who the bloody hell are you?" he yelled. Nelson fled

to the basement, streaking away at a speed one would have to see to believe, making a beeline for the back door.

Arnott descended the last few steps and introduced himself, explaining away his presence as having been sent by the solicitor to help Miss Pullen check out the Juniper place. Basil Meek calmed down, smoothing the lapel of his blazer, and invited Arnott into the recently vacated Osima flat. He left the door ajar, keeping an eye open for anyone who might try and slip past unnoticed.

"Take a pew, squire. Sorry about all that row, but it had to be sorted out. My cousin was running some sort of private refugee camp here. Went to some Pan-Africa jump-up and invited the Nigerians to move in. As her house guests. I just told the council the Osimas were their problem not mine now Lady Bountiful was no longer issuing complimentary tickets. Silly girl. What a stupid thing to do! Once you start handing out that sort of charity the house ends up nothing but a squat. Let's have a drink."

Basil Meek opened an airline bag and produced a bottle of gin and some vermouth. With all the expertise of a professional barman he soon had Arnott seated with a large dry martini clinking with ice in his hand. It took the edge off what had started as a funny old Monday morning.

"Cheers."

"Bottoms up," Meek replied, relishing the first slurp of the day. He was a cheerful-looking guy, deeply tanned, his hair expertly styled. Had a good set of teeth an' all, Arnott admitted, and his brusque treatment of the Osimas was no black mark as far as he was concerned. Basil sipped his aperitif, keeping a weather eye on the passage outside, and quizzed Arnott for a first-hand account of his cousin's suicide. Arnott spared none of the details.

"Pity you couldn't get back for the funeral, Mr Meek. Not a bad show, all things considered."

"Just couldn't get away," he answered, far from defensive, confident of Arnott's understanding when it came to priorities. "Anyhow, I'd been back here just a month before filling in a spot of unexpected leave. Two flights stateside in four weeks would have dented my piggy-bank."

"You kept in touch then?"

"Only since my aunt died." He winked. "She gave me a belly-ache if you must know. You ever cross swords with the old girl?"

"Once or twice. I don't think she liked men full stop. You got on with your cousin though?"

"Oh, Ellie and I rubbed along. No-one else sitting on the jolly old family tree, was there? Blood tells in the end."

"Aye. Good berth here when you was on leave, though."

"Not likely. I've got a shipmate who's got his own place in Notting Hill. As it happens—"

Meek suddenly broke off and leapt up as a shadow passed the door, collaring Mikki Ferrero. The man squirmed, shouting obscenities, finally managing to wrench himself free to run outside as if he had a force ten gale behind him.

Meek returned, grinning, and emptied his glass in one gulp.

"Easy come, easy go," he said, nodding towards the street.

"Another charity case?"

"Not intentionally. Just three months behind with the rent. Don't suppose I'll catch sight of him again. I slipped an ultimatum under his door last night. Pay up or ship out. He's not Spanish, you know, not even called Ferrero." Basil leaned across, confiding in Arnott as one man of the world to another. "Moroccan. Not even a current visa, I bet. No point in running a place like this for the benefit of a bunch of illegals, is there? I've got plans," he said, holding out his hand for Arnott's glass. "The other half?"

"No thanks, lad. Got to take these keys back to Miss Messop. They're the only set."

"I thought that caretaker, Barnes, had duplicates."

"Not for the top floor. There *were* some. But your cousin said she'd lost hers and whipped the spares off the jazzman. Wise move if you ask me."

"Something I should know?"

"No business of mine. But security here's not what you'd call cast-iron, is it? Best if any spares were under lock and key if you're not living on the premises yourself. What about these plans of yours?"

"Too early to say. I've got to see the figures first. But I won't re-let this flat," he said, frowning at the Victorian furnishings, all very much the late Mrs Juniper's choice. "I'll take those

146

keys off you, Mr Arnott, and save you a trip. I want to scout round upstairs myself in any case. I'll probably get Barnes to run a paint roller over the top flat when he's finished doing Miss Pullen's ceiling. She away?"

"Gone down to see her mum, I reckon. Back at the weekend she told me." He handed over the keys and got Basil Meek to scribble a receipt. Always a belt and braces man, Arnott had no wish to ruffle Veronica Messop's feathers. A kick like an ostrich, a big girl like that.

He left Basil Meek totting up his rent books and was crossing the hall just as Mavis Clements crashed through the front door, her plump cheeks pale as milk. She almost collapsed in his arms, grasping his jacket. For a moment he thought she was going to faint.

"Oh, Ralph. Thank goodness you're here. I've just heard the lunchtime news on my little tranny. I was so upset Mr Harris sent me straight home. Poor Mr Fielding's been found dead!"

"Aye, I heard. T'was an accident. He was clambering about in a quarry in—"

"Buckinghamshire! But why was he there?" she croaked, her voice breaking. "He was supposed to have been in Scotland! With his field study group."

"Happen he changed his mind, lass. Here," Arnott muttered, drawing her inside. "Let's go up to your place and I'll make you a nice cup of tea. You've had a nasty shock."

She allowed him to lead the way and opened her door with shaking fingers. They went through to the kitchen and Nelson appeared at the window, glad to see a friendly face at last. While Arnott filled the kettle Mavis unlocked the window and, clasping the cat to her chest, subsided into her favourite chair in the sitting room, goggle-eyed, like someone who had narrowly missed being knocked down on a zebra crossing.

After a cup of tea, her colour returned and she started to gabble about a typescript. Arnott's attention had been elsewhere, his mind veering back to the dilemma of what to do about the cassette from the answering machine. Pullen had dumped the whole mess in his lap, expecting miracles. He didn't want to lose face and admit he had got nowhere with it. Nowhere at all. And now, the only new evidence he had discovered, the damage to a door in the attic, was likely to be mended and painted over before he'd got the chance to put the forensic boys onto it.

"Eh, what did you say, Mavis? I'm a bit deaf on my left side."

She patiently repeated her story, her second delivery a dramatic improvement on the first.

"You see, Ralph," she said "You don't mind me calling you Ralph, do you? . . . Well, Ralph, you won't believe this but only this very morning my friend Cynthia at the library brought in this typescript for me to pass on to Mr Fielding."

Arnott perked up, taking an interest at last.

Mavis continued, straining to expose the amazing coincidences of life. "Mr Fielding had mentioned he was writing a book and, naturally, I was very excited about it. Fancy that, a real author living in the house! Flavia would have been *so* proud. Well, as I was saying, Mr Fielding used to discuss his work with me and just before Easter he asked if there was anyone at the Society who undertook freelance typing. There isn't, of course, not in the normal way, but Cynthia was saving up to visit her sister in Australia and when I mentioned it she simply jumped at the chance. It was awfully lucky Cynthia being keen to take it on – she's used to scientific work, you see, has deciphered the most execrable handwriting in her time. Some of these geographers, Ralph, are—"

"Go on, Mavis! Did your mate Cynthia say there was something she found out about Fielding?"

"Oh, no," Mavis replied, not at all sure what Arnott was suggesting. "It was an entirely satisfactory arrangement to both parties. The sad thing was, Cynthia brought the typescript in for me only *this morning*. All 100,000 words of it! Something about sedimentology and—"

"About what?"

"Soil analysis." Mavis's eyes began to fill with tears and Arnott, already familiar with the disposition of the grog, swiftly emptied a tot of brandy into her teacup from the decanter on the sideboard.

She blew her nose. "What shall I do with it, Ralph? Cynthia's not been paid. And it's his life's work, poor man. Should I take it to his department and let them deal with it or post it on to his widow? It seems absolutely tragic that all that study was for *nothing*. He would have become a professor eventually, you know. I'm sure of it." She drew a bulky package from her shopping bag. "On this body of research alone," she added, touching the parcel with reverence.

That did it for Arnott. He rose to the occasion and met her brimming eyes with his own unflinching gaze.

"Don't you fret, my lass. You've done your bit. Leave the rest to me. I'll take this lot straight to Birmingham and hand it to the lady in person. I see the Fieldings' address is on the flysheet."

Mavis sighed with relief, clasping the cat to her. "Oh, *would* you, Ralph? You are a *tower* of strength!" Touching his sleeve, she whispered. "There's something dreadfully wrong in this house, isn't there? Ever since Flavia died. Now two more tragic deaths . . . Do you think the Osimas dabble in black magic? I feel as if we have all been put under a curse."

Nelson leapt off her lap and streaked to the door, his fur bristling. Arnott jumped up, poo-pooing her silly fancies, promising to take her down to see his boat at the weekend. All she needed was a breath of sea air. Soon put her right.

He fled with Fielding's masterwork under his arm and didn't feel at all his old self until settled in Mortlake with a glass of whisky at his elbow and the incomprehensible graphs and diagrams of Gus Fielding's complex research project spread before him.

His mind was made up. Checking out Basil Meek's movements over Easter could wait. First things first. He would tackle Fielding's grieving widow before common sense got the better of her. Arnott was like an undertaker. He knew full well that you only did the best deal before the tears had dried.

CHAPTER SEVENTEEN

After supper Arnott packed an overnight bag and drove to Birmingham, booking into a motel overnight to be first in the queue at the Fielding wake.

He didn't telephone first: no sense in giving the opposition the chance to fend him off with any shadow boxing. After a shower and twenty minutes availing himself of the trouser press and valeting facilities in the room he presented himself at the Fieldings' front door and rang the bell.

The house was a big ranch-style place on what developers call an executive development. The lawns were landscaped in the American style with no fences or privet hedges to spoil the view. All the curtains at the windows of the Fielding homestead were drawn.

He rang again, the chimes decorously unperemptory. Arnott fixed his eye on the peephole in the door, Gus's typescript parcelled under his arm, trying to arrange his craggy features in sympathetic mode, fully aware that it was an outside chance Cora Fielding would let him over the doorstep even if she was at home at all.

Before leaving London he had made a few phone calls and pencilled in some sort of background information. Gus Fielding had not, as he supposed, been a penniless idler living off his wife's money. Arnott got the low-down from a pressman who had had good reason to keep in with the inspector in the old days and was still in the market for tip-offs. Apparently, Fielding senior farmed in Suffolk and was a barley baron with political influence and not inconsiderable means. He was far from delighted when his only son married a divorcée nine years older than the bridegroom but had not cut him off entirely and was, in fact, extravagantly proud of his academic achievements. It was whispered that Cora was persona non grata down on the farm but as someone who had her own success, was far from disappointed. Cora's boutiques were advertised in *Vogue* and *Harper's* and being situated in the provinces had been less affected by the yo-yo fortunes in London.

Arnott stayed rooted on the doorstep, feeling a bit of a mug but determined to hold his impatience in check. The door finally opened a few inches and a thin-faced woman peered round, gripping the door as if expecting Rape & Pillage.

"Yes?"

He swiftly removed his trilby and explained his mission, tapping the brown paper parcel under his arm with emphasis and underlining its importance as if the woman was sub-normal. In fact, she didn't seem too bright and Arnott knew he would have to tread very carefully if he were to get his foot on the welcome mat.

"Oh, I'll have to ask my sister," she whispered, noiselessly closing the door again. Arnott stood his ground, hatless and feeling the cold, unused to dancing attendance on weeping women. As he waited, his mind drifted back to Mavis Clements, wondering if he had overplayed the sympathy there, given the poor cow a false impression. Who'd have thought an ugly brute like himself would have to worry about middle-aged spinsters getting the wrong idea? Being a widower had its down side and no mistake.

The door opened again and the skinny bird in the glasses invited him in, taking his hat and raincoat which was a good sign. At least they weren't tossing him out on his ear like a bike-messenger. He kept a tight hold of the parcel which he guessed was the only reason Cora Fielding was giving him the time of day and followed the sister through to a conservatory at the back where the widow rose to offer her hand and a fleeting smile.

Arnott took to Cora Fielding straight off. Well used to what he called "Sloaney tarts", women involved in the fashion game generally gave him the pip: too thin, too acid and too jumpy. Cora wasn't a bit like that and he could see why Gus Fielding had refused to let her go. She was "all woman" as they say, tall and attractively well covered, smart as paint in her black dress, the warmth of her personality shining through like candlelight at Christmas.

The skinny sister vanished like a puff of wind and they settled down in two basket chairs, Arnott's creaking like a volley of machine-gun fire as he settled, the typescript on his knees.

"My sympathy, Mrs Fielding. A terrible tragedy."

Tears welled up and she quickly blew her nose and hurried to put him at ease.

"You knew my husband?"

"Met him only the once but from all accounts," he said, tapping the parcel on his lap, "Gus was a real trailblazer. This book of his will break new ground so I'm told."

"I know nothing about geology, Mr Arnott. But it's such a relief to know his work was finished before this terrible accident cut everything short. His publisher phoned me last night . . ."

As soon as she spoke Arnott knew for certain the voice on the Juniper tape was not Cora Fielding's. The inflections were pure Brum, no question.

He handed over the parcel and she held it in both hands for a moment before putting it aside to turn her attention back to the man sitting opposite.

"Forgive me, but I'm still confused. How exactly did the manuscript come into your possession? Was it at Rectory Gardens? You don't live there yourself, do you?"

"A former colleague of mine does. Judith Pullen?"

Cora shook her head, none the wiser and Arnott explained about Pullen having been his sergeant before his recent retirement from the force.

"I was with Pullen and your hubby the night poor Miss Juniper committed suicide. That's when I met him. We had a very interesting chat about geology."

Cora's eyes lit up and she patted his arm. "Poor you. Gus could be a terrible bore about it."

"No way. Any road, the reason I got the manuscript was through another lady who lives in the house, Miss Clements. It was Mavis who arranged for it to be typed up. A friend of hers at work." He paused before adding, "I hope you don't mind me mentioning it, Mrs Fielding, but the typist hasn't been paid and she won't send a bill because she don't want to intrude on your grief." Arnott was pleased with the way he put that. No point in beating about the bush when it comes to money.

"Thank goodness you reminded me! Of course, she must be paid. Do you have her address?"

"I'll ask Mavis – Miss Clements – to get a bill from her friend and post it on, shall I?"

The sister came in with a tray of coffee and Cora introduced her, placing an arm affectionately round the scraggy shoulders. "Daphne's staying with me for a bit. It's been such a terrible shock . . . I had to identify his body, Mr Arnott and—"

The tears fell, this time unchecked and Arnott stood awkwardly between the two women, feeling the initiative sliding away. Dare he bring up the subject of Rectory Gardens again?

Cora managed to pull herself together and while her sister poured the coffee, busied herself unwrapping the parcel. She flicked vaguely through the sheets and sheets of data, as bewildered as Arnott had been, her red-rimmed eyes scanning the incomprehensible thesis as if hoping a trace of her husband's presence was still discernable in all this scientific verbiage.

The doorbell chimed and Daphne went to answer it. After a minute the house was again silent.

Cora stared out at the garden where a man was trimming the edges of the lawn, her cheeks chalky under a thin film of sweat. Suddenly, she left the room and Arnott wondered if that was that. Was he expected to see himself out? He heard her speaking to her sister in the hall, insisting she would see no-one else. Then she returned, holding a bulky folder and sat down again, pushing aside the tray to make space on the low table between them. No-one had touched the coffee and it remained, gradually getting cold as Cora Fielding unfolded an extraordinary story.

"I feel I can trust you, Mr Arnott. I am at my wits' end . . . With your police experience you'll be able to advise me what to do. I haven't slept a wink, worrying about this on top of everything else. Since Gus died, everything's changed you see . . ." She took a deep breath and plunged on.

"You know all about Ellie Juniper. I'm not a vindictive person, Mr Arnott but when I heard she had committed suicide I couldn't summon up a moment's regret. I was *glad* she was dead. That's a terrible admission, isn't it? Do you believe in evil, Mr Arnott?"

His rough hands opened in mute response, not daring to break in.

"Well, I do," she insisted. "We are all bad to some degree. And perhaps the evil in me had to be paid for by losing Gus. I loved that man with all my heart—" Her voice faultered but she clung to Arnott with a frantic determination to unburden herself.

"Gus was no saint – no-one knew that better than me. But we were very happy and there wasn't a grain of sin in that man, not real sin, not the blackness Ellie Juniper and those friends of hers were into. Easter is a busy time for me. It's the beginning of a peak selling period, you see. Spring weddings, going-away outfits, special once-in-a-lifetime spending sprees for the races and holidays . . . Marketing designer clothes in the provinces is very much a seasonal affair, you understand. Women up here are willing to spend and have the wherewithal all right but they want value for money and judging the market is vital. I was up to my eyes and buzzing up and down the country making sure all my outlets were geared up for spring. Gus and I were not planning anything special until the Bank Holiday Monday when Daphne and Arthur were coming over with the twins. We had no kids so "family" means a lot to me."

Arnott nodded, the picture filling out, wishing now he'd had more chance to get to know this geology bloke.

Cora continued, anxious to get her story out in the open, confident of her instinctive trust in this stranger who had turned up out of the blue.

"Gus arrived home about four a.m. which surprised me as I wasn't expecting him till mid-morning on the Monday. I woke up when I heard his car and went downstairs to make some tea. We hadn't seen each other for a couple of weeks and though it might sound odd to you, our marriage was a good one. He loved me, you see. I never doubted that even after—"

She suddenly stopped, picking at a loose button on her cuff and biting her lip. Arnott waited. She looked up, waiting for Arnott's response but his face gave nothing away, he just sat there, solid as a wall, silent. Cora picked up the thread of the story, determined to bring it out in the open once and for all.

"Gus was in a terrible state. I thought there'd been a traffic accident on the motorway or something. He was trembling, desperately upset. He told me he had planned to tackle Ellie before coming home. She was trying to blackmail us – she had all these porno pics she had taken of Gus and a lot of other VIPs from a country club they used to go to to play tennis."

"The Domino?"

Cora nodded, brushing the sweat from her top lip with her fingers. "We'd had a row about it weeks ago. At first he said he'd call her bluff, it was madness to start paying up, but I said no. Buy back the polaroids he appeared in and that would be the end of it, the money wasn't important and it could only be a one-off payment. I hadn't seen them then or I might not have agreed but there you go . . . Anyway, he had made up his mind to settle with her before he came home but it all went wrong. He told me everything. We were up all night. That woman was a monster! Gus would never have got involved in a filthy thing like that if she hadn't dragged him into it. He was careful though, so he wasn't entirely innocent, was he, Mr Arnott? Called himself George Prentice he said, just in case anything leaked out."

"You mean he used a false name?"

She nodded. "Ellie invited him down to this smart country club a couple of times when I was abroad on buying trips. He had a good time, made a lot of new friends and he's always been mad keen on tennis. I think the initial attraction was getting away from the university crowd at weekends, taking a break from all that in-fighting. They can be very spiteful, you know, those bookish people. Crabby and envious."

"So I've heard," Arnott agreed, not an habitué of academic circles himself but well able to appreciate the universality of professional jealousy.

"Ellie's boss and his wife Helen Janssen introduced her to the club as a thank-you for helping out with their horses. Ellie could never have afforded to join a place like that on her salary but Helen was lonely and persuaded the doctor to fund Ellie's membership so when he was on call she had someone to keep her company. They used to ride a lot and Ellie sometimes stayed at their cottage looking after the stables when they were on holiday or stuck in London. Ellie seemed to be able to take time off whenever she felt like it and I suppose the doctor was glad his wife had some company. But that was only the beginning. The Janssens started having parties at the cottage and things got pretty wild Gus said. He didn't go that often but Ellie used to take people from town, girls she'd met at clubs, that sort of thing. Quite a lot of drinking went on and although Gus didn't spell it out to me, he hinted that cocaine was the Janssens' idea of an ice-breaker. A few of the people from the Domino who joined in were well-known – on the social circuit anyway – and they didn't have the sense to use a pseudonym like Gus did."

"George Prentice?"

"Exactly. Gus didn't want to get caught up in any newspaper gossip. These people move in a bunch, Mr Arnott, and Gus was worried it was all getting out of hand."

"Did both the Janssens participate in these parties?"

"Oh, yes. I'll have to show you the pictures. Ellie took them on the sly with her polaroid. That's what trapped Gus in the end."

Cora spilled the contents of the folder onto the table.

"And he showed you all these when he got back in the small hours after that Easter Sunday, Mrs Fielding? It was the pictures that put him in such a state?"

"Oh no. Gus had seen most of them before when Ellie had threatened to expose him to the university. He thought she was just kidding at first."

Arnott was baffled, dragging his attention from the eye-popping porno snaps to stare at the poor woman twisting her hanky into a rag.

"As I said, Gus intended to see Ellie that Sunday night and have it out once and for all. He thought everyone was out, you see and it wouldn't matter if it got to a shouting match. But your friend – Judy? – caught him on the landing on the way up and he had to put it off until later. He didn't want anyone in Rectory Gardens to guess he was involved with that creature."

"Oh, aye." Arnott relaxed, getting events in focus at last. "So he didn't have his row with the Juniper woman till after midnight – after he left me and Pullen?"

"There was no row. That was the terrible thing. He slipped up there to have it out with her after the house went quiet and found the door open and all the lights on. It was Gus who discovered Ellie in the shower!"

156

She shivered, reliving the dreadful moment in her mind. "It was a shambles, Mr Arnott. And water running everywhere, he said."

"He didn't touch nothing?"

"No, the girl was obviously dead. He could see that from the doorway – he didn't go right in. Then he searched for the photographs. That sounds dreadfully callous, doesn't it? But Ellie was dead. He didn't want any filthy blackmailer's material coming to light. Gus wasn't the only one involved you know, Ellie admitted that. She said she needed money urgently, to pay a debt she had run up during her holiday in the States. I didn't believe it – she had been living way beyond her means for ages but Gus was taken in, said he almost felt sorry for her, would you believe?" She frowned, determined to defend the man even at this pitiful stage.

"Of course, of course," Arnott reassured her. This was no time to start blaming anyone. "Gus knew where Juniper kept her dirty photographs?"

"She'd shown him before, like I said. They were in a shoe box in the dressing table, all mixed up with lots of other old snapshots. She didn't lock them away or anything."

"You think she was using these to blackmail other people. People who went along to these coke parties at the Janssens' cottage?"

"Oh, yes. The Janssens, too, I expect. Ellie was perfectly open about it to Gus. She didn't think it particularly bad, battening onto rich people the way she did. They had money, she wanted her share. Simple as that."

"You're saying Gus found the body, skimmed off the evidence and then drove home?"

"Yes, he did. As a policeman I can't expect you to approve of that. But he was scared stiff, Mr Arnott. A lot was at stake. Reporting the suicide would have meant saying what he was doing in Ellie's flat at one in the morning. He'd have to explain about the photographs, the blackmail, drag in the Janssens and all those other people. What good would that do? Ellie Juniper was dead. She had caused enough grief already. He walked out and took everything he could lay his hands on which pointed a finger at Ellie Juniper's extortion racket." She pronounced these last words flatly, with defiance, as if the suicide victim should be grateful for leaving her character intact.

"Did your husband turn off the lights before he left?"

Cora's mouth dropped, her astonishment almost comic. "Turn out the lights? In Ellie's flat? How would I know? Are you some sort of energy-saving freak, Mr Arnott?"

Arnott brushed this aside, immersing himself in the polaroids, firing questions at Cora and forcing her to examine the photographs closely to see if she recognised anyone. She didn't, apart from a prominent TV executive who was almost unrecognisable in a strange leather outfit and a blond wig. The poses seemed standard porn stuff to Arnott, poorly lit, the glimmer of chains and bondage paraphernalia weirdly appropriate against a background of Christmas glitter and baubles. Ellie looked as if she was enjoying herself but Cora was deluding herself if she thought the Juniper woman was the only person in the party mood. Gus didn't look too brassed off with the antics either. It didn't seem to have occurred to Cora Fielding that Ellie's camera might not have been the only one in action or, at best, Ellie Juniper was not the only one clicking the shutter. He studied the faces in detail, their boozy expressions leaving little chance that the funlovers would recollect next morning that any record existed.

"Well, as a month's gone by and no-one's heard a whisper of any of this, I'm sure you can just forget all about it, Mrs Fielding. Let your husband rest in peace."

"And say nothing about Gus discovering the suicide and not reporting it? And these photographs. Should I destroy them? Aren't they some sort of insurance for me in case any of these revolting people try to blacken Gus's name? Ellie Juniper knew the power of threats, Mr Arnott and so do I if driven to it. I don't want to give the go-ahead to publish his research if someone is just biding his time to take pot-shots at the poor man. The dead can't take out a libel case, Mr Arnott, and plenty of people out there think the Fieldings are rolling in money and will do anything to protect the family name. And there's something else I have to show you. Something I only discovered yesterday when I recovered all this from Gus's desk. It got jumbled up with the snapshots in his hurry that night to grab everything quickly, I suppose. He didn't even bother to show me this before."

She produced a typewritten invoice from an office in Washington DC, a bill for a considerable amount addressed to Miss Elinor Juniper at Rectory Gardens. She passed it over, dry-eyed, stronger now she had someone with whom to share Gus's secret. The demand was from a detective agency and gave no details. Just "For Services" and the date, January 3rd.

"I have cash flow problems myself in my business, Mr Arnott. If a bill's not paid there's always trouble. Creditors don't go away. Should I settle it myself? If this agency was hired by Ellie to investigate Gus's university work when he was in Georgetown in September it could lead to embarrassment at the very least. My husband's academic reputation is at stake here."

"Do you know of anything harmful Ellie might have discovered, Mrs Fielding?"

"No, I don't. But that doesn't mean none exists. Gus liked women. And women sometimes thought he was flashing a go-ahead signal when he was just flirting a little. I understood my husband very well and when he showed me all those horrible pictures I was terribly distressed, of course I was. Any wife would be. I threatened to throw him out when he first mentioned it after Christmas but our relationship was strong enough to come to terms with it and Gus was sure once he paid Ellie off that would be the end of it. He promised never to go down to that country club again. I forgave him, Mr Arnott, and if I accept that damage was done and we were working at repairing it why should I wait for more bricks to be thrown now he's dead? I can't go ahead and publish this book of his knowing his credibility is about to be destroyed by academic mud-slinging from the States."

"Don't get involved, Mrs Fielding. Your husband was canny enough to call himself George Prentice, chances are the folk in these pictures never knew his real name or even want to. You don't even know if this bill from the detective agency has already been paid. Once you start issuing cheques to settle up for things which are no concern of yours, warning bells are going to start ringing. I'll hand this to Juniper's solicitor." He scribbled Veronica Messop's business address in his notebook and tore out the page, passing it across the table. "Play dumb,

Mrs Fielding. You know nothing about this US investigation Juniper was involved in and I'm sure Miss Messop won't be interested either. I'll tell her I came across the bill when I was checking out the flat for Pullen – as a matter of fact I have had a little recce so she won't question it. Your name won't come into this at all. Miss Messop's dealing with the Juniper estate, this demand from the detective agency can be settled with all the others, no questions asked, merely a covering note from the solicitor to confirm Elinor Juniper is dead. OK?"

"What about the photographs?"

"I'll keep those if you don't mind. If you have any unwelcome callers just give me a ring and I'll deal with it. I very much doubt you'll hear any more about these saucy sex parties at the Janssens' place. Water under the bridge, Mrs Fielding. You take my word on it."

Cora looked dazed, totally confused by Arnott's facility to belittle her fears.

"There is one thing though," he said. She sagged, waiting for the inevitable price to be quoted. Nothing ever came free in this life.

CHAPTER EIGHTEEN

Arnott took the cassette from his breast pocket and asked if they could try it in her answering machine. She nodded and led him through the house to an office along the hall. It was a small room, jammed with filing cabinets and a workmanlike table spread about with a litter of bills and bank statements, very similar to the state of Ellie Juniper's desk the night he and Pullen had discovered the body in the shower.

He explained the origin of the tape and asked her to hear the last half-dozen messages. The machine worked perfectly and they juggled the playback while she listened intently, before turning back to Arnott with a shrug.

He said, "You didn't recognise any of those voices then?"

"No. Should I?"

"The woman near the end, the one offering to make a deal. An obvious victim of Juniper's little sideline, wouldn't you say?"

"How many of us were there for God's sake?"

"Well, no-one's going to put their hand up now, are they? Might be four or five people who sleep better since Juniper cut herself up."

Cora shivered, clasping both arms to her chest. Arnott pushed ahead with his questions.

"You never heard Gus mention anyone called Stig? Or Steve?"

She shook her head.

"And you never left any message for Ellie Juniper yourself?"

"I've never spoken to that bitch. Threatened to often enough. When Gus first told me about the blackmail I wanted to get on the phone straight away, tell her she was wasting her time thinking she could bleed him dry like that. But I didn't."

"Did he know that?"

"I'm not sure he trusted me not to lose my temper and give her a piece of my mind. He was like most men. Gus liked a quiet life, hated rows. He insisted on dealing with Ellie himself, tried to make me promise to keep out of it. But I've always acted for myself, Mr Arnott. I'm not the sort to hide behind a husband if the going gets rough and to be honest I didn't like Gus telling me what to do."

"He suspected you'd given her a piece of your mind then?"

"In fact, I didn't, but I wouldn't give him the satisfaction of knowing for sure."

Arnott removed the tape from the machine and she patiently reset it with her own. Wearily, Cora Fielding slid onto a chair and started to weep, very softly into her hands, despair claiming the last of her endurance.

He left without another word, tipping his hat to Daphne on the way out. He had left the van in the main street, its peeling paintwork seeming an affront to that smart cul-de-sac with its multi-garage complexes and striped lawns. He climbed into the van and drove back to London, feeling curiously uneasy after what should have been a very satisfactory excursion.

He drove straight to Cale Street and found a meter near Veronica Messop's building. He barged straight through the outer office ignoring the secretary's strangled cries, which insisted his quarry was in an important meeting with a client. The client was Basil Meek whose important business was the expedition of probate. Two angry people rose to protest at Arnott's intrusion but he took no notice, banging the detective agency's account down on the desk and getting stuck in with no preamble.

"Your late client, Miss Messop, was a blackmailer. This well-known American enquiry agent has been conducting an investigation on her behalf and supplying information which may well come within the category of secret data." Arnott let this little bit of invention sink in and extemporised some more, encouraged by their confusion, even Veronica Messop uncertain of the exact status of this former CID inspector whom she had met when Pullen was his sidekick. She decided to hear him out. Basil kept mum, for once genuinely knowing nothing.

"Sit down, Mr Arnott," Veronica snapped, "and tell me what this is all about."

She snatched up the invoice and scanned the printed heading and was, in fact, one up on Arnott in that she knew of this agency and had good reason to respect its reputation. It was on Veronica's recommendation that Ellie Juniper had contacted the Power Agency in the first place, confiding in her solicitor that she was trying to trace a missing relative in the States. Veronica felt herself on shaky ground and tried to retrieve the initiative, challenging Arnott's right to have possession of this confidential item and questioning the legality of the method by which he had acquired it.

Arnott, raising a hand in curt dismissal, ploughed on. "The estate owes money here and I have good reason to believe Ellie Juniper's activities were under police investigation before she cut them off at the knees by killing herself. Your cousin was dabbling in murky waters, Mr Meek, and as a friend of yours I think the sooner this mess is cleared up the sooner we can forget all about her nasty little game."

Basil, not at all sure how far he would be held responsible for Ellie's debts, grabbed the account from Veronica's hand. He handed it back. "Pay it," he said.

"But we don't know what it was for," Veronica persisted. "Or even if any other fees are outstanding."

Basil started to argue. He had the crock of gold practically within his grasp and was in no mood to have things snarled up in legal niceties. They *owed* him. The Junipers owed him. Now it was *his* turn to call the tune. He had put up with being treated like flotsam by that sanctimonious gin-bag and her oily husband, the unlamented Commander. Uncle Basil. He'd even put up with being lumbered with his stupid name and a fat lot of good it had ever done him.

"Oh, Basil, my boy, joining the Mercantile Marine, I hear." Just as if he'd gone and got himself booted up the gangplank by a press gang. They *owed* him! Ellie understood that. Ellie and Basil had each been tarred and feathered by the bloody Junipers in their time, all those old has-beens looking down their long noses at the dregs of the clan.

The voices in the solicitor's office became louder, Basil leaning across the desk, his fists clenched.

"I've got a suggestion here," Arnott interjected. "Mr Meek's right. Pay up. No sense in attracting attention. Telephone this agency and offer a full settlement if they tot up the outstanding expenses and send a new invoice straight off. As the Junipers' legal representative it is your duty to inform them that their client is dead and any business arrangement is therefore cancelled."

"That's what I just said," Basil expostulated.

Arnott glared. "I hadn't finished, had I? I'll phone the Power Agency head man myself and explain the background first. Say a full and final settlement will be in the pipeline but as Miss Juniper's sudden death is still the subject of police investigation the coroner's officer will require a copy of all the reports supplied by his agency."

"Why bring the Coroner's Office into it? Surely, if any reports are going anywhere that's the last place! *We* want to see them first," Veronica spluttered.

"That's why we've got to box clever, missy. They ain't going to fall over themselves to go public on a private investigation. But the Yanks are always impressed by a rubber stamp and will be only too quick to wipe their hands of it if it sounds official. As soon as they cooperate and send full copies to prove work's been done for your late client the estate can settle any outstanding bills. How does that sound?"

"Whatever happened to client confidentiality?" she groaned.

"You pay for it," Arnott retorted, grimly eyeing his reluctant fellow-conspirators.

Basil Meek hastened to agree with Arnott's proposal but Veronica was far from happy, humming and hawing as lawyers do. Arnott sat back and let the muck swill about, both the solicitor and the beneficiary tempted by the need to wrap everything up as soon as possible, both privately disconcerted by a growing suspicion that Ellie Juniper's activities would bear little investigation. Arnott had his own reasons for wanting any reports faxed from the Power Agency to go to Bernie Allen's office. It would then be for his eyes only, not blocked by Veronica Messop. But that was his own little wrinkle and he'd have to get his skates on to put Bernie in the picture.

Veronica reluctantly admitted there was something else which had to be taken into account. She had received a curt note from the manager of the Domino Country Club attached to an alarming list of items retrieved from Ellie's locker. It didn't look good. Arnott insisted on seeing this list and was still wondering if the amount of cash had been a typing error when Basil Meek curtly instructed his solicitor to stop prevaricating.

Arnott grinned and reached for the telephone. With the wonders of international communication at his fingertips the proprietor of the Power Detective Agency was soon on the line. Arnott introduced himself as an associate of Miss Juniper's lawyers and outlined the recent history of their late client.

Veronica tensed, marvelling at the sheer audacity of this pushy Yorkshireman who had taken over her office. She listened while he ran through their proposals. The extent of the Power Agency's brief was not questioned, the important matter under discussion being the final settlement of all outstanding accounts. This certainly smoothed the negotiations and Arnott's confident batting of the coroner's officer into the debate and his own attachment to Mr Allen's department went over without so much as a hiccup. It was agreed a complete copy of their findings, together with an updated and final invoice would be faxed immediately, the former marked Strictly Confidential and addressed to Arnott c/o Bernie Allen and the latter sent to Veronica Messop at her office. Arnott put the woman on the line and she assured Mr Humphrey Power that her firm was anxious to expedite matters and, after a further flurry of polite assurances, the phone was replaced.

Basil Meek looked mightily relieved; Veronica, far from happy, wished she had taken the easy option and specialised in divorce law; Arnott had the greatest difficulty in curbing a desire to kiss everyone in the room. He glanced at the time and bolted.

He went straight off to Bernie's office and was informed he was out on a case which was a stroke of luck. Arnott was all too familiar to the girl working the fax machine and put on a spectacular show of temper, a real fireworks display.

"Bernie said he'd be here without fail, Tracey! Now where the bloody hell is he? It's very important. We're expecting a fax from Washington about the Juniper case. Didn't he tell you I'd be in this afternoon? Bugger me, I've just driven all the way from Birmingham for this!"

He blazed on, strutting about the office, throwing his weight about and when the fax did come through the poor kid practically fainted with relief. He jotted a note to Bernie and shot off with the vital information before you could say "knife". As he told Pullen: What are old pals for?

It wasn't until he was back home and sitting with a double tot of Islay malt in his hand and the fax on his lap that he realised what a dung heap he had stumbled into. Ellie Juniper had moved on from small-time blackmail of susceptible bondage fans caught on film at naughty parties. She had hit the jackpot. Ellie Juniper had discovered what had happened to a certain paramedic called Mark Trujina who had disappeared in 1978.

The doorbell rang. Bernie Allen was standing on the doorstep, red as a turkey cock, his temper, so underused, a match for anything Arnott could produce. As soon as he opened the door, he knew Bernie was going to put up with no tap-dancing. He would have to come clean. He took him into the stuffy little living room and let him shuffle through the faxed reports while he poured Bernie a stiff whisky. Then he told him the rest of the story.

"And you believe this Mrs Fielding?"

"Why should *she* drop her husband in it? Say he withheld evidence when the poor sod's only just been dragged out of a quarry?"

"She didn't push him, did she?"

Arnott laughed, slapping Bernie on the shoulder. "'Course she didn't, Bernie. Poor woman's really cut up about it. Why? You heard anything different?"

"Not my case," he snapped. "Let's get back to this other business. What put you onto it?"

"Been buzzing about in the back of my old brainbox for weeks there was something I'd overlooked. You remember I asked you most particular when you and Coles first got to Rectory Gardens to run a nit-comb through all Juniper's personal effects?"

"Her glasses, you said."

"That's the ticket, Bernie. You never got back to me about that, did you, chum?"

"No need once the pathologist's report came out. I gave you a copy myself. She wore contact lenses."

"Not *all* the time, she didn't. In fact, Judy Pullen says different. She says Juniper wore big tortoise-shell jobs. We even found a photo of her wearing 'em."

"Where?"

"Pullen's got it. Found it under the wardrobe when she was clearing out the top floor after the funeral. Funny thing, now you come to mention it, that poor bloke Fielding was in the picture with her . . ."

Arnott shook his head, worrying at these complex relationships all surviving under the same roof at Rectory Gardens.

Bernie pressed home his point. "So her weren't there. So what?"

"Well, no-one pinches somebody else's glasses, do they? No bloody good to anyone else. Pullen cleared the flat after you lot picked it over, like I said. She didn't find 'em neither."

"Juniper could have *lost* her glasses! Or chucked them out when she got the contact lenses."

"But Pullen saw her wearing the glasses only a few hours before she croaked. How *could* she lose them, Bernie? She didn't go anywhere that night."

"We don't know that." Bernie was becoming mulish, well aware of the one-way street Arnott was forcing him into.

"Come off it, Bernie. You was first on the scene. You made the list and I asked you most particular to keep your eyes skinned for her big tortoise-shell glasses. They wasn't there, was they? Admit it! The poor bitch was blind as a bat without them, she wouldn't toss her glasses in the dustbin just because she'd got herself some pricey contact lenses. Too mean to waste a good pair of glasses I'd say. Any road, stands to reason she'd give herself a bit of a go with the new lot first, just in case they didn't suit. Then she'd have something to fall back on. Blimey, I'd be a goner without mine."

"What are you getting at, Ralph?"

"Ellie Juniper was playing a very dangerous game. She made enemies. *Someone* came to her flat that night and the poor bitch was knocked down and murdered. She was left-handed, Bernie. I only found that out after the inquest and the pathologist never knew. Those neck injuries given in the pathologist's report don't quite square with a suicidal left-hander. The only other pointer we've got that she wasn't alone is the missing glasses. P'raps they got smashed during the attack and the killer daren't leave evidence of any fight. He cleaned up good as new apart from a bloody great dent in the door which still has forensic evidence sticking to it that Coles didn't find. There was nothing Juniper's boyfriend could do with a busted door panel at short notice so he taped it over with a pop poster – and you'd better move quick on that an' all before the new landlord puts in a new door. That pathologist needs to take a second look, mate. That was no suicide."

"What are you asking for?" Bernie said with weary resignation. "Just as if I didn't know."

"An exhumation order."

CHAPTER NINETEEN

Judy Pullen surfaced from unconsciousness to find herself in a hospital bed.

Her head felt double the size and in the semi-darkness she cautiously explored her injuries. This was very difficult as she only had the use of one hand. She closed her eyes and the familiar swirling motion started up again. She vomited on the floor. Judy hung over the side of her hospital cot, the bed seemingly churning beneath her, feeling like a shipwrecked mariner on a raft, adrift on the ocean. She raised herself and slumped back on the pillows, her hair wet with perspiration, and bravely took another peek.

It was a standard issue iron bedstead all right but the place was unlike any sanitorium she had ever even heard of. The worst forebodings about Rumanian lunatic asylums couldn't match this. Her throat felt like a nutmeg grater and she fished about on the floor for the plastic bottle of water glimpsed as she was spewing up. After a long draught she felt saner and lay on the bed taking in her surroundings. One thing was certain: she was going to have to get used to using only one hand. Her left wrist was handcuffed to the metal rail of the bedhead.

The bed stood in the middle of a basement lit by a single light bulb hanging from the ceiling. Judith was glad the light bulb hung well clear of the bed: Rectory Gardens had left her with an abiding horror of any dangling light flex above her pillow. Several leather sofas were placed about the extensive floor space and here and there thick rugs made things seem almost cosy. But as a design feature, the hospital bed posed a problem even in a minimalist interior such as this.

It was deathly quiet, only the occasional swish of cars on a wet road giving a clue to her possible whereabouts. Judy recalled her last moments before blacking out and if she had not, while unconscious, been transported elsewhere, chances were she was immured in the cellar of Borodino Lodge. Had she disturbed some sort of gang in the course of turning over the big house? Stumbled upon a hideaway taken over by bank robbers? Escaped convicts even? Judith had to laugh at this flight of fancy, the most likely scenario being the bang on the head having seriously dented her powers of detection. Detection! Her hollow laugh rang out in the emptiness. What a ridiculous gumshoe Judith Pullen had turned out to be. Her first lone exploit and she gets banged up in a cottage on the edge of a country estate miles from anywhere. These things never happened to those American heroines with their little hand guns and their judo.

She sobered, listening hard, wondering if her captors, whoever they were, had scarpered and left her to be rescued by the Janssens on their return from Italy. But they weren't coming back for another week, were they? Who *was* supposed to get her out of here?

She sat bolt upright, stiff with fright, her head throbbing like the neck of a bullfrog. The only window was shuttered on the inside and, if her memory served her, barred and wired to boot. There were still no sounds from outside, not even a dog barking. She peered at her watch, a cheap Rolex copy which kept perfect time. It seemed to be four a.m. on Sunday. She sniffed at strands of her hair, aware of a strange metallic smell, and wondered if she had been chloroformed. Surely, the egg-sized bruise on her forehead plus the more serious contusion at the back of her head would hardly have paralysed her for seven hours . . .

Judy experimented with her range of movement and discovered that apart from the business of her wrist being clamped to the bedhead, the handcuffs were welded to eighteen inches of chain which could be manoeuvred along the metal rail giving her access to a lidded china bucket on the other side. She cautiously removed the lid and disclosed an inner saucer moulded with a large central hole. This porcelain bucket prettily decorated with a design of pink roses and fitted out with a basketwork handle was a convenience fit for Marie Antoinette. Her gaoler had thoughtfully provided a commode.

She spent some minutes juggling with the pants of her cherry-coloured trouser suit and fervently wished she had worn a skirt for that excursion to the Domino Country Club. But even a capsule wardrobe could hardly be expected to include prison garments and being pinioned was something even lifers were not subjected to. Having availed herself of the fancy bucket, she felt too exhausted to struggle back into her trousers, lay back on the bed, closed her eyes and pulled up the counterpane. The groundswell under her imaginary raft surged, and Judy gave herself up to the waves and drifted back to sleep.

Suddenly startled awake, she reared up, momentarily losing her bearings. Her watch now registered well after ten and, with a mixture of relief and terror, she recognised the rasp of a chair scraping the floorboards overhead. She started to shout, bawling for help at the top of her voice, finally subsiding into feeble cries. No-one came and with a feeling of total abandon she heard a door slam. She strained to catch footsteps, voices, anything . . . But silence descended again and angry tears burned her cheek.

Taking another swig from the bottle, she tried to pull herself together. When she eventually escaped from this freaking rat trap she'd have to confess to Arnott that she'd behaved like a total nutter. The thought of his grim satisfaction that his distrust of women officers was entirely justified, stung her to take fresh stock of her horrible predicament.

She plumped up the pillows and crossed her ankles, jiggling the handcuffs along and down the rail so she could rest her arm in a more or less normal position. Rubbing her cramped wrist, she blessed her good fortune in that she at least had her *right* hand free and wasn't gagged.

Also, the place was warm and clean, was quite hot in fact, and the floor expensively laid with sprung wooden laths like a dance studio. The basement was soundproofed and one end fitted out with stereo equipment, amplifiers and what looked like strobe lighting. It might have been used as a recording studio of some sort or even a party venue guaranteed against complaining neighbours. Judith had seen a set-up like this before. In Sweden where houses were frequently built to incorporate a sizeable cellar used as a games room.

Apart from the hospital bed which struck a bizarre note, Judy realised this place *was* a games room, though not for table tennis or snooker. Chains and dressing-up gear, leather masks and sundry fun items falling within the category of playful flagellation equipment hung over a folding screen. Judy stifled a giggle, feeling a bit like a white slave awaiting a fate worse than death. Perhaps the bed was for playing doctors and nurses.

Her fleeting amusement was broken by the unmistakable sound of her own racketty VW being driven up the lane, presumably to join the Volvo in the barn or hidden in one of the outbuildings. Thinking back to her last moments of freedom when she was peering into the Janssens' car, Judith guessed it had been one of the stacked logs which had been used as a bludgeon. Gingerly, she touched her matted scalp and wondered if she should make some attempt to clean the wound with some of the precious water. But who knew how long they would leave her festering in this dungeon? She decided to play safe and save the water for drinking. Toying with the urgency of her need to use the commode again, she decided against it. If these crazy kidnappers were not checking on her welfare, she could envisage questions of hygiene looming large on the horizon. Being at sea on a real raft would at least have solved one of her problems.

The sound of a key in the lock galvanized her terror and instinctively she sprang into a sitting position, grasping the rail, swinging her legs over the side of the high bed, ready to kick out. The door swung open and an emaciated figure stepped inside, the light from the cellar steps streaming in from behind, her face in shadow. The woman paused on the threshold, surveying her prisoner, then bobbed down to pick up a tray she had placed on the floor before unlocking the door. In the crook of her arm she balanced a shotgun.

She moved within the nimbus of the hanging light bulb and spoke.

"Hello, Judy. Sorry about the cuffs. It'll only be till Stig gets back tonight, then we'll phone someone to come and let you out when we've gone."

Judy shrank back, fingering the darkening bruise on her forehead, her face ashen.

It was Ellie Juniper.

CHAPTER TWENTY

Ellie Juniper had lost a lot of weight since Judith saw her last. Her skin looked opaque and the mauve track suit did nothing to warm her unhealthy pallor. The woman had an air of exhaustion about her; like a perished rubber band, there was no resilience left. Ellie's long fair hair was as pretty as ever and swung against her thin cheeks as always, leaving an impression of shyness. But her grey eyes, magnified behind the lenses of the tortoise-shell glasses were now feverish in their intensity. She didn't look well. Even so, she looked a whole lot better than the corpse buried in the Juniper family plot.

"You're thinner, Ellie," Judy said at last. "Have you been alone here all this time?"

"Stig comes when he can."

"Stig?"

Ellie smiled. "Philip, of course. Who else? He identified the body after all. But then so did you, didn't you, Judith?" she said, fussing in a hostessy way with the teapot. She offered a plate of sandwiches but Judy shook her head. It was true: she could have sworn the body under the shower was who she had expected it to be. Substitution had never entered her mind.

"Don't blame yourself, Judy. People look different when they're dead. After all, it's only natural no-one would want to take a second look at a girl with her throat cut. And Helen and I were always alike. It wasn't your fault, dear."

The flat dismissal of Judy's colossal error of judgement, couched in the polite phrases Mrs Juniper must often have expressed in the course of many a conversation over the coffee cups, was positively eerie. Was Ellie barking mad?

"And Stig is due back tonight," Judy said in what she hoped was a normal tone of voice. "Does he know I'm here?"

173

"He phones me every day. He's due home this evening. You arrived a day too soon."

Judy began to shiver, her fear impossible to disguise. If "Stig" had murdered his wife and persuaded Ellie to go away with him and pose as Helen, the arrival of a witness at his weekend cottage was not the best news he'd had since Christmas.

She clung to Ellie's reassurance that she would telephone someone to fetch Judy just as soon as they were safely out of the country. But would they? Would such foolishness be tenable when he had nothing to lose by disposing of one more inconvenient female? After all, it was only her presence here which spoiled their clear getaway. Perhaps Ellie was suffering from the delusion that they could live together always as Doctor and Mrs Janssen. And before she had burst in on Ellie's hidey-hole perhaps they could have . . .

"What did he say about me?" Judy blurted out.

"Well, we have to revise our plans a little. In any case we intended to leave at the end of next week when his contract expires. Stig insists he behaves normally, sees through his Venice conference and completes his tour of duty before handing over to the New Zealander. It might have aroused suspicions if he'd cut short his work to rush abroad straight after his typist committed suicide. That's why I've been stuck here."

"It must be over a month. Why didn't you leave immediately and wait for him there?"

Ellie's face hardened. It was clearly an argument she had heard before. "I *won't* go without him. He knows that. He *needs* me, Judith!"

Judy drew back, knowing she had touched a raw nerve, saying softly, "But hiding out here in the dark must have been terrible for you. How do you get food and everything?"

"He brings stuff for the freezer and I *do* get out sometimes. I went for a drive only the day before yesterday," she said with defiance. "If I wear my sunglasses and a headscarf I can drive through the gates in the Volvo without anyone taking much notice. At a glance, I can easily pass off as Helen."

"Of course you can. But then you *did* pass off as Helen! Everyone was fooled – even the pathologist. After my first identification nobody thought to question it."

Ellie frowned and Judith hastily added, "She must have been very like you, Ellie."

"Well, *you* thought so, didn't you?"

As if to prove this, Ellie produced a passport from her zip pocket and proudly displayed the photograph. It was Helen Janssen and it had to be admitted the likeness was striking. It was only Ellie's glasses which gave the game away.

"Where shall you go?"

She gave a sly smile and sipped her tea. "Somewhere nice where nosey people like you won't be snooping around."

"But you can't spend the rest of your life masquerading as Helen Janssen to protect this man."

"I *can* be Helen," she snapped, noisily gathering up the crockery onto the tray. "We shall live in Europe for a year, travelling about while he completes his studies. And then we shall go back to America." Her tone brooked no argument and Judith nervously eyed the shotgun propped up in the corner. She was clearly dominated by the handsome doctor, determined to stick by him at all costs. It was like something from *True Romances*! Mind you, she had always thought Ellie Juniper pretty immature, putting it down to that gorgon of a mother. Judith could imagine her own mother's facetious response: "See what happens when a girl has a conventional upbringing, Judith!"

It struck her that Ellie could be lying. It was entirely possible she had not spoken to Janssen the previous night after all, had perhaps been out of touch for days, her insistence that Stig was constantly ringing her and was already on his way home merely wishful thinking, a figment of her fevered imagination. Clearly, Ellie thought kidnapping a police officer a minor hiccup in their arrangements and that they could live happily ever after as planned.

She went upstairs, leaving the door ajar, and Judith struggled to formulate some sort of plan. The woman was unaware she was acting independently for a start. If Ellie thought about it, the police might already be encircling the cottage. If she had spoken to Janssen since Judy's capture such an eventuality would immediately suggest itself to him. The man wasn't a fool. But even Arnott had no idea where to look for her. Or even that she was missing. Judy felt even more like a shipwrecked sailor adrift on the open sea – and she hadn't even thought to alert the coastguard before setting out. Oh, silly old me!

Her head ached abominably and the fear of being locked up again made her heart race. She was relieved when Ellie reappeared with a bowl of hot water to mop up the vomit. She made a wry face at Judith marooned on her hospital bed amid that expanse of dance floor and retrieved the commode. Judy could hear her sluicing away at the sink upstairs and decided the best bet would be to establish some sort of rapport with this crazy female. If Philip Janssen had decided to do a bunk on his own, Ellie would need a sympathetic ear. The poor creature had, after all, been a prisoner here herself for more than a month. Judy had only a few hours before Janssen did or did not reappear. Either way was bad news for an inconvenient hostage: Ellie's state of mind would not improve if she discovered her paramour had left her in the lurch.

Judy's mind flickered back to the funeral and the abiding fantasy that she had been attending some sort of black wedding, the body in the coffin a star-crossed bride. She pushed this bizarre notion aside, seriously concerned that the bump on her head had wreaked more damage than bore scrutiny. She definitely needed all her wits about her to talk her way out of this *oubliette*. Even persuading Ellie to leave the door open would be something – then at least the soundproof basement would have its chink.

Ellie returned and put the Marie Antoinette bucket back by the bed. Judith touched her arm.

"Don't leave me, Ellie. Stay and talk. There's no sense in us both sitting on our own. Tell me about Mark Trujina."

As soon as the words were out of her mouth, Judith knew she had screwed up. Ellie's reaction was electric. She stiffened, her mouth curling with sarcasm as she replied.

"Well, who's a clever girl then! You've been through my locker – so what? What makes you think I owe *you* any explanations, Judith Pullen?

"Well, of course you don't!" Judy stammered, scrabbling for the words to placate her. "Ellie, you've been so clever in all this. Nobody suspected a thing. You must have been planning it for months—?" This last was a shot in the dark and sensing Ellie's temptation to confide, swiftly followed it up with, "And I suppose this Trujina guy helped to set it up?"

Ellie's eyes darkened and her clouded response suddenly cleared. She let out a gust of raw laughter, her thin shoulders shaking with genuine amusement.

She slammed out of the room, locking the door behind her, leaving Judy in despair, straining for any signs of life upstairs.

The hours dragged by and Judy began to feel seriously unwell. The plate of sandwiches had been left by the bed but the bread stuck in her throat like lumps of bitter regret. How could she have been so stupid? What on earth had she hoped to gain barging down here, snuffling about like a truffle pig?

It had to be admitted, she had seriously underestimated Ellie Juniper. For stamina alone, the woman deserved a Duke of Edinburgh Award, sticking it out alone for weeks on end, knowing herself to be officially dead and buried. Judy had had enough after twenty-four hours! Janssen could dispose of both of them and escape scot-free without a single person alive to put the finger on this wife-killer. Certainly, in the murder business, doctors had an unfair advantage when it came to the disposal of bodies. Had Ellie never considered the dangerous tightrope she danced?

Gradually, another explanation emerged even more sinister than the first. Perhaps Ellie had no reason to fear her lover. Suppose *she* had killed his wife and was now insisting she take Helen's place . . . a sort of incubus . . . If so, Judy's chances of escaping alive were seriously diminished.

She broke out in a sweat, scenting the sourness of her fear as the nightmare took shape. Why would a successful consultant allow himself to be dragged into Ellie's fantasy? What possible hold did she have over Janssen? Judith couldn't bring herself to accept Ellie's version: that they were in love, that "Stig" desired to replace one wife with a look-alike. A look-alike with homicidal tendencies.

Despite her panicky reappraisal, Judith drifted into a fitful doze, her mind exhausted by the proliferating possibilities. Truth was, she just didn't know enough about these people. If Janssen did turn up she would find out for sure one way or another. No sense in banging her head against the wall. "Bide your time, lass." How often had Arnott said that to her? And the canny old devil was generally right.

Sunday night drifted by like a bad dream. At one point Judith woke to find a saucepan of cold soup on a tray on the floor by her bed. Ellie had evidently slipped in while she was asleep. She dozed off again and later woke shivering with the cold. It now was well after five in the morning and she was feeling distinctly worse. She reached for the saucepan handle and, ignoring the dish, spooned the soup straight from the pan, forcing herself to drink the stuff, to muster some strength to get her through. Her rage simmered, fuelled not only by the realisation of her own impotence but anger that she had placed herself in the power of such a feeble opponent. About seven she heard the boiler start up again and the temperature rapidly rose.

Eventually, mid-morning, Ellie reappeared. She had changed into a mini skirt and a cashmere jumper, her hair tied back in a blue ribbon as if she had made a supreme effort to look attractive. But the fresh clothes looked as if she had slept in them and the gauntness of her frame was accentuated by this show of bravado. The skirt, tightly belted, was several sizes too big. It was all rather pathetic. Judith's anger seeped away as she realised this wraith standing before her had obviously had a sleepless night, a worse night than her captive, in fact, her eyes bloodshot and puffy behind the thick lenses.

Judith roused herself to accept a mug of coffee, forcing a smile as Ellie pulled up a chair to sit almost within range. Judy felt like a dangerous dog, chained to a kennel, all too well aware what a sorry sight she must present lolling on the bed in her knickers and stained jacket. The basement was now unbearably hot, presumably housing not only the Janssens' fun equipment but the central heating boiler.

"Could you help me out of this jacket, Ellie? It's a hell-hole down here with the door shut."

Her wardress looked anxious, sizing up the difficulty of removing Judy's coat without unlocking the cuffs. In any event, it might be tricky getting close to a policewoman who had presumably trained in one-armed combat.

"Sorry. You'll have to bear with it till Stig gets here."

"He didn't turn up last night then."

"There must have been a flight delay. He'll phone."

Judith didn't know if she was sorry or not. It all hinged on whether the bloody man was a goodie or a baddie. Well, he *must* be a baddie, she supposed, but if he was as much Ellie's victim as she herself, this would be his big chance to walk away, his career intact and only the ravings of a madwoman to contend with. But he *had* identified the body, after all. And even if he claimed this was a mistake – and Judith herself had performed no better – how could he explain the disappearance of his wife?

She had played safe too long. If she was to fall prey to a pair of nutters, she might as well speed things up and, at least, get some answers before they finished her off.

"We *must* talk, Ellie. Stig won't be coming back. Ever. I spoke to Mrs Quick on Saturday afternoon. Ellie, you've got to face up to facts. Phone the surgery yourself if you don't believe me. Janssen never went to Venice at all. He's disappeared. Ask Mrs Quick."

Ellie sustained these blows without flinching, hardly blinking even, and Judith held her breath waiting for her bluff to be called.

Ellie's response was cool.

"You know I can't do that. Mrs Quick knows my voice. I couldn't ask a thing like that."

"Let me telephone her for you then and pass it over so you can hear what she says. I wouldn't lie to you, Ellie. I know how long you've waited and . . ."

Her words faded. Perhaps she had guessed the truth already. Ellie had a lifetime's experience of being cheated.

She sighed. "I knew Stig wouldn't come as soon as I told him about Gus. He isn't brave like us, Judy. I should have kept it a secret. I thought he would be glad, you see. Gus Fielding was the last obstacle. Until you came. It was all too much – why the hell couldn't you all leave us alone?"

Ellie slid onto the floor and crouched there, sobbing like a child. Judy breathed more easily. The rock had been cleft. All she needed now was a wedge to break Ellie Juniper into a million pieces. She felt no pity.

"What happened to Gus?" she coldy enquired.

"He's dead, Judith. I didn't kill him. He fell, I swear. I explained how it happened but Stig didn't believe me. He thought we could just ignore Gus. But that's not possible, is it? That man wouldn't just forget about us, would he? Any more than you."

179

CHAPTER TWENTY-ONE

If Ellie Juniper had been perfectly sane when she decided to place herself in Helen Janssen's shoes, a month in hiding had unhinged her. It would unhinge anybody – Judy would be the first to admit that. Ellie lay on one of the leather sofas and the words spilled out. It was if she needed to put the record straight, tell her side of the story for once.

"I got involved with the Janssens soon after I went to work at the consulting rooms three years ago. They asked me to go down to the cottage to look after the horses while they were away. They exploited me really but I liked the horses and was glad of the opportunity to get away from London and the claustrophobia of living with Mother. And I got paid for it.

"The pair of them fascinated me right from the start – starstruck you might call it, a teenage crush when I was past thirty years old. Can you believe it, Judy? Not that I was a virgin before I got mixed up in it but there was no tricksy stuff. In the beginning Helen was a real friend and lots of fun. I was crazy about both of them so it was easy for things to take their course. I was gradually drawn into an intimate threesome – both Helen and Stig were so gentle and uninhibited – it was an exciting contrast to the boring life I was leading at Rectory Gardens. They bought me clothes and paid for me to join in their social life in the country, dished out money as if it blew down from the sky – all absolutely secret from that nosey old bag, Mrs Quick, of course. That made it even more thrilling. To be taken up, a plain, not very sexy thing, by such a glamorous cosmopolitan couple and taught all sorts of fancy ways to enjoy myself was absolute heaven. Not just the sex: books and art and foreign movies.

"It got so I had to make a terrific effort to stay looking plain

old Ellie Juniper for the office – and at home, too, especially when Mother was alive. We had to be careful, you see.
Stig didn't want anyone to guess . . . Helen taught me about
clothes, make-up, making myself sexy. Stig was really fascinated. Loved to see me change into some sort of beautiful,
strange creature as soon as I got away from Rectory Gardens. It's easy, Judith – I could show you. It's nothing to do
with all this silly stuff in the magazines. Helen knew everything. It's a sort of secret power we all have – no-one is really
plain, you know. Sometimes," she confided, getting up to move
closer to the bed, "I longed to show Mother how changed I
was, how lovely underneath. Just *show* her. But Stig made me
promise . . ."

Ellie drew away, lost in her own reverie and Judith watched
her like a rabbit in a hole, waiting for the stoat to make a move.
If she could just keep her talking . . . She cleared her throat and
was about to speak when her captor picked up the thread of her
story again.

"No wonder it went to my head, Judith. You can see how it
was, can't you?" She shrugged. "They used to drink and dope
at the cottage and I pretended to go along with that too but
I needed no stimulation – they were like champagne to me.
Eventually, they coaxed me to bring friends back from discos
in town, on a no-names basis. I was drawn into threesomes
and foursomes – not always with an extra man – Stig liked to
be outnumbered.

"That hurt me at first – we were head over heels for each
other by then – but he explained that his love for me wasn't
rationed. There was plenty to spare for fun which could only
make things even better for us. He took some videos and
photographs on the quiet. He keeps them in the safe at the flat
in town and when they were all boozed up I took a few polaroids
myself and Cindy borrowed my camera and did some snapping
just for laughs. There was no harm in it – we were all revelling
in the total freedom down here. Helen had this basement done
up specially like a sort of private nightclub, and no-one ever
bothered us. Sir Guy's hardly ever in the country and the staff
turn a blind eye if they're kept sweet.

"But that's when it all started to go wrong. You see, I had
fallen for Stig in a big way. Before that it was only a crazy

freakout at weekends, innocent larks. Stig felt the same way as I did but we managed to keep our feelings a secret from Helen.

"After a year or so my rôle as the novelty number in Helen's cabaret began to wear off and she was starting to cut me out, invite new chums she had met in London. Don't be taken in by what you hear about Helen Janssen. She's no quiet, horsy Englishwoman like they say. Stig met her in New York when she worked for an escort agency and, believe me, she must have been worth every penny. She was a real enthusiast, knew every kinky trick in the book. A golden girl. It was Helen that got my darling hooked on the bondage game and, to be fair, we all craved it at the start. Nothing sadistic – not horror movie stuff. I brought Gus down here a couple of times but for the past nine or ten months Helen was getting itchy feet, wanting to move on. They're not married, you know. Helen Janssen's her real name. Stig promised he would leave her but I found out she was planning to drag him off to Switzerland for a year so he could write this medical book. Helen made it quite plain my time was up. The writing was on the wall and I began to panic. I trusted Stig but he couldn't bear to upset anyone and was used to being led by the nose by Helen.

"I spent a few weekends down here on my own while they were on holiday last August. That's when I found the press cuttings about Mark Trujina. She had hidden them inside her stable account book with all the feed bills and vets' receipts and so on. I thought it was a very funny thing to do as they both made such a thing about this open relationship of theirs. I thought at first it must be some old sweetheart of hers but it seemed odd stuff to hide away like that. It wasn't even current, the cuttings were years old and all tatty. Secrets are always potential ammunition – I learned that from my sainted mama who squirrelled away old sins against people in case they might come in handy some day if only to demonstrate her wealth of Christian forgiveness. Knowing Helen was trying to shake me off, I decided to look into it, just in case I needed a weapon of my own if she tried to throw me out. I didn't mention it to Stig. He would never hear a word of criticism of her even though he knew she was dictating where he should work, where they should live, every step of his career.

"Helen was a woman who got bored very easily, you see. London had become stale for her and she couldn't let her hair down there, the wife of a fashionable consultant and all – chances were the high life was too close to his patients to risk any scandal. It was only when she got down here they could party in the style which thrilled her and even this place was becoming a drag. I took the cuttings into Bray and made copies before putting them back where I found them.

"I was the perfect companion for Helen while I was still starry-eyed. But she had taught me too well. Stig hinted I was getting too close to the spotlight, best not to upstage her. Helen could turn at a flicker of an eyelid. Hit out. She knew how to really hurt. You know, the funny thing was, the longer this charade went on, the more I began to realise that Helen and Mother were the same – pretending to love you while forcing you back against the thorns. Have you ever read about those birds that do that – shrikes I think they're called." She shuddered. "Horrible. It turned my stomach, I don't mind admitting. I could see what Helen would do to the poor man in the end, flatten him out and prop him up at the table like a cardboard cut-out.

"Then Mother died in September. Everyone was very kind – even Mrs Q. My cousin, Baz, arranged for me to go out to Miami and wangled a free cruise on a sister ship of the same line. It was wonderful. But the prospect of coming back to Rectory Gardens and that stultifying typing job was hellish and I knew, deep down, Helen would soon drag him abroad with her. That man is all heart, too kind for his own good. He couldn't see what she was doing to his life, organising every move he made. I decided to strike back, show Stig what a double-crossing cow Helen really was.

"I took some extra holiday and set about looking for Mark Trujina. No luck, of course. What hope did I have in tracking the man down after so long? But the idea of having a hold over Helen really appealed to me – it could tip the scales against her and then Stig wouldn't feel so bad about leaving her flat. I had some bits of jewellery from my mother and decided to blow the money on some professional detective work. It had been in my mind ever since I found the cuttings but until Mother died I was hamstrung – I've never been good at saving money. I consulted this firm in Washington before I flew home, left them all the details about Helen I could muster – and Stig, of course – and asked them to track down this guy, Trujina, from the archives. It was my only chance. I wasn't going to be taken off the shelf like that, dusted off, given a whirl and then put back in stock like the fairy off the Christmas tree, getting tackier and less fanciable every year.

"Weeks later I got my first report from the American detective agency and it really blew my mind. Nothing much about Trujina except he'd had his squint fixed before leaving the army but they'd unearthed a whole rat's nest in just their initial investigation.

"I took a day off work – said I had to have a tooth out – and arranged to meet Helen in a café in Windsor. I didn't want to risk seeing her privately – you could never tell what Helen would pull. Actually, I was scared of her in a funny sort of way. She was like one of those spitting snakes sunning itself on a rock – looking so calm and beautiful – but poised to get you in the eye in a flash. Anyway, I plucked up courage and confronted her with the dossier and offered to keep quiet about it if she pushed off and left me and Stig on our own.

"He would have been more than generous – how else could he be? They had been together for years. Helen was really shocked – I've never seen her turn white like that. It was as if I had managed to strike first for a change. I got brave and spelt out my terms. I had nothing to lose and she knew I must be desperate to threaten to blow the whistle like that. Stig was away at the factory redesigning a new back corset they are to market in the autumn and I told her not to mention our meeting to him. I had to tackle Helen myself – it was no use asking Stig to face up to anything. I said nothing about Mark Trujina." She started wandering about the room in a distracted tour, touching chairs and tables, perching here and there and Judy strained to catch the indistinct phrases as the insubstantial figure paced about in the gloomy recesses.

"That's where she underestimated me. Everyone does, of course. It's wearing glasses – people think because you're shortsighted you can't spot a situation that's staring you in the face. I passed over the agency report – after all, I had copies – but didn't mention the Trujina cuttings in my locker at the club.

184

She didn't know I'd even heard of this guy Trujina and there was still a chance my American detective would come up with something solid, given time. I suspected she had married this man when she lived in New York. It might just be enough to show Stig that Helen hadn't been as straight as she pretended – she was always going on about being the only woman since Eve to own up to everything. Hiding the stuff in the stables where Stig never went just had to be suspicious – I had a gut feeling about Trujina. Helen was not a sentimental type, the sort to keep old Valentine cards. She thought I only had the evidence against Stig."

Judith grasped the bedrail, steeling herself not to interrupt, the volume of unanswered questions piling up in her mind like snowflakes on a windscreen. Ellie's voice pattered on, soft and light, eager to expose her torment, to display the stigmata on her innocent palms.

"Helen took the agency report from me and read it through. After a minute she looked up and just laughed in my face. Offered me a bloody fortune to forget all about it, enough to set myself up well away from Rectory Gardens, start a new life in the sun if I wanted. It was quite a package. A year before I would have snatched at it. But she was too late. We were in love. She couldn't see that I had changed. He wanted me to take her place. I could give him a real home, a settled life at last instead of this gypsy traipsing around Europe to satisfy her wanderlust. Why should I be the one to be shoved aside, even with her golden handshake – it was like being offered redundancy money!

"Helen spelt it out. I knew then I should have confided in Stig first. Helen would make my meeting with her sound ugly, like blackmail. I had to talk to him, explain why I had gone behind his back and set this horrible investigation in motion, put it to him that my motive was purely to give us a means of escape. I persuaded Helen not to panic him – no need to upset everything at this stage – and to make it a secret between us two women while I thought her offer over. She had her faults but you could make a deal with Helen Janssen and she wouldn't cheat on it. That was my big mistake. I needed time to plan my next move but she wouldn't wait. She gave me twenty-four hours to decide. Later she left a message on my answering machine and insisted on calling at the flat for a final answer. It was obvious she had made up her mind that I would be dazzled by the money – possibly my last opportunity to break out of Rectory Gardens. The trouble was I hadn't had a chance to speak to Stig, to explain my side of things. I phoned her back and she told me a bank account in my name had already been opened abroad somewhere and I'd better make up my mind damn quick before she changed her mind. After all, she said, I wasn't getting any younger. That hurt!

"Easter Sunday night she bounced into my scrappy little pad looking wonderful as usual, all glammed up and wearing this lovely short chiffon sarong dress, all floaty and soft green like that expensive bubble bath stuff that's always being advertised in magazines. Helen said they were going on somewhere, joining friends at a new club in Grosvenor Street – Stig was waiting at home for her to pick him up after she'd sorted me out. Made me feel like a minor inconvenience that had to be dealt with before they could get on with the rest of the evening.

"Helen had broken our agreement and showed him the agency report. That was mean of her, wasn't it? I might have known she would try to set him against me. But she wasn't altogether fireproof – Helen had her little weaknesses the same as the rest of us – she couldn't resist the gin. Gin and water was her thing – a real boozer's tipple, no wonder she got on so well with Mother. I'd got it in specially and kept refilling her glass. Helen insisted on putting on some rock-and-roll tape she'd brought round with her, said she'd lived in a house like Rectory Gardens before, places like that were always full of peeping toms and old pussies with their ears pressed to the wall. What she had to say was strictly private.

"She made it plain Stig wasn't going to leave her for me and rang home and made him spell it out to me that the honeymoon was over. He was scared to leave, poor lamb, devastated that his secret was out, terrified at the prospect of Helen out on her own, rolling about like a loose cannon, her spite and jealousy infinitely more dangerous than any threat I might be. He knew I would never destroy him by disclosing that report. I worshipped the man, you see.

"I was overwhelmed with loathing for her at that moment. Stig is a weak man but left to decide for himself he could never abandon me. I was totally numb, didn't really believe it was all over. She sat in the flat downing the gin like holy water and I wondered if I was expected to ring for a taxi for her afterwards as if I was still just her husband's little typist. We exchanged the papers and she gave me the details of a bank account in Luxembourg which was mine. It was an Easter egg of Mother Goose proportions, believe me, all that money tied up with ribbons. I wanted to break her smug face in half, smash all that bloody self-confidence. People like Helen Janssen think they can drop all the little people that get in the way like so much unnecessary baggage. 'Not wanted on the voyage' was the message and she made no effort to hide her contempt of my puny effort to break up their cosy nest.

"I had one last shot to play. I showed her the Trujina press cuttings and waited for Helen to crumple up. She just fell about laughing. Didn't I recognise the man I was supposed to be in love with? It was Stig. That silly nick-name of his. He'd never explained it to me, had probably forgotten its origin years ago. It was a cruel tag he'd picked up in the army and, as usual, such things stick. Astigmatism. He'd been born with a squint, not a bad one but enough to cause teasing, and Stig was something he'd got used to; didn't bother him a bit. His real name's Trujina. The press pictures were years old. She didn't care that I'd found out about it. What difference did it make to our little arrangement?"

Judith could contain herself no longer.

"Let me get this straight, Ellie. The old press cuttings you found in the stables were about Philip Janssen? He changed his name?"

"Helen organised it. They met when he was just a simple paramedic in a singles bar in New York." Her voice softened, imagining, Judy guessed, the immature young soldier in his uniform.

"Why should Helen do that?"

Ellie smiled. "I told you, silly. Helen was a real live fairy godmother. She could *transform* people. Really, Judith. Helen had a gift, sort of second sight. She could spot the potential in quite ordinary people. The only trouble was, once she'd made a person over she thought they *belonged* to her and when she got bored they could be tossed out like toys in the attic."

"She made Mark Trujina into Philip Janssen?" Judy mouthed the words with incredulity.

Ellie became tetchy, irritated by the stupidity of her listener. "Not at a single stroke, Judith. No, of course she didn't! It took ages, years even – I don't know. She made him leave the army. He had so much to learn in so many ways, poor lamb. But Helen worked it out, kept him studying at home, using her own earnings. She certainly had the money, even in those days. And she had peculiar friends he told me, people she met when she was working for the escort agency. Government people some of them, willing to provide references, pointers, all that sort of thing. She changed him, gave him power. Helen had a strength which simply poured *into* a person. Can't you see?"

Ellie became impatient and thrust aside Judy's next question, delving back into the narrative before Judith had started on her stupid side issues.

"As I was telling you. There we were, in my flat at Rectory Gardens, she was sloshed and we were arguing. Then suddenly, Helen sobered up. God knows how she did it. It was if she'd just been coasting along and then accelerated away like some sort of racer, changed up into a different gear. Her mood turned really ugly. She grabbed my arm and gave me the full eyeball treatment, no more messing about, her mouth all twisted up in a smile about as funny as a crocodile on heat. She said as I had been such a pal she and Stig wanted to leave me with an extra farewell gift, a special bonus, something personal they had been saving just for me. A dose of HIV.

"I knew immediately Helen wouldn't lie about a thing like that, even drunk. Only *she* could sink to such black comedy. That they had both deliberately exposed me to *that*! It was incredible, even coming as it did from a witch like Helen. She was choking with laughter, rolling about on my sofa, busting with the joke of it. She burbled on about having shared every-thing with me just as I longed for – all the spoils of a successful career, clothes, money, clubs, horses – even their disease. That set her off on another fit of giggles. And there I was, she said, mumbling on about Stig settling down! A boring little semi in Wimbledon I'd got my eye on no doubt. He'd told her all about it, she said. I'd scared the poor darling out of his wits, she said he'd called it a suburban Valhalla more terrifying than

188

full-blown AIDS. Helen told me that if I had any sense at *all* I would grab this chance of a short life and a merry one as they had decided to do. Take the money and run. Enjoy life to the full while we all had the chance. No point in tiptoeing through a minefield of useless treatments, scrabbling for cures."

Ellie had stopped speaking and lay on the sofa like a patient on a psychiatrist's couch and Judith, cross-legged on the hospital bed, dared not move. The silence dragged on and for a moment Judy panicked, thinking the woman had passed out. Ellie had obviously not eaten a decent meal for weeks, her arm hanging to the floor like an anorexic teenager's.

"Ellie! Are you all right?" she ventured at last.

The figure on the black leather sofa unfolded and started pacing the room, frowning at the floor.

Judy said, "Do you think I could have a cigarette?"

Ellie flinched, as if she had completely forgotten her existence. Like a sleepwalker, she picked up an onyx cigarette box and a matchfolder from one of the tables and placed it on the bed. Judy reached out and took a cigarette. She lit up more for something to occupy her shaking hands than anything else but when Ellie's back was turned she slid the heavy box under the bedcover. It was an unlikely weapon but, so far, the only one to come to hand.

Judith scrabbled about for something to keep Ellie talking, terrified of what the woman would get up to if she went back upstairs and left her alone again.

"Tell me about Basil Meek. Why did you decide to leave everything to him in your will?"

"Basil?" she murmured. "Well, why not? That bossy friend of yours, the solicitor woman, Messop, went *on* and *on* about the problems she had sorting out Mother's affairs. I agreed to make a will and couldn't think who else to name. I could hardly leave everything to Stig, could I? Even if he needed the money. Poor old Basil never had any luck. Chances are he'll not outlive me anyhow." She sniggered, tickled at the thought of that last surviving remnant of the Juniper line. It had just worn out like a threadbare old flag.

"You were fond of your cousin?" Judy prompted.

She shrugged. "We were in the same boat really – both my parents and his regarding us as inexplicable runts in a pedigree

189

litter. Anyhow, after Mother went, he wangled a free holiday on one of the cruise liners for me, you know. Wasn't that kind? Made a bit of a fuss of me, hoping I'd got some spare cash after the estate was settled I expect, but there weren't any savings, of course. My parents' generation lived on past glories, Judith, no substance there at all."

Her voice was flagging and introducing the dismal subject of the Junipers had probably, Judy decided, been a mistake. She tried something else.

"You must have wondered who it was when I drove up the lane," she ventured.

"I was upstairs changing when I heard the car. As I looked out the lights were doused and I watched the torchlight weaving through the trees. My God, Judy, you practically freaked me out creeping up on me like that! I knew it wasn't Stig – I'd only just spoken to him on the phone. The most obvious stalker was Basil; he'd been following me about before Easter, nosing at the country club, checking up on me, trying to find out where I'd got the money to join an outfit like that, dying to get in on the act if he could, I suppose. He suspected I'd been holding out on him about Mother leaving no savings but when he saw me at the club, he realised that wasn't so. He's always on the make, that bloke." She smiled indulgently, like a fond parent. "We understand each other – it must be a fault in the family genes, two duds in the same generation. Anyway, Basil touched me for a loan, said he had to rustle up the air fare to meet a guy in Amsterdam and, quick as a flash, I paid up. It was the only way I was likely to shake him off and seemed cheap at the price. I didn't want my cousin poking his nose into my little clique at the Domino. He could find his own little scam."

"Then Basil pushed off and you never saw him again?"

"That's right. He phoned me from Amsterdam about eight o'clock Easter Sunday night and said he was enjoying a bit of a binge before rejoining his ship."

"You sure he was abroad?"

"Oh, yes. I had to ring him straight back. He said he didn't have any loose change for the pay phone. Typical Baz, the mean bastard."

Judith plumped up her pillow and forced a smile.

"You never told me how Gus fell," she said.

"You believe me, don't you, Judith?"

"Of course I do. Tell me about it. I didn't even know there'd been an accident."

Ellie brightened, drawing on Judy's encouragement like water in the desert.

CHAPTER TWENTY-TWO

"What about Gus?" Judy persisted.

Ellie had perked up since the subject of the Janssens had been dropped and she flopped on the chair she had brought as near to Judith as she dare. She became animated, embellishing the story with lively gestures and smiles.

Judy let her run on, marvelling at the many-faceted persona of this strange person. At first, Ellie had seemed just an ordinary, rather soppy female, but, as she said, everyone underestimated her. Judy's understanding of what had gone on had been well off the mark. She thought, at first, Janssen had been the Svengali but the more that emerged, the more the roles reversed, Ellie being the one to force the issue.

"As I told you, Gus came down here to the cottage with me a couple of times. We stayed at the club – Helen covered all my expenses at weekends and encouraged me to make up a party. It was all anonymous – Gus called himself George Prentice and he only guessed who Stig and Helen were quite recently when I showed him the polaroids one night at the flat. Dear old Gus was a nice enough guy but slow on the uptake. He used to come to the flat now and then when Mother was at one of her church meetings – just to air his socks you might say. Gus was always good for a laugh. Did you ever get to know him? He wasn't at Rectory Gardens much, just once or twice a week. Gus took to the Janssens' alternative lifestyle like a duck to water.

"Anyway, when I was feeling matey one night soon after I moved upstairs, I got the polaroids out just to hype him up a bit, I suppose. He got pretty excited by that sort of thing and one or two featured Gus in all his glory. There were several of Stig, of course, and one of the four of us: Gus, Helen and us two. You know the sort of silliness a few bottles of champagne can lead to at a party. Gus Fielding's a boring sod, takes everything so seriously it would make you weep. That was his trouble. Fill the man up with bubbly and he's a barrel of laughs but get him back to London and his rock samples and he turns into a real old worryguts – terrified his wife would find out. Those pictures gave him the shits and I knew I'd made a terrible mistake showing him. I swore it was a secret between us, not even Helen or Stig had seen the polaroids. He wanted me to tear them up there and then but I said they were my insurance in case Stig wanted to give me the sack. But I promised to put them under lock and key and he had to be satisfied with that.

"Turns out, sod's law as usual, Gus Fielding trundled up to see me that Easter Sunday night after I'd left. Totally taken in, poor bloke. Thought I'd topped myself and, typically, his first priority was to take his fat bum out of there damn quick, to keep right out of it. Then he decides to make quite sure I hadn't left a suicide note incriminating him or blaming the parties at the cottage for my death wish. Worse, he imagines the polaroids will surface and heave everyone into the mire, including the Janssens. So, playing the Good Samaritan, Gus does a quick recce and sifts the naughties from the family snapshots in the shoebox I keep in my dressing table and runs home with his tail between his legs. If he'd had any sense he would have set light to the lot there and then and put the whole episode out of his head but academics get the palsy when it comes to destroying evidence of any sort.

"Being the worrying type and slow to make up his mind Gus eventually decides to warn Stig and Helen, tell them about me disclosing their real identities to him and tip them off he had these polaroids, and that there might be more under lock and key somewhere.

"He phoned Stig at the surgery and suggested they meet at the country club. You see, Gus had this idea I had more photographs in my locker and wanted Stig to make the manager empty the locker before the police cottoned on to it. Stig was absolutely thunderstruck that his cover was blown but at least we knew why the porno pics hadn't featured in any police report or surfaced at the enquiry. Gus had done us all a big favour lifting those photographs overnight. If Stig had known that he would never have shown up at the flat early that

Monday morning and got involved in the official identification of the body.

"I was lying low in London till later that Monday when Stig drove me down here. If there had been a hue and cry over the identification, we were ready to take off – Stig hinted he had an old passport that would see him safely through the barrier at the airport."

"How did he get the Janssen passport?"

"That was all part of Helen's package deal. Through her contacts in the States from her escort agency days. That sort of thing's dead easy if you know the right people, Judy. You've no idea!"

Judith shifted awkwardly on the bed, wondering if this second wind of Ellie's would last. The woman had the stamina of a marathon runner, able to jog on with no sleep and little nourishment. If she pegged out upstairs after this little burst of liveliness, there might be a slim chance of raising the alarm. It was a pity she was teetotal, a few gins would have put her out like a light.

"Anyway," Ellie said, "there was no need to take any emergency action after all. Stig did the identification and the inquest slid through as smooth as silk. He's been able to carry on perfectly normally at the surgery and, as luck would have it, was due to take a sabbatical soon after this Venice trip in any case. Gus stumbling on Helen's body in the shower and removing the polaroids before the police got a sniff was the luck of the gods as far as Stig was concerned. And Gus was utterly convinced of the substitution. He was as sure as you were that I was the corpse. Only goes to show how people shy away from looking closely at dead bodies, even someone they know intimately. People like Gus at any rate. When my poor mama was laid out in Shiner's 'Chapel of Rest' as he calls it, she looked a different woman – younger, all ironed out. Almost a stranger. Odd isn't it?"

"Gus wasn't trying to blackmail the doctor with the polaroids?"

"Absolutely not! Quite the reverse, in fact. Stig couldn't believe it. But there was no way he wanted to get involved with 'George Prentice' – Gus kept up the pseudonym and I never told Stig he rented a room at Rectory Gardens. He thought

Gus was just some bloke I'd picked up. Driving over to the country club with 'George Prentice' and bribing the manager to empty my locker was the *last* thing poor Stig wanted to get involved in. Anyway, I told him there was nothing in the locker to worry about. To be honest, Stig poking about in my sports bag wasn't a good idea for me either. You see, I'd accepted help from a few of Helen's friends, to cover all my extra little expenses, and naturally I didn't want Stig to know I had side bets as you might call it."

Judith blinked at this assessment of the bundle of cash Ellie had squirrelled away but let it pass. No sense in getting on her high horse about it.

"Gus really should have called it a day but he was obstinate as a mule, determined to tie up all the loose ends. He kept phoning Stig at Harley Street and made himself an awful nuisance but Stig was adamant, quite determined to keep right away from the club. He didn't trust Gus, of course, that was the trouble. He couldn't believe he wasn't trying to corner him in some way. But I know the man and insisted Stig really should see him if only to satisfy himself Gus really had only those silly snaps up his sleeve and wasn't trying to put the bite on. Stig reluctantly agreed to meet him on the quiet a week ago and Gus suggested an abandoned quarry not far from here, an isolated place where he collects fossils. He promised to bring all the polaroids and turned up as arranged. But Stig got cold feet and stood him up. You see, Judy, he felt if he could put Gus off long enough we would be well away, out of the country, and just keep our fingers crossed that Gus wasn't the vindictive type. After all, Gus was in the pictures too, at least the ones that featured Stig. For all he knew I *did* have more snaps tucked away. But I had this sneaking suspicion Gus knew more than he was admitting on the phone. I begged Stig to fix up another meeting and warn 'George'."

"Warn him about the HIV infection?"

Ellie curled up with laughter, almost hysterical. Judy waited, tense with apprehension, knowing it was all too easy to blow Ellie off course. At last, she contained her amusement and went on.

"Gus was never in any danger in that way! You don't know Gus Fielding, Judith. He's the most careful calculating bugger you could imagine. He'd make love in a full-length raincoat if it was put out as a safety factor. Gus *never* performed without a condom. Probably couldn't get it up unless he was medically fireproof – not just with me and Helen, mind you, probably with that wife of his too. No, Gus was the last man to ignore public health warnings. He didn't even smoke!"

Judith practically passed out with relief. If Gus Fielding, bless his cotton socks, had been hermetically sealed from any direct contact with the Janssens' party folk, she herself was in the clear. She offered up a prayer of pure thanksgiving. Life, after all, was back on the rails and even her present predicament paled in contrast to a future overshadowed with doubt. Judy brushed aside Ellie's assertion that Gus was also a non-smoker as old news. The poor chap had obviously had an attack of nerves since stumbling across the girl in the shower. Who wouldn't?

She harried Ellie, anxious not to let her off the hook. "So Stig kept his second appointment at the quarry."

"No. I did." She paused, watching for Judy's reaction and, encouraged by her bright-eyed attention, continued.

"Well, what else could I do? Stig phoned to tell me he had decided to ignore Gus's persistence and leave for Venice straight away. So I drove over to the quarry myself. I'd been there once before with Gus when we were staying at the club one weekend. The place is always quiet on weekdays, especially late afternoons. It's not exactly a beauty spot and because the slopes are insecure the council fenced it off to everyone except the boffins. It was almost dark by the time I arrived. I parked the Volvo well out of sight and clambered through the fence where Gus had explained to Stig he would leave his scarf tied to a break in the wire.

"Gus had been there for hours messing about with his equipment and had probably given up hoping Stig would make it. He must have decided that from the first because afterwards I searched his stuff just to make sure he'd brought the polaroids and there wasn't a sign of them. I slithered round to where he was working on the other side of the quarry before he realised I was even there. He'd expected a man, you see, and when I called out and waved my scarf I'd quite forgotten what a shock I would be to him. Stupid of me, I know, but it hadn't really sunk in that I was supposed to be dead and I was really looking forward to seeing him. I hadn't spoken to a soul except Stig for weeks. I called out to him again and ran down the path. It was awfully steep and I nearly fell over. The sun was low down on the horizon behind me now I think back, and Gus looked up. He probably only saw the dark outline of a woman scrambling down, bringing a shower of loose gravel and stones on his head. I shouted to him and he stared up at me in pure terror. Before I could reassure him, he stepped back and caught his feet in one of his bloody surveyor's poles and went crashing down, setting off a landslide. He disappeared in the water, Judith, and sank like a stone!"

"He didn't swim or splash about?"

"Not once. He must have hurt himself falling, bashed his head or something. The water was awfully deep. No wonder the council put up the barbed wire and the danger notices."

Judy grasped the bedcover, mute with shock.

"You do believe me, don't you? I told Stig the whole story but he just got really angry with me. Said I'd ruined everything. It would start up a whole new police investigation. That's what I thought you had come about when I found you checking the Volvo in the barn. I just panicked. I thought if I kept you here till Stig got back he would know what to do."

"Ellie! Forget about me." Judy burst out. "Didn't you go in after him? Gus was probably just knocked out by the fall, Ellie!"

She looked up with surprise. "But I can't swim."

There was nothing you could say to that, Judy decided. How could you criticise a "dead" woman for refusing to risk her life?

She slumped back on the pillows and said with weary resignation, "Why don't you go and make us a pot of tea, Ellie? You look absolutely done in. See if you've got any aspirins while you're about it. And get something for us to eat, for God's sake. And when you come back, we simply must get ourselves out of this mess. Stig isn't coming back for you. Let's face it. We might as well both give up."

The truth of it seemed to hit Ellie like a slap in the face to a hysteric. She flinched, her mouth sagging in shocked disbelief.

Then she turned and went away and Judith grimly assessed the odds against ever seeing Ellie Juniper again.

She couldn't have been more wrong. In fact, she quickly reappeared and after a scratch lunch of crackers and cheese and hard-boiled eggs, Ellie ran upstairs with the crockery and didn't come down again. She had left the door ajar but taken the shotgun. Judith crouched on the bed straining to catch the merest movement from above, dreading the sound of the Volvo starting up. Would Ellie really just take off? Leave her here like so much dirty washing? Judy tried not to think about it and spent the silent afternoon exploring every possible means of escape.

With the utmost care she manoeuvred the chain on her wrist to the end of the rail so she could get a grip on the bedstead. The boarding school issue bed was on castors which moved easily enough but made loud squeaking noises on the wooden floor. Inch by inch, Judy edged the bed back until it stood under the window and, using the free handcuff, tried to prize open the interior shutter. It seemed to have been screwed to the framework of the window, a precautionary measure for the parties, she imagined. After thirty minutes' serious jabbing one of the shutters groaned and then split, and Judy saw daylight at last. The window *was* barred but at least she could break the glass and shout or wave a flag or something. Some member of the staff was bound to patrol the estate bounderies at some time. Even a Rottweiller's would be a welcome face at the window.

She listened hard, terribly afraid that Ellie would just walk away and yet just as scared she would return. The woman was volatile, her state of mind weakened by enduring so many weeks alone and now having to face up to the fact that the man for whom she had suffered this ordeal had deserted her. With a passport and money in a numbered bank account waiting for her in Luxembourg there was really nothing to stop Ellie from walking away. It would be nearly another week before Judy was even missed at work and Arnott had no reason to guess she had landed herself in trouble.

Judith decided her best chance of survival was to play on Ellie's vulnerability, ally herself to the woman, ladle out the sympathy and try to persuade her into giving herself up.

After all, what had she done? Unfortunately, the answer was patently obvious. Ellie Juniper had probably killed one woman and, faced with having to handle her escape without Janssen, might well decide to kill again. Or at best leave her hostage to scream her head off with nobody within earshot.

Reluctantly she decided to play safe and closed the shutters, painfully shoving back the bed to its original position. Still, there was no sound from upstairs and, with luck, Ellie had flaked out on the bed for the afternoon. The longer this cat and mouse game was played out, the greater Judy felt her chances to be. If Ellie won hands down in the stamina stakes, her tortured recollections were playing havoc with her ability to make any logical plan.

After all that furniture moving Judith crashed out herself, mercifully annihilating six hours. She woke to hear queer noises in the central heating pipes and guessed Ellie was running a bath or, better still, cooking supper. Some hopes! The woman had spent weeks here living like a bag lady. Feeling better for her extended siesta, Judy tried to smooth out the crumpled sheets in an effort to make her "raft" less uncomfortable.

She would kill for a tall glass of Campari soda with a sliver of lime and clinking with ice. Being in chokey had its little routines like everything else in life and already, Judy admitted, she was getting better at it. Sleeping a lot helped to pass the time and planning an escape took up what wasn't concerned with banalities like the level of the water in the plastic bottle. One's imagination was tested to the full and she tried to remember how those poor wretched hostages had spent their years in Lebanon. Trouble was, she was no stoic. Even so her priorities had whittled down to (i) eating, (ii) the Marie Antoinette bucket and (iii) an urgent desire for a wash and brush-up. Her mouth tasted like a silage heap, dry and faintly rancid.

She determined to test Ellie's goodwill by demanding a basin of hot water and a clean towel and wondered if the afternoon sleep had improved her captor's attitude of mind. Perhaps, having confronted the likelihood that Janssen would never surface again as far as she was concerned, Ellie would respond to a little gentle bullying, some manoeuvring in the right direction.

But by the time Ellie did put in an appearance, it was almost midnight and Judy had long since given up hope. Intermittent sounds from the rooms above reassured her that she had not been totally abandoned but, with growing hunger and despair, this seemed little comfort. It dawned on her it was entirely possible Ellie's mind had snapped and she had totally forgotten about Little Miss Muffet in the basement.

When footsteps clattered on the cellar stairs, Judy could hardly bring herself to raise her head off the pillow.

Ellie approached the bed and held out a peace offering. It was a warmed-over frozen pizza, almost hot, and sticky with melted cheese. Judy took it without a word and struggled to sit up. She eyed her fellow-prisoner with the wary regard of a beaten cur. The fight had gone out of her, there was no strength left even to plan a way out. The eyes which stared back at her were equally lifeless, like a winter sea.

Judy took bites from the soggy pastry, leaning her head against the cold metal rail of the bed, chewing slowly, saying nothing.

When she had finished, Ellie produced a damp face flannel and wiped her face as if she were a child. Judith slumped back, no longer afraid but tired to death of it all. She sensed a rawness about Ellie, a new, harder spirit, nothing like the scatty girl in Rectory Gardens she had thought she knew.

Ellie started to speak, explaining that she had decided to drive to Heathrow. Very soon now. Judy's brain registered this with little reaction. It was only what she had expected after all. Ellie seemed troubled by this lack of response and her words tumbled over themselves in the urgent necessity to justify herself.

"What nobody understands, Judy, is that Helen asked for it. She deserved nothing less. When she told me she had deliberately allowed me to contract their appalling infection, it was as if she'd handed out an order of execution. And for what reason? Why me? She wasn't jealous – I'm sure she didn't really consider I had any right to feel bitter. Helen was pretty boozed when she arrived and after a hour of my ministrations with the gin and water was very drunk. How dare she shrug me off like that! How would you feel suddenly to be told you had no future, nothing to look forward to but disease and a slow death? I lost my temper and flew at her. Helen dropped her glass in the hearth and it smashed all over the place. I grabbed the biggest piece and went for her.

"We struggled as she tried to get away and I grabbed her chiffon dress. It tore right off her shoulder – the skirt was just a wrap-around affair but the top was in ribbons. She swore at me and we bundled into the little hallway, me threatening to cut her face with the broken tumbler. She raised her hands to fend me off and there was a bit of a fight. Nothing serious but it gave me a thirst for blood. Justice? Retribution? You name it. I could have killed her there and then. All this time that terrible rock music of hers was pounding out, driving me crazy. I hurled myself at her back as she tried to open the door and get out and her head smashed into the plywood with such a wallop she dented it.

"Then she passed out. More from fright than anything, I suppose. In one clear bright moment I knew I had my chance. It was the only way Stig and I could possibly be together. He could never shake off Helen, not in a million years. I tried to drag her into the bathroom and her dress ripped even more. There was no way it could have happened except in a brawl. And yet, seeing her sprawled out with her hair all over the place, I kept seeing myself. That's when I knew I really would take her place. *I* would be Helen Janssen."

Judy drifted in and out of consciousness and Ellie became impatient, pulling at the pillows, forcing her to sit up and listen. She splashed her face with water from the bottle. Judith opened her eyes like a china doll.

"*Listen* to me, for Christ's sake! She *deserved* it, Judy. You know she did. Letting me play about with them all that time without so much as a warning! I took off my jumpsuit, pulled Helen into the shower, wrapped my hand in a face flannel and made a few experimental cuts and then slashed her throat, finally cutting away that rag of a dress and leaving her propped against the wall like a Barbie doll waiting to be dressed up.

"Then I turned on the water and cleaned everything up, taped over the damned door with a poster and collected the broken glass, placing it in the bathroom with the gin bottle. I left all my own clothes behind, put on her coat and shoes and made sure I had everything of hers – apart from her undies. I couldn't bear to touch her beyond stripping off the torn cocktail dress. There were no car keys in that silly little evening bag. I hardly expected there to be, she must have had a skinful at dinner before she even left Harley Street. I crept downstairs and walked to Exhibition Road and picked up a taxi. From start to finish that final bust-up between us was over in minutes.

"Stig was waiting at the flat over the consulting rooms and pretty well freaked out when I told him what I'd done. Even threatened to walk out on me, said he would only be exchanging one harpy for another. Eventually, I calmed him down and sketched out my plan. We sat up all night trying to decide how to play it. I had to tell him about the disk hidden in one of my suede boots – the only thing I'd forgotten. He knew the police would almost certainly find it and was terrified those people listed, many of them influential, would be questioned about their connection with the suicide victim. Also there were the wretched polaroids still in the shoebox. Stig was convinced the police would identify all of us and put two and two together. He decided there was nothing for it but to go back and see for himself, recover what he could and make sure I hadn't left any other evidence. There was a chance he could get into the flat and retrieve everything before the body was discovered – we didn't know Gus had already lifted all the photos and the disk on its own would mean absolutely nothing. After all, the info by each name was all in my own little coded symbols.

"But he still needed an excuse to call at the house. I hit on the idea to telephone and leave a message on the answerphone to say he'd be there Monday morning to collect his typescripts. That was in case he arrived too late and the body had already been discovered. How else could he explain being there? He'd never even called at Rectory Gardens. Helen used to drive me home sometimes and took delight in winding up Mother with all her travel rubbish and photo albums but Stig never had any reason to be there. We had to put off his visit till a reasonable hour but I said the house was practically empty over Easter and he could be in and out without anyone seeing a thing. I'd got a set of spare keys in my desk at the office and he took those to get in. But when he spoke on the entryphone, just to be on the safe side in case anyone was watching, he found the police were already there. The rest you know. He had to play it by ear and as it happened it all worked out perefectly.

"It would have been a wonderful solution, Judy. We could have gone abroad and lived without a care in the world apart from the virus and that might have lain dormant for years. He could have worked even. There was no stain on his career, you see. He's a wonderful doctor."

"But you may not even have HIV, Ellie. You could be perfectly fit. Helen was being terribly cruel saying a thing like that. In any event, people testing positively don't necessarily develop AIDS. Why risk your life staying with Stig?"

Ellie shrugged, the effort of explaining her feelings for the man quite beyond her.

"Why tell me all this?"

Ellie stood absolutely still, staring at Judy with a fierce determination. "You are the only one here *to* tell. If I leave now without putting my side of things no-one will ever know how it happened. Or why. I've got to go, Judith. Forgive me, please. I'll try to send someone later, I promise I will. But you'll have to give me a day or two to get right away. I've got money now, I can buy an entirely new life for myself, a new name even. It's all been set up for me. Stig explained everything. Perhaps he knew I'd have to make it alone. I was fooling myself, it was Gus's accident turned him against me. He thought I'd killed Gus too. Me! My attack on Helen was entirely justified. You could call it self-defence, after all she hit me first by exposing me to that filthy disease." Her voice rose, ugly with recrimination. "It wasn't *his* fault he caught it from her. I'm not some sort of maniac, Judith."

Ellie was breathing deeply, her rage like a burning incandescence. "I can do *anything* she did, no question about it."

Judy felt the situation was beyond saving, no amount of smooth talk would be enough. So she pushed ahead, knowing this was possibly her last chance with Ellie Juniper.

"But how did Helen exert such tremendous power over him if Stig was in love with you?"

Ellie looked across at Judith, her glance bitter. "Ah, well, one could say Helen invented the man. Stig just stepped into his shoes. You see, Philip Janssen never existed. He was never a doctor. He was a total fiction."

"You mean he never qualified?" Judy gasped.

Ellie nodded. "That was the only reason Helen kept hold of him all these years. She sculpted a medical consultant out of thin air, exactly the sort of man she wanted. A successful practitioner with hundreds of grateful patients."

"But how?"

"Oh, it's not unknown even here. Honestly. But it's easier in the States. As you know Stig started out as plain Mark Trujina, an army paramedic and, to give Helen her due, she recognised a wonderful intelligence just wasting away. She hatched the whole scheme, helped him forge qualification certificates from a non-existent medical school in Mississippi using forms available at any US newsagent. Yes, really, it's absolutely true, Judy. Stig obtained his registration by posting a notarised photocopy of a forged medical degree even though the medical council regulations say applicants should produce original documents only. The council required no proof of identity other than a signed statement that the facts were correct. Even when checks were run with the council's overseas registration department when he applied for his first post, he got the all clear. I think Helen had some powerful contacts from her time in New York and she was never one to pass up a tool. Administrative cock-ups are by no means uncommon, Judith, and once a man is accepted, going private and setting up your own consulting rooms is a doddle. Helen kept behind him, wouldn't let him lose his nerve, I'll give her that. Stig has been a huge success in his field, hundreds of people have reason to be grateful to him and few highly qualified practitioners could boast an absolutely blameless record like that. If it hadn't been for Helen's predilection for high jinks, not to mention gin, he could have got away with it for ever."

Ellie touched Judy's cheek but she seemed to have heard none of this, snoring gently, a loose feather from the pillow rising and falling with her breath. Ellie pulled up a coffee table beside the bed and set out an unopened litre of water and a motley collection of biscuits and apples.

Then she quietly left, went out into the darkness and drove away.

CHAPTER TWENTY-THREE

During the course of Tuesday evening at Mortlake, Arnott and Bernie Allen agreed on a plan.

Arnott would deal with Veronica Messop and Bernie would show copies of the detective agency reports to Coles and insist on the reconsideration of the new evidence, underlining the urgency to examine the door in the Juniper flat. No-one could claim *when* the poster was taped over the damage – it could have been done well before the woman died, she hadn't just moved in. If the examiner was sufficiently convinced by the samples taken from the flat, backed up by Mavis Clements's assurance that Juniper was left-handed – this fact conflicting with the pathologist's observations about the entry wound – he might be persuaded to call for an exhumation. *Then* they could satisfy themselves whether the victim's injuries were, or were not, self-inflicted.

Arnott explained to Bernie why Mavis Clements's information was an important factor in any fresh forensic reappraisal, her evidence an additional reason for any re-examination of the case, all of which Bernie must stress. Exhumation orders were not issued lightly and the possiblity of overturning a coroner's verdict and a pathologist's opinion on the strength of a single hair stuck to a door which may, or may not, belong to the victim and which may, or may not, have been there for days before her death, was by no means certain.

Even with proof supplied by the American agency that Janssen was a fraud, that no doctor of that name had been registered with the US authorities and, indeed, the medical school quoted on the fake documents did not even exist, there were still several avenues to be explored prior to prosecution. But, having acquired this astonishing information about her employer, Ellie Juniper presented the classic profile of a blackmailer and showed every sign of having money to burn. It was a start.

"Where's Judy Pullen?" Bernie asked, rising to go.

"Search me. I phoned her ma but she's heard nothing for over a week. I'll put out some feelers in the morning. Her sister might have something. Pullen's taken the week off so she could be anywhere. She was doing some freelance legwork for the Junipers' solicitor. I'll see Miss Messop tomorrow and find out if she knows anything. It could have been Pullen stirring up that Domino Club manager. He wrote a stinking letter to the solicitor about the muck left in the dead girl's locker. These people make you laugh, don't they, Bernie? A sports bag stuffed with twenty quid notes and he gets all sniffy about the dirty washing the poor stiff left behind."

"If I take the Power Agency report now, Ralph, I'll have copies ready first thing in the morning. Eight suit you?"

"By 'eck, I'd give a tenner to see Coles's face when you show 'im what we found out about that quack. Bloody Harley Street an' all! Where do you think he's scarpered off to – the Cayman Islands? Phoned his office yesterday and the poor cow on the desk had spent all weekend cancelling his appointments at short notice. No better than being on the panel if you ask me. All the same, these medicos, think they can do as they like."

They parted on good terms, Bernie's burst of temper well doused and the trust between them re-established. Arnott was absolutely tickled pink with their progress and only wished Pullen was around to celebrate. After Bernie had gone, his mind was still fizzing, and he sat up late making notes in his slow, crabbed hand. Next morning he was up and revving well before seven and took pleasure in ringing Veronica Messop at the home number Pullen had given him and guessed by her brisk response, the great lummox wasn't even out of bed. He refused to discuss the reasons for the urgency of mounting a fresh enquiry into the death of Ellie Juniper but hinted that an exhumation order was in the pipeline. That woke her up all right and she put no objection to meeting him at her office at eight-thirty.

Their discussion was curt and to the point and they got on a lot better with Basil Meek out of the way. The Power Agency's findings came as a great shock to her and, after a quick run-through, Veronica agreed that they must come clean with Coles about the fraud.

"I've already arranged an interim payment with the agency from Basil Meek's account. He insists we invite no trouble from that quarter and I tend to agree with him. The police will encounter little opposition from Power now a settlement has been reached. Do you know anything about the other man whose name crops up in the original brief, Mr Arnott?" She checked the file. "Mark Trujina?"

"No, I don't. It might have been a lead about Helen Janssen's private life Miss Juniper was following up. Quite separate from the husband's little scam. If you phone this man Power, ask him to keep looking. Coles will want all the facts Power can dig up and if Mr Meek's happy to foot the bill, we might as well enjoy his hospitality."

She looked up sharply, far from comfortable with this blunt Yorkshireman who had a nasty habit of trying to push her along. Veronica's response was defensive. Arnott fired another set of questions about her private deal with Judith Pullen. Well, why not? In for a penny . . .

"She was really far too diligent, Mr Arnott. I arranged with Mr Meek that he would redecorate her flat and Judith very kindly offered to clear out Ellie's personal items for us."

"Aye, she's a bonny lass and no mistake," he said, his eyes under the terrier's brows levelling with the solicitor in a gaze she found very disconcerting. She hurried to justify herself.

"It was a speedy solution to a difficult situation. Judy had to put up with a ruined apartment and insurance claims are always a bit of a rigmarole as you know. Mr Meek was more than happy to cooperate and Judy was naturally anxious to hurry things along. A mutual arrangement which suited everyone."

"So what's all this about clearing out a locker at Juniper's sports club?"

Veronica looked evasive. "That was entirely Judy's idea. I think she was curious about the place as much as anything. She had a few days due and wanted to pop down to check nothing of Ellie's was in store there. In fact, as you know, she kept a considerable amount of cash in her locker."

"A float?"

"A what?"

"Never mind. Just my little joke, Miss Messop. I think I'll just have a run down there meself before Inspector Coles starts nosing round. You realise that once he reopens the case we shall have to put all our cards on the table."

She drew back as if Arnott had emitted a very nasty smell.

"You don't have to tell me my duty, Arnott! I am always more than happy to cooperate with the police."

He smiled, nodded curtly at a very worried Veronica Messop sitting behind the mountain of correspondence on her desk, and saw himself out.

Arnott drove straight down to the Domino Country Club, parking the rusting van smack bang outside the Georgian portico. He introduced himself as the solicitor's enquiry agent and Jacqueline heard him out before showing him into the manager's office, well out of sight, while she sent one of the gardeners to look for Mr Brooke. Arnott expanded in the lush surroundings and relaxed in an armchair while he waited, smoking one of his vile roll-ups.

Brooke hurried in, towelling the sweat from his tanned forehead. He wore an indigo track suit with "Domino" tastefully embroidered on the pocket.

"My usual work-out," he said brusquely by way of explanation, wasting no pleasantries on the scruffy looking man lounging in his office, fouling the air with a cigarette smelling like charred seaweed.

"I suppose Miss Messop's sent you down about that Juniper business," he said, flopping behind his desk to sift through the morning's post. "There's nothing more I can tell you. We made a list of the entire contents of that locker and as far as I'm concerned, that's that. I can't be held responsible for what members get up to. I've already sent one itemised copy to Miss Messop, you know. Do you want another?" he said wearily.

"No, I don't, Mr Brooke. I reckon I'm already a mile up the road in front of you with Miss Messop. No, what I need to know is what was said to Sergeant Pullen. She's disappeared, sir. And as we have good reason to believe the dead woman, Elinor Juniper, was blackmailing some of your members, a little cooperation might save a lot of embarrassment. There's likely to be a fresh investigation of this Juniper case. If a blackmailer dies sudden like, the police start looking under the carpet."

That made the poncey sod sit up and take notice, Arnott reflected.

"Have you anything to go on? Has a member of this club registered a complaint?"

"Now, you know full well we have to be discreet when it comes to such investigations, Mr Brooke. Protect the identity of the victims, an' all."

"Of course," Brook replied, now looking distinctly sickly. "What can I tell you? Sergeant Pullen came, emptied the locker and we talked about the Juniper woman's circle of friends here. That was all there was to it."

Arnott tended to believe him but with Pullen on the loose, Brooke seemed to be the last port of call.

"Pullen didn't mention where she was off to?"

"Naturally not. Why should she? We had finished our business. In fact, I got the impression she was taking a few days' leave. She did make a note when I told her Ellie Juniper sometimes stayed with friends nearby."

"Oh, aye?" Arnott tensed, waiting for more details to dribble out but Brooke had shut up shop and was attempting to lead Arnott to the door.

Arnott didn't budge. "And what friends would they be, sir?"

Brooke became truculent. "Is all this part of the enquiry? I have to protect the confidence of our members, you know."

"*Everything* about Miss Juniper is under scrutiny at present, Mr Brooke." Arnott lowered his voice and drew close to his reluctant confidant. "Strictly between ourselves, Mr Brooke, there's likely to be a murder enquiry. The police have reason to believe Miss Juniper did not cut her own throat." He spoke these last words slowly, with dramatic emphasis.

Brooke leapt back, colliding with a bag of golf clubs leaning against the wall. They clattered to the floor. "Really? Oh, come off it. You're pulling my leg."

"I'm not given to jokes of that nature, sir. You'd better expect a visit from an Inspector Coles. Take a bit of advice from an old hand, sir. Get your facts off pat before he comes sniffing round. The inspector's a man with a short fuse, not an amiable chap like meself. Watch yourself, Mr Brook. Coles is a right little mustard pot."

Arnott drove away still grinning to himself, a copy of the Juniper membership form safely under his belt and a thirst raging in his gullet. He made straight for Reapshaw, the nearest village to the Janssens' country cottage.

The sun sparkled on the van's flyblown windscreen and he decided Pullen was on to something picking this week to take a break, the first decent bit of weather for weeks. He should have asked her down to the boat for a couple of days. Now it was away from the boatyard, he could enjoy little excursions up the coast. Do her the world of good to get some fresh air in her lungs after all that trouble at Rectory Gardens.

He drew up outside the Slug & Lettuce just at opening time and stamped into the dim saloon bar, ready for a pint and a pork pie. Maggie was serving and only one other customer had beaten him to it.

The barmaid glanced up as the red-faced bloke with the big nose blew in, and summed him up straight off. Big drinker. No doubt about it. She'd seen noses like that before. She smiled and moved away from the barfly at her elbow to take Arnott's order.

In no time at all another pair of thirsty customers trooped in and Arnott sat up at the bar, sipping his ale and taking it all in. He ordered another half and drew the Domino membership form from his pocket to check the Janssens' address. Borodino Lodge. Funny old name and no mistake. Maggie took his money and Arnott invited her to have one herself, chirpy as a robin on a Christmas card. She warmed to the man, her regulars mostly snooty buggers who thought living within spitting distance of Smith's Lawn gave them royal blood.

"You on holiday, love?" she said.

"Retired. Retired copper."

Maggie's thin pencilled eyebrows raised but her response remained friendly. Arnott leaned across the bar and tapped her arm. "I'm looking up some folk I know who live round here. A Doctor Janssen. You know 'im?"

"You'll never catch him here weekdays, he's got this smart practice in London, see. You got a bad back then? Need a nice corset on the quiet?"

Her loud belly laugh made heads turn but when she'd quietened down, the general talk resumed. Arnott grinned, wondering what the joke was.

"Not me, lass," he said. "Back like an iron rod."

She winked. "Your missus is a lucky girl then."

Arnott gave up and tried another tack.

"The doctor's not the only one I want to see. His wife'd do. She's here most of the time, ain't she?"

"Can't say I've seen much of her lately. But that big bloke sitting at the end of the bar works for Mr Guy. Brian. He'd know. Borodino's on the estate. Hang about. I'll ask him if you like."

Arnott waited, mentally flicking out the bait like a fly fisherman, careful not to disturb the water. He was on a delicate line here. Whoever killed Juniper was dangerous and still on the loose. And Pullen had been nosing about a bit too much for his liking.

Maggie came back, shaking her head. "Brian reckons the doctor's away on a course. Italy somewhere. His wife's been in and out the cottage but she's none too popular with Brian and the staff up at the house. Mrs Janssen complained in the past to Mr Guy about them poking round the Lodge when she had guests. Likes her privacy, you know. Mr Guy gave Brian a real flea in his ear about it so now he keeps well clear when Mrs Janssen's down. They've got this place in London, you know. Over the shop as you might say. If you wanted to see the doctor, you'd be better off trying his surgery, got a flat upstairs, so she told me."

"What do you reckon about Mrs Janssen then? Fiery tart, is she?"

Maggie shrugged. "Not really. Brian's touchy. Mrs Janssen's always been all right to me and the doctor's a very nice man. Comes in regular when he's at the cottage. Loves his pint. Funny you asking about her though. I had a young girl in here on Saturday night; she was a friend of hers an' all."

"Blonde with brown eyes?"

Maggie sniggered and turned to serve another customer, and Arnott had to curb his impatience till she had time to get back to him.

"You keen on blondes then?" she said, fingering one of her

211

earrings and giving Arnott a sideways look.

"Not 'alf! Still, if this girl you said was 'ere at the weekend come to visit Mrs Janssen, she must be up there on her own while the doctor's away. P'raps she stayed over?"

"Your friend wasn't staying at Borodino. As a matter of fact she let me down. I was quite upset about it. Can never tell with people, can you? Do someone a favour and it blows up in your face."

"What happened?"

"Well, this young woman said she was on her own, see. Her boyfriend's in America she said. Wanted a room here but Mr Smith don't take guests. So I fixed her up with a B & B at my friend Beryl's place down the road. But she never showed up. Bloody typical with these young girls! Beryl was really annoyed with me but how was I to know she'd let her down?"

"When was this you say?"

"Saturday night. Said she had a date so Beryl waited up but she never come."

"Tch, Tch," Arnott sympathetically responded. "Tell me about the big house. Guy's place. Did the girl say she had a date with the bloke up at the manor?"

"Mr Guy?" She smothered a fresh attack of giggles, clamping her hand over her mouth, her eyes dancing. "You must be joking, love. He don't want to be bothered with blondes, take my word for it. Apart from the other," Maggie leered, "he's too old for it."

She got a black look from the barfly whose glass had been empty for a full minute and a half. Maggie moved away to take his glass, gliding behind the bar as if mounted on castors.

Arnott pushed through the lunchtime crowd to the other end of the saloon, the Slug & Lettuce now doing a roaring trade in counter snacks. He approached Brian, a moody looking chap with a low forehead, and offered to buy him a pint. Brian accepted first and smiled later.

"Stranger here?" he said, sipping his bitter.

Arnott trotted out the usual pleasantries and then drew the man to a quiet corner.

"I'm looking for my daughter. She said she was visiting some people called Janssen who rent a cottage on the estate. Right?"

He eyed Arnott suspiciously and waited.

"Blonde kid with an old green VW. Seen it running about, lad?"

"Might've."

"Maggie says my girl was in here Saturday night. I'm worried about her, see."

"And well you might be if she's going to parties at that place," Brian retorted.

"Well, that's what I thought. Any chance you'd take me over there? See what's what? Silly girl said she was coming down for the weekend and it's bloody Wednesday and she ain't come home. How about it, son?"

"It's none of my business." Then after a moment, he added. "How old is she, this girl of yours?"

"Old enough. Still, I expect you've got kids yourself. You know how it is."

Brian eyed Arnott with suspicion and, after a minute's consideration, said, "Tell you what. Every car passes through the gates gets clocked on the magic eye. You can come up to my office if you like and take a dekko at the video. See if the VW's been through. Can't say I heard any goings-on at Borodino this Saturday though. Sure you've got the right weekend, Pop? Been pretty quiet up there ever since that time we got snowed up in February. These party types ain't so keen once the weather gets rough and last Saturday was the first decent day we've had here for a month."

Arnott waved to Maggie and left with his new mate, far from being really anxious about Pullen who was well able to take care of herself but keen to see who *was* going in and out of the Janssens' place. Never know your luck. You might spot a familiar face. Once you'd got yourself a fake doctor running what Brian hinted was a weekend brothel, you could be in business. Arnott's real aim was to be one jump ahead of Coles. Was that such a lot to ask?

Arnott sat in the stuffy estate office with Brian and ran through all the video recordings of the comings and goings through the entrance gates.

"Not exactly Piccadilly Circus this place, is it?" he said as they trawled through miles of identical shots of the empty drive. The Volvo appeared a couple of times and Arnott craned his neck, stopping the film, trying to get a better look at the driver in her headscarf and dark glasses.

"That's her. The Janssen woman. No wonder the doctor travels a lot."

"Spend her time alone here, do she?"

"Mostly. When the weather's good she goes up to the country club quite a bit."

"The Domino?"

"Yeah. But the parties are only when *he's* here."

"No private nooky then? No special boyfriend?"

"No, I can't say that about her," Brian grudgingly admitted. "P'raps she's a dyke."

"No staff neither?"

"Does the lot herself. You'd think they had a goldmine at Borodino the way she locks up, shutters an' all. You should see the—"

"Oi! Stop it right there, mate! Look, there it goes. Little VW."

"That your gel's? You sure?"

Arnott nodded and they ploughed on. It took some time and he insisted on seeing every inch of footage.

"Ever think of getting yourself a job in this security lark?" Brian said, genuinely impressed.

"Oh aye. Once or twice." Arnott leaned back, flexing his shoulders. "Any other way off this estate, lad?"

"Not a chance. All bricked up except for the main gates. Even the oil lorry has to come up the drive."

"Well, if Judy came here visiting on Saturday night, why didn't she go again?"

"P'raps she did. The Volvo's still in and out all hours. She could've gone with the Janssen woman, you can't always see everything when it's dark."

"Can we have a scout round?"

"More than my job's worth as a rule. But since we know Lady Bigmouth flashed out of here last night and the Volvo's not been back since, no harm in having a sniff. By the look of your kid's old banger, it's more than likely it wouldn't start."

"You ever heard of one of them Beetles not starting up first time? Bloody miracles them little engines."

Brian laughed and reached for his coat.

As soon as they got near the Lodge they could see the smoke issuing from the basement through a broken pane of glass. Arnott rushed forward, kneeling at the barred and wired-up window, coughing his guts out. It was impossible to see anything. Brian ran back to the jeep and put through a mayday call on his intercom, his mind whirling with the desperate likelihood that the Borodino was about to blow up – the bloody boiler was in the cellar! If the old busybody hadn't been trailing his stop-out of a daughter it could have been another hour before the smoke had been noticed. And that was being optimistic.

Arnott slammed at the window with a brick but the wire made it impossible. He threw it down and belted round to the back and Brian broke in.

They found Judith crouched on a hospital bed which had been pushed under the window, a heap of sheets now well alight on a makeshift bonfire. The atmosphere was thick, the two men choking, their eyes blinded by a pall of smoke. As Arnott attempted to lift her away he saw that her wrist was chained to the bedrail. He stared at the handcuffs in panic. How was he supposed to get her out?

Brian emptied the bottle of Perrier on to a blanket and threw it over the blaze, then flew upstairs, coming back with a small household extinguisher from the kitchen. He quickly had the flames under control and once the fire engines arrived, the girl was cut free. An ambulance took her away and Arnott slumped against the wall outside, utterly done in. Judith had been out cold, only coming to as they lifted her into a hospital bed. She unaccountably started to scream, fighting with the nurses to get away. They sedated her and it was twenty-four hours later before Arnott was able to get the full story. By then she had discharged herself. She was allergic to hospital beds, she said.

Judy Pullen hit the headlines and her ordeal percolated to the embassy in Washington where Laurence Erskine was barely occupied ensuring the safety of a visiting politician. And Judy thought *his* job was dangerous. He got leave and arrived in time to share the excitement of the exhumation.

The body was that of Helen Janssen, her dentist proudly identifying his beautiful bridgework. Some time afterwards, Shiner's Funeral Service disceetly returned the coffin to the

Juniper family plot, not wishing to waste a prime situation. After all, Ellie, the last of the Junipers, was unlikely to be complaining, was she? Basil Meek was more than happy to acquiesce, preferring cremation himself.

"But, Judy, why did you set the place on fire, for Pete's sake?" Laurence couldn't stop himself asking. "Weren't you in enough trouble already?"

"OK. *You* tell me how to get out of a trap like that! I'd tried everything else. All I had was a cigarette box and a Domino Club matchfolder. How was I to know Arnott was already bringing up the Cavalry?"

Laurence didn't spoil the yarn. Truth was, Ellie Juniper had already telephoned the police as the fire engines were passing through the main gates at Reapshaw. To warn them, she said, that a policewoman was being held prisoner in Borodino Lodge.

It had been a close call.

EPILOGUE

As Arnott finally departed from Borodino Lodge, Ellie Juniper was joining a flight out of Amsterdam for Chicago. Later, they found the Janssens' Volvo in the long term car park at Heathrow but that sunny day in April marked the final departure of the elusive corpse from Rectory Gardens.

Basil Meek came closest to this "corpse" one Christmas Eve, spotting his cousin entering a hotel lobby in New York. He followed her into the piano bar and watched as the svelte creature in the full-length chinchilla greeted a middle-aged Italian wearing gold-rimmed spectacles.

The woman was Ellie all right. Basil Meek was not a man to make mistakes. He still had bad dreams about that lady, dreading her recapture. He'd had to keep on his job with the shipping line but Messop was pulling out all the stops to make some special arrangements for him and, in the meantime, he at least had the best flat in the Kensington house on indefinite free loan in exchange for acting landlord, collecting the rents and keeping an eye on the ball. Things were settling down nicely at Rectory Gardens. It was no time for Ellie to pop up and upset the apple cart.

He sneaked a view of his elusive cousin. Her hair was different; reddish and cut close to the head. And she had finally got used to wearing contact lenses. She was still on the wanted list and from time to time a sighting was claimed but it always turned out to be a hoax or an innocent look-alike. The police efforts to trace "Doctor Janssen" were less energetic. He was a fraud but no-one had complained about his professional treatment and he had disappeared leaving no debts. He had harmed no-one and the medical authorities were none too anxious to publicise their own poor vetting of his qualifications or the loophole through which such confidence tricksters could creep. Janssen was no sort of political terrorist and, all things considered, his name, or whatever it was now, was unlikely to assume any priority in any international police dragnet. Scotland Yard would just have to bide its time, wait for the man to make a mistake, repeat the pattern and get caught up in a routine police trawling exercise. Or someone sometime would turn him in.

Basil ordered a martini and watched Ellie for nearly half an hour, impressed by the attention she received from the restaurant manager who came over to greet her and her escort, whinnying like a lovesick hyena.

Basil sidled up to the bar and slipped the barman twenty dollars, grabbing the man's startled attention with a discreet gesture towards the laughing redhead in the fur coat. The barman was relieved to find the money was to be so easily earned and, in an undertone, filled in the details. The woman was a comet, newly arrived on the Manhatten skyline.

"And?" Basil prompted with a curt nod.

The man shrugged, subtly inferring such shooting stars were well beyond the scope of such as Basil Meek. He murmured a name, glancing nervously along the bar.

"Works for an escort agency," he muttered. "Very expensive, sir." He produced a selection of business cards from under the bar, swiftly scanned them and slid one across to him under a bowl of peanuts.

Basil passed him another ten dollar bill, slipped the card in his pocket and drifted back to his seat at the side of the room. He was in a quandary. If he reported the discovery to the police and his cousin was eventually extradited what good would that do? And when she found out who had pointed the finger, Ellie Juniper would instantly tear up the will and even the distant prospect of an inheritance would vanish into thin air. But the Junipers *owed* him.

He stared morosely into his glass, pondering the options. He could, of course, approach her directly at her place of work. The Polly French Agency. A woman on the run with money in the bank wasn't going to risk everything for the sake of a decent pay-off. Would she agree to make a legal deed of gift, passing the house in Rectory Gardens to her cousin? It *was* his by rights – Ellie could have no further use for it, especially if she remained at large. Would such an arrangement even be legal while she was sought by the police? Would she fall for it? And even if it were possible in law, would he not find himself investigated for collusion, for withholding evidence – for God knows what else?

He shrugged impatiently. It wouldn't wash. The authorities would do their utmost to throw the book at him even if Ellie could be persuaded to cooperate.

It rankled. Had rankled ever since he could remember. The Junipers *owed* him. The conviction had festered for years, cut deeply into his life, soured his career – such as it was – trapped in a job at the beck and call of rich old women like his late aunt, bloody Flavia Juniper.

He stared at Ellie, chatting to her well-upholstered friend, her profile a replica of his own. She looked expensive, like an enamelled box, all shiny. His courage failed. He had tried putting the squeeze on Ellie once before. At her smart country club when he realised, for the first time, his shy cousin Elinor was not what she seemed.

He covertly studied the woman in the chinchilla coat, marvelling at the transformation. Ellie had already killed once. She also looked as if she had powerful friends, hard men well able to squash a middle-aged ship's steward on the make. But Basil consoled himself with the knowledge he had her new *name*. Also, he knew where to skewer her if necessary. Escort agency? Wasn't that the game Helen Janssen had been playing when she met her paramedic? Did Ellie still want to play at being Janssen's wife? He smiled grimly, taking a nervous gulp of martini. At least, he could now pinpoint this glittering star on his horizon.

Basil suddenly knew he had too much to lose. Why rock the boat? The hue and cry had died down, the mysterious Mark Trujina, alias Philip Janssen, had vanished like a puff of smoke and Ellie Juniper was no longer of serious interest to anyone. Not even to Inspector Coles who'd had a bellyful of Arnott's criticism of his handling of the case which must inevitably remain on file, a stain on his career, a painful reminder of unfinished business.

The place was crowded. Basil signalled a waiter and quietly ordered another drink, re-positioning himself behind a pillar,

219

never taking his eyes off her. Perhaps it was the intensity of his stare or a sixth sense, but Ellie quite suddenly swung round, breaking off her conversation. They exchanged one brief moment of recognition. Basil raised his hand and smiled before walking out into Fifth Avenue without a backward glance.

He strolled into the nearest bookstore and bought a lavishly illustrated guide to New York: a present for Nick, the friend currently sharing the Osimas' old flat on the ground floor with him. He filed away the memory of the woman in the chinchilla coat as if he had undergone temporary amnesia. After all, if it hadn't been for Ellie he wouldn't have a home to go to, would he? And, who knows, someone as partial to bad company as Elinor Juniper would come to a sticky end before long. He'd have to think about that one. See what ideas Nicky might have . . . If a girl from the Polly French Agency had a fatal accident, Basil Meek could help the police clear their filing system . . . An anonymous tip-off to the press would be enough. New York was a more likely setting for a short life than any other place he could think of. Basil was prepared to bide his time. After all, as the good book says, "The Meek Shall Inherit the Earth."